Also by Tom Turner

Charlie Crawford Mysteries

Palm Beach Nasty

Palm Beach Poison

Palm Beach Deadly

Palm Beach Bones

Palm Beach Pretenders

Palm Beach Predator

Palm Beach Broke

Palm Beach Bedlam

Palm Beach Blues

Palm Beach Taboo

Palm Beach Piranha

Palm Beach Perfidious

Nick Janzek Charleston Mysteries

Killing Time in Charleston

Charleston Buzz Kill

Charleston Noir

Savannah Sleuth Sisters Murder Mysteries

The Savannah Madam

Savannah Road Kill

Dying for a Cocktail

Matt Braddock Delray Beach Series

Delray Deadly

Broken House

Dead in the Water

DELRAY DEADLY

_____

MATT BRADDOCK DELRAY BEACH SERIES BOOK 1

TOM TURNER

TRIBECA PRESS

JOIN TOM'S AUTHOR NEWSLETTER

Get the latest news on Tom's upcoming novels when you sign up for his free author newsletter at
tomturnerbooks.com/news

ACKNOWLEDGMENTS

To my friend, Phoebe, and highly-esteemed but unpaid editor, Alex.

ONE

Larry Carr rolled off the zaftig woman's body and glanced at his watch.

"Oh, Jesus, I gotta be on the first tee in ten minutes."

The woman smiled as he sprang out of bed and pulled on his boxers. "I guess you stayed a little longer than expected, big boy."

Carr smiled. "Yeah, and I hate like hell to leave."

She shot him an air kiss. "You don't have to. Just call the guys and say you pulled your...whatever."

Carr laughed. "You know what? I actually think I might have pulled my whatever," he said, his eyes darting around the carpet next to the bed. "Where the hell's my shirt?"

The woman saw the corner of a sleeve and slid it out from under a pillow. "Is this yours...or Dan's?"

"Not funny, the man's a thousand miles away. Better be anyway," Carr said, putting on the shirt she tossed to him.

"Don't forget your socks," she said, pointing at them. "Can't leave any evidence behind."

He nodded, walked over to her quickly, and kissed her on her sweat-glistened cheek.

"Well, as usual, it was fantastic," Carr said. "You're amazing."

"That's what they all say."

*****

Carr walked barefoot through the house and into the garage. He hit the button that opened the garage door, then popped the trunk of his black Audi. He reached in for his golf shoes, opened the Audi front door, sat in the driver's seat, and tied his shoes. He figured it had taken him five minutes so far and it was another five minutes to the club. He threw the car in reverse, turned around in the driveway, then drove fifty-five in a thirty-five and was at the club in four minutes. No time to hit balls on the range, but he'd made it on time. He walked quickly to the first tee.

"Well, well, Last-minute Larry," Matt Braddock greeted Carr on the tee.

Chris Coolidge, always a stickler about time, glanced down at his clunky Rolex as if to say, "you just made it." Jack Vandevere simply gave him a smile and a little wave.

"The usual?" Carr asked Braddock.

"Yeah, you and me against the right-wingers," Braddock said. "A hundred a side."

Carr said under his breath, "Can Coolidge afford that? Might have to mortgage his condo if he loses."

"You mean, *when* he loses," said Braddock.

Carr nodded and smiled.

"Quit your mumbling," Vandevere said. "By the way, I'm feeling lucky today."

"Well, I'm feeling good," Carr said.

"I'll take luck any day," said Vandevere.

"And the banter begins," Braddock said to Carr. "Tee it up. We already hit."

Carr took a ball and tee out of his pocket and turned to Matt. "Yours was long and straight, I assume?"

"Sorry, not so long and first cut of the rough," Braddock said.

"All right," Carr said, teeing up his ball. "Guess I gotta bail you out...as usual."

Carr waggled his driver a few times and took a ferocious cut at the ball. It was long and straight.

"Nice goin' partner," Braddock said.

Carr and Braddock walked off the tee together, right behind Coolidge and Vandevere.

Vandevere turned back to the other two. "Who is it who smells so good?"

"I noticed that, too," Braddock said. "You wearing your Chanel No. 5 today, Larry?"

"No, I think it's called 'Good Girl Gone Bad,'" Carr said, remembering his lady friend's perfume.

"A subject you're quite the expert on," Vandervere said.

"What's that, Jack?" Carr said.

"Making good girls into naughty ones."

*****

The men were playing the challenging course at the prestigious Island Club in Delray Beach, Florida. It wasn't challenging because it was long and narrow, but because it was short and wet. Meaning a lot of shots splashed down in one of the many water hazards. Usually, men who play golf in a foursome are jovial and genial, swapping stories, hurling jokes and lighthearted insults back and forth. But not always. No, this was a cutthroat team match between men who knew each other but didn't necessarily go to the same cocktail parties.

The second hole at the Island Club was a par three over a lagoon that had swallowed up its fair share of golf balls over the years. Largely because there was a steep bank right before the green. If you landed on it, your ball often backed down into a watery grave.

Vandevere had teed off first and landed on the far edge of the green, a long way from the hole.

"Looks like three-putt territory to me," Carr jibed him.

Then Coolidge teed off. It was a towering shot that looked good at first, but then a stiff breeze caught it, and it landed on top of the bank.

"Uh-oh," said Carr, seeing his opponent's ball slowly rolling backward toward the water. "Going..." he said, as the ball picked up speed. "Going..." he said, as it raced toward the water. "Gone!" he said, as the ball disappeared into the water.

"Glug, glug, glug," Carr added.

Coolidge turned to Carr, who was doing a poor job of suppressing a grin. "Asshole," Coolidge hissed. "It was going to be in the hole if it wasn't for the wind."

"*If*," Carr said. "You always have an *if*, don't you, Chris?"

Carr turned and teed up his ball. As he did, a family of four Egyptian geese slowly tramped across the green. With brown plumage and a splash of white on their feathers, the geese had a smug, haughty look about them. The father, slightly larger, led the way, with the mother a half step behind, trailed by two smaller geese.

Carr took two practice swings and looked ready to drive.

"Whoa, whoa," Braddock said, putting up a hand. "You might hit 'em."

"Don't worry, I'm aiming for the other side of the pin," Carr said.

"Just hold off a sec, will ya," Braddock said.

Carr put up a hand. "Okay, but I'm a deadeye from this range."

A minute later Carr hit his ball. It was a hook and landed only ten feet from the geese who were waddling along to the left of the hole.

"Deadeye, huh?" sneered Coolidge.

Braddock was next and his ball landed ten feet from the pin.

Carr bumped fists with Braddock as they walked off the tee behind Vandevere and Coolidge.

Carr lowered his voice. "Might've pissed off ol' Chris."

"Nothing new about that," Braddock said, walking past the lagoon as three black turtles on the bank slid into the water.

Carr pointed. "They're going after your ball, Chris."

Coolidge heard him but just kept walking.

Carr and Braddock won the hole as Braddock two-putted and Vandevere, true to prediction, three-putted.

There was no blood on the third hole, even though Vandevere hit a screaming slice that bounced off three trees and came to rest next to a fallen coconut. Coolidge saved them by scrambling for a par to tie Braddock and Carr.

On the fourth hole, all four hit good drives that ended up close to each other. As Braddock and Carr walked down the fairway side by side, Carr pointed at a statuesque snow-white stork. "I love the looks of that thing. Skinny, long, lithe…and such regal bearing and posture."

Braddock shook his head and laughed. "Jesus, man, do you see women in everything you look at?"

Carr chuckled. "Guilty."

The hole they were on had a large, yawning trap on the left that caught about as many balls as did the lagoon on the second hole. That was where Chris Coolidge's second shot landed.

As Coolidge walked up to the trap, he saw a common sight: an antediluvian spiny-tailed iguana easily four feet long and probably weighing close to fifteen pounds, slink across the fairway.

Then he saw that the iguana's weighty tail had left a deep rut in the trap which is where his ball had ended up.

"Son of a bitch," Coolidge said, pointing at his ball. "I get an unplayable," meaning he wanted to move his ball to a more favorable lie.

"Why?" Carr said, walking up behind him.

"Why do you think?" Coolidge said. "'Cause that fuckin' iguana left a goddamn crater in the trap."

"You move it and it's a one-stroke penalty," said Carr.

Braddock, next to the trap, shook his head. "Don't be such a ballbuster," he said to Carr, then under his breath, "he sucks at sand shots anyway."

As it turned out, Jack Vandevere holed a long putt to win the hole, so Coolidge's double bogey was no factor.

Next was the fifth hole that ran along the Intracoastal.

"Nice putt," Coolidge said to Vandevere, as they walked to the fifth tee. "But, Christ, we'd be one up if you hadn't Lorena Bobbitt-ed your drive on the second."

"Lorena what?" Vandevere asked.

"Bobbitt. A 'nasty slice...' Get it?"

Vandevere looked blank.

"Come on, Jack," Coolidge said. "The woman who cut off her husband's...you know. Jesus, never mind."

Coolidge walked away from the others to try to find his drive which he had hooked into a stand of trees alongside the Intracoastal.

Carr picked up where Coolidge had left off. "Know what a Mary Jo Kopechne is, Jack?"

"No."

"When your ball goes down to Davy Jones's locker."

Vandevere frowned. "That's a little sick."

"How 'bout an Elin Nordegren?"

"Who?"

"Tiger Woods's ex-wife who—"

Larry Carr never got a chance to finish the sentence as suddenly he lurched backward, let out a loud groan, and hit the ground with a thud. The club in his hand almost clipped Braddock in the back of his leg.

"What the hell?" Vandevere said, glancing down at Carr, who was flat on his back, eyes slammed shut, a patch of bright red spreading across his chest.

Braddock got down on his knees and grabbed Carr's wrist.

"Call 911!" he shouted.

Vandevere pulled his cell phone out of his golf bag and dialed, then suddenly fearing for his own life, ducked for cover behind his bulky golf bag.

Braddock felt no pulse. "Christ, he's not breathing."

"What in God's name happened?" Coolidge said, having run over to them from the trees.

"Someone shot him," Vandevere said, his eyes wide with disbelief at seeing the prostrate, seemingly dead man at his feet. "Get down, for Chrissakes!"

Coolidge crouched down low. "Yeah, but how…where?" he asked.

"Fuck if I know," Vandevere said, waiting for someone to pick up on his 911 call. "Yes, hello, this is an emergency. A man has just been shot on the Island Club golf course. On the fifth hole, runs along the Intracoastal. I think he might be dead."

"What is your name, sir?" the voice asked.

"What the hell does that matter? Get emergency help here right away. Fifth hole of the Island Club."

"Okay," said the voice. "Stay right where you are. First responders and the police will be on scene shortly."

"We'll be here," Coolidge said, clicking off and shaking his head. "I mean, what the hell's she think, we're gonna take off and leave him?"

Shock and disbelief registered on Vandevere's and Coolidge's faces.

Braddock was the only one who seemed to be alert to their surroundings, looking around in all four directions. First, out on the Intracoastal, then at the cluster of trees close by where Coolidge had hit his drive, then at the looming condominium complex to the east and south. But nothing caught his attention.

"Incredible," he mumbled to himself. "Just incredible."

Five minutes later, they heard the first siren. It would be the first of many. It was almost as bizarre as witnessing Carr fall to the ground with a bullet in his heart, seeing two shiny red fire trucks weaving across fairways at breakneck speed.

Braddock started waving down the two fire rescue trucks, and a minute later they skidded to a stop on the soft zoysia grass.

It said *Boynton Beach Fire Rescue Station 4* on the side of the trucks. Three men with emergency kits jumped out of the first truck and were on their knees next to Larry Carr's body within seconds.

"What the hell happened?" asked the driver of the first fire truck as his two coworkers went to work. With quick, skillful action, one opened a defibrillator kit and started pasting on the two pads. The other had cut Carr's shirt up the middle with big shears, baring his chest and abdomen.

"One minute I was talking to him," said Braddock, "the next he was on his back. Shot in the chest."

"By who? Where?" the driver asked.

"Straight line, no heartbeat," said the EMT on the defibrillator. His partner had already started chest compressions, while the driver applied an O_2 face mask, and was squeezing the Ambu bag.

Braddock shook his head. "No idea. We didn't see anyone."

"Just that boat out there," Vandevere said, pointing at the Intracoastal.

"I didn't see any boat," Braddock said.

"'Cause you were busy trying to help Larry," Vandevere said. "There was a white boat with a black hull out there."

One of the EMTs looked up at the three golfers, "We got a flat line. Gonna shock him. Step away!"

Carr's body lurched with the voltage. More compressions, followed by even more shocks. Still no response.

The driver stood. "I'm afraid he's dead, gentlemen."

But they knew that already.

Matt nodded grimly, as a black and white SUV hurtled across the golf course.

"Guys are really tearing up the course," Vandevere muttered to Braddock.

"Christ, Jack, that's the least of our worries," Braddock said.

TWO

It was the next day at the pool of the Island Club, which over-looked the ocean.

"Just horrible," said a woman in a zebra-striped bikini on a chaise lounge next to the pool.

"Did you know him at all?" another woman in a black one-piece asked.

"Not really," said zebra-striped bikini, lowering her voice. "Just that he was a real, um... womanizer."

A bald man on the other side of the pool, out of earshot of the woman, had a slightly different take. "Guy was a major league ass-shagger," he said to his friend. The men were playing backgammon, facing each other.

"What the hell's that mean?" the friend in green trunks asked with a perplexed frown.

"Come on, Steve, an all-world skirt chaser."

Steve nodded. "Oh yeah, so I heard. Still, what a way to go."

"Hey, quick and painless," said the bald man, whose name was Bill. "Better than a lot of other ways."

"Yeah, but he was only fifty."

On the other side of the pool, the woman in the zebra-striped bikini, Stephanie, said, "I heard he had...shtupped his fair share of women in the club."

"Not me," said her friend, Ingrid, in the one-piece.

"But did he ever, you know, come on to you or anything?" Stephanie asked, propping herself up on one elbow.

"Well, I guess you could call it that," Ingrid said. "Asked me to dance at that New Year's thing and was kind of a grinder."

Stephanie laughed and squeezed out some sunscreen from an orange tube.

"A grinder, huh?" Stephanie said. "I've never heard that expression."

"It means—"

Stephanie held up her tanned arms. "I got it. It's very descriptive."

Ingrid took a sip of lemonade from her plastic cup. "It kind of makes me have second thoughts about going out on the golf course any time soon."

"I hardly think what happened is going to be an everyday occurrence."

"Yeah, I know, but, I mean, the fact that it happened at all…"

Stephanie yawned and nodded. "I hear you."

On the other side of the pool, Steve asked, "So, do they have any idea where it came from?"

"What?"

"The shot that killed Larry Carr."

"Oh, all I've heard is they don't have a clue… Guy was a hell of a shot, though."

"You mean, got him right in the heart?"

"Yeah, exactly," Bill said.

"How 'bout… They got any suspects?"

Bill looked up after picking up his dice. "Why you asking me? Not like I was there or something."

Steve shrugged. "I don't know. Just…you're always on top of everything."

Bill rolled his dice. "I'd say the guy to ask is Matt Braddock. He seems to be playing…what's his name… Hercule Poirot?"

Steve, not a big reader, looked up. "Who?"

THREE

Matt Braddock was in line at the Publix supermarket. A man he knew slightly from the Island Club was right behind him.

"Terrible thing about Larry," the man said.

"Yeah, sure was." Braddock was not keen on making it a public conversation.

"They don't even know where the shot came from, right?" the man said.

Braddock nodded again. Publix was not the place to talk about the brutal murder of his friend.

"Well, see you around," the man said, walking out of Publix with his groceries.

Braddock drove across the bridge, back to his condominium on North Ocean Boulevard in Delray Beach and put the groceries away. Then he went out to his terrace overlooking the ocean and sat and watched the crashing waves.

He put his hands on his face, over his eyes and replayed the moment Larry Carr was shot, much as he had done a dozen times already. It was just so unreal. He had come up with every conceivable cliche to describe it in his head. *Like something out of a movie. Like a really bad dream. Like... The list went on and on.*

Larry Carr could be tough on people but had a good heart. He was smart, he was funny, he was opinionated, and he did not suffer fools gladly. Which made some—who were none of the above—fear they might become the target of his acid humor. And now...Larry Carr was dead. Damn, he was going to miss him, flaws and all.

He was *really* going to miss him.

Braddock was forty-six years old and retired. He had graduated from Princeton in three years and immediately started as a trainee at Blackstone at age twenty. It had been nose to the grindstone for twenty-five years until he retired from Blackstone as a Managing Director, a rich man…a very rich man. His partners had tried to talk him out of retirement, but he was done. He had worked his ass off for twenty-five years and now wanted to play his ass off for the next twenty-five. He did the math: *no, make it fifty.*

Braddock was not a flashy or ostentatious man, but he bought himself a two-million-dollar sport fishing boat, planning to catch himself lots of swordfish and marlins. And he had, but after about six months and lots of calluses on his hands, it had gotten old.

Golf was next on his list, and though he had gotten decent at it and enjoyed it, it was not going to become his new passion the way it seemed to have become for certain friends. Like Larry Carr, who'd played eighteen almost every day and watched golf tournaments on TV all weekend long.

Braddock had been divorced for two years and had an amicable relationship with his former wife, Jennifer. But why wouldn't he? She came out of the divorce with seventy million dollars. Braddock had had a son and daughter from his marriage to Jennifer. The daughter had graduated from a boarding school and was now in her junior year at Stanford. His son had been killed by a drunk driver at the age of eighteen. Matt had weekly nightmares about that, and it had left an irreplaceable void in his life. He had a house in Christmas Cove in Maine, where he liked to get away from it all, not to mention the Florida summer heat.

Some people said Braddock looked like a young Jeff Bridges, minus the beard but with bright blue eyes and a cleft chin. When asked, he said he was six feet tall, but at his last physical, the nurse had said he was five-eleven. He made her remeasure him, but she said five-eleven again and added, "Men start shrinking at your age, better get used to it."

After his divorce, Braddock had been barraged with offerings from what was dubbed the "casserole brigade," i.e., single or widowed women showing up on his doorstep—literally—with various casseroles. It was the first step in what some of the women hoped might blossom into a burgeoning romance. Most of the women, though, did it simply as a nice welcoming gesture.

No romances came out of the brigade's offerings, not even any dates, but Braddock was happy to meet the women anyway, and one taught him how to play croquet, which was not at all as he remembered it when he played the game as a kid. Everyone wore white, and nobody knocked their opponents' balls into the pucker brush...which was what had made the game fun back then!

Matt made plenty of friends at his new club and knew many others who had winter homes in the Palm Beach area to the north. Some of them had introduced him to single women and, as a result, he had gone out with a number of them. One relationship in particular—with a thirty-eight-year-old woman on the tail end of her modeling career and just beginning as a real estate agent—was pretty torrid at first, then leveled off, then started to crater when Braddock realized they had almost nothing in common except sex.

As he was wading back into the past, his cell phone rang. He looked down at the display: *Catherine Carr.*

He had sent her a large bouquet of flowers and a long note but had planned to call her after she had a few days to process life without her murdered husband.

"Hi, Catherine, I am so sorry about Larry."

"Thank you, Matt. Those were such nice flowers," she said, then got right to the point of the call. "What do you think happened? You were right there?"

He had no idea how to answer the question and was silent for a few moments. "Oh boy, I really just don't know, Cath. I asked the Delray detective to contact me when he had anything at all but haven't heard back from him."

She sighed deeply. "I mean, it's just so beyond real to me. Being shot like that. When it happened, did the detective theorize at all about where the shot may have come from?" But before Braddock could answer, Catherine let loose with a torrent of random thoughts. "I mean, I know about Larry's affairs. He thought I didn't know, but I knew. And reneging on buying that company. But were those reasons to *kill* him? Larry was such a good father and, except for the women, a good husband too."

That was a pretty big *except*, Braddock thought.

He knew of at least three women Carr had had affairs with in the last four years—two married and one single. It was quite possible he had missed a few.

"I wish I could give you some answers, but I just don't really know anything," he said, choosing to keep the subject on Carr's murder instead of his affairs.

"But did the detective say where he thought the shot came from?"

"Well, he didn't know for sure yet. But it must have come from one of the club's buildings."

The Island Club had a long, four-story building overlooking the golf course to the south and another one, also overlooking the course, to the east.

"Maisie and Bobby Hudson live in the top floor of the one overlooking the fifth hole," Catherine said matter-of-factly, leaving Braddock to fill in the inference. Maisie Hudson was, according to the not-always-reliable rumor mill, the woman currently having an affair with Larry Carr.

"I know." Braddock actually had considered the possibility of Bobby Hudson being the shooter. But the man was just so docile and meek. Maybe that was the problem with his marriage to Maisie. "But I can hardly see Bobby getting out a rifle and waiting for Larry to come along... Can you?"

"No, not at all. But maybe another man whose wife was—"

"We can speculate all day long, Cath, but why don't I call the detective—I have his card—and ask him what he knows at this point. I can get back to you after I speak with him."

"Oh yes, would you? I was thinking of calling myself, but I'd trust you to know better what to ask."

"I will, I promise. I'll call him right away."

"Thank you so much, Matt. I really, really appreciate it. By the way, I'll let you know about the service here. He's going to be buried up in Connecticut. Family plot."

"Thank you, Cath. I'll be in touch soon."

*****

He went back to watching the waves crash.

Then he walked back inside to what he called the den, his daughter called the library, and his short-lived model girlfriend called his man cave. He took out his MacBook Air and wrote down a list of questions he wanted to ask the Delray detective, Jason Fisher, whom he had met briefly after Carr was shot. He had learned subsequently that Fisher was the lead detective on the case. When it came to asking questions of Fisher, Braddock didn't want to wing it; he wanted to be deliberate and specific with what he asked.

The den was his favorite room in the large condominium, unless you counted the sun porch which was not really a room. In addition to two floor-to-ceiling walls of books, it had a lot of plants and small trees: two bougainvilleas, two silk trees, a six-foot golden cane palm, and a four-foot lemon tree. All fake. When he was living with Jennifer, everything in the room was live and real, but she'd had a green thumb. Braddock did not. Plus, he was a lousy pruner.

He spent the next twenty minutes typing questions on his MacBook Air, reading them over, making a few changes, then he dialed Jason Fisher's number.

He fully expected his call to go to voicemail, but instead Fisher answered in a deep baritone. "How can I help you, Mr. Braddock?"

"You remember me, I was playing golf with—"

"I remember. How can I help?"

"Well, I was wondering if you have any suspects yet."

"As I'm sure you can appreciate, I can't go into great detail at the moment. It's an active investigation and I don't make a habit of disclosing information to the public."

"Detective Fisher, I'm hardly 'the public.' Larry Carr was a good friend of mine. I was by his side when he died, and I'm hoping his killer can be caught as soon as possible."

"Okay, Mr. Braddock, without meaning to sound like a wise guy, that makes two of us. Catching him as soon as possible, that is. I can tell you this, in addition to me, our top homicide detective is also working the case and we'll be going full speed ahead until we catch the perpetrator."

Braddock glanced down at his computer. "Good to know," he said. "Do you want me to fill you in on Larry's personal life? I know quite a lot about him. It might be helpful."

"All in due time, Mr. Braddock. We're working the case the way we always work a case. But I'll make note that you're a source to talk to about Mr. Carr's personal life."

"You don't want me to tell you now?"

"No, Mr. Braddock. I've got my hands full at the moment."

"It'll take no more than ten minutes to give you some information that I think might be vital to you."

Fisher sighed deep and dramatically. "Mr. Braddock"—a long, dramatic pause—"you are very persistent. So I want to say this as diplomatically as possible: the last thing we need is a bunch of amateurs gumming up the works."

Matt chuckled. "Not too diplomatic, Detective," he said. "But I don't need diplomacy. For one thing, I'm not a *bunch*, I'm one man.

Second of all, I need you to solve my friend's murder, and all I'm trying to do is offer you some background that might be helpful."

"I have your number, Mr. Braddock, and I will get back to you. I have to go now," Fisher said and clicked off.

Matt stared down at his MacBook Air. He still had eight more questions to ask.

FOUR

"How long's it been since it happened?" Ingrid asked her friend, Stephanie. They were in their usual chaise lounges at the pool.

"Since Larry Carr got killed, you mean?"

"Yes."

"Um, about three days."

Stephanie sat up and hiked up her zebra-striped bikini top. "I read somewhere that if the police don't catch the killer in the first forty-eight hours, chances are cut in half they ever will."

Ingrid chuckled. "Another subject you're an expert on?"

"No, I'm serious. I haven't heard about any cops on the case. Except right after it happened."

Ingrid turned to Stephanie and squinted. "That's actually not true. This morning two detectives—I think there were two—went door to door in my building. They talked to everyone who was there."

"Oh, really, that's news to me. What did they ask?"

"I don't know exactly. I was at Pilates. But Burt told me that one of the things they asked was if he had heard any kind of a loud noise or pop on Monday morning."

"Like a gunshot, you mean?"

"Exactly."

"And what did Burt say?"

"He said no. We both were in the condo when it happened and didn't hear a thing."

"What else—" Stephanie was suddenly distracted by a shirtless man in a blue bathing suit. "Who's that?"

Ingrid swung around and looked. "Oh, he's a new guy. Single, I'm pretty sure. I met him at croquet. He said he was trying to meet women."

"He actually told you that?"

"Not me. He told Burt. You know, one of those things men say to each other with that pathetic little wink of theirs."

"I hate winkers. What did Burt say?"

"Told him his best bet was on the beach. Early morning yoga. The guy—his name's Todd—said, 'Forget it, I don't get up before nine.'"

Stephanie gave Todd another look. "So much for yoga, he clearly spends some time in the gym… Where were we?"

"So these detectives were there for a while asking questions."

"Well, that's good to hear," Stephanie said. "I'm not too keen on their being a killer running loose."

Ingrid laughed. "You can say that again."

Stephanie didn't.

*****

Detectives Jason Fisher and Tambor Malmstrom were back at their station after spending two hours questioning residents of the south building at the Island Club. They had split up when they were at the building and were now comparing notes. They didn't have much to compare because they hadn't come up with anything. No one had heard a shot. No one had seen anything unusual. Just another day at the south building.

"But his widow was kinda hot," Malmstrom said to Fisher.

"Easy, Tam," Fisher said. "That's not the way to describe the grieving spouse."

Malmstrom raised his hand. "Sorry, man. But did you get the sense that maybe the husband, the vic…played around a little?"

"How'd you come up with that?"

"I don't know…when you asked her if he worked or was re-tired and she said he sold his company a little while back, she added something like, 'He spent a fair amount of time away from home.'"

"She could have just meant playing golf."

"Maybe. But I didn't get that feeling."

Fisher nodded. "Actually, now that you mention it, I kind of got the same vibe from another woman in the building. I asked her if she knew Carr and she first answered 'no', but then said, 'But I know *about* him.' I asked her what she meant by that and she said, 'I just heard he liked the ladies.'"

"There you go," Malmstrom said. "So now maybe we got the jealous husband or boyfriend angle."

"I guess so," Fisher said. "I'm gonna get that guy Matt Braddock from Carr's foursome to come in. He seems real eager to tell me all about Carr."

"Why's he so eager?"

"Beats me," Fisher said. "Maybe wants to play amateur sleuth or something."

FIVE

Frank Diehl owned a large portfolio of commercial and residential buildings stretching from West Palm Beach up to the Jupiter area. Included in that was a thirty-story building in West Palm Beach where a nightclub called Narcissism, owned by Diehl, occupied the first two floors. Aside from being a real estate investor and club owner, Diehl was also in the dating site business and owned a company called dreammates.com—like match.com or eHarmony.

Diehl's private club, Narcissism, had a separate address on Narcissus Avenue. Diehl loved having the custom address and he knew full well that it was because, in fact, he indeed possessed a considerable amount of narcissism. Not only that, he viewed narcissism as a good thing, not a character flaw, as some did.

It was Tuesday night at Narcissism and Diehl was expecting all the regulars plus some new couples that came highly recommended as possible new members. Couples began drifting into the bar at around nine o'clock—no dinner was served on Mondays and Tuesdays—but drinks were free, which members took full advantage of. Dues, however, were three thousand dollars a month. Nobody complained about that, though, because members got their money's worth in…less tangible ways. Champagne was a drink favored by much of the clientele, and Diehl didn't scrimp or serve the cheap stuff. Veuve Clicquot, Louis Roederer, and Dom Perignon were the brands the bar stocked.

If Narcissism only broke even, that would have been fine with Diehl. But it didn't. It did way better than break even. He referred to it as his *side hustle*, and what a hustle it was.

*****

Cindy and Karl Doheny were sitting at a table with Gary and Anneke Melindez.

"How's business, Karl?" Gary asked.

Karl shot Gary a thumbs-up. "The market may be down, but people are spending like crazy."

Karl Doheny owned a third-generation jewelry store on Worth Avenue in Palm Beach. Those in the know preferred it over Tiffany and Cartier, also located there.

"How 'bout you?" Karl asked. "How's the chopping business?"

Gary was a thoracic surgeon who had a thriving practice in West Palm.

"Good. Still banging out the triple bypasses," Gary said.

"Please, Gary," Anneke said, feigning shock. "I don't think your patients would like to hear you say you're *banging* 'em out."

"Aw, screw 'em if they can't take a joke," Gary said and laughed heartily as Karl raised a champagne flute.

"How 'bout you, Anneke, you're still flying, right?" Karl asked.

Gary Melindez had met his wife, Anneke, in the first-class section on a flight to Amsterdam. She was a flight attendant. She was thirty-nine years old, buxom, and had a beautiful wrinkle-free face, which she spent a fortune on maintaining.

"Yes, Gary wants me to stop, but I love it," Anneke said with the trace of a Dutch accent.

"It's those layover nights in Amsterdam, after she's had a couple of pops, that I worry about," Gary said. "An old boyfriend or someone putting the moves on her."

Karl turned to Gary and lowered his voice. "I don't blame you; I might worry too."

But Anneke heard him. "Oh, stop, you two," she said. "In case you've forgotten Gary, I took a vow. Remember?"

Gary put up his hands. "Yeah, yeah, yeah. Which all of us honor…most of the time."

All four laughed.

"Speaking of which," Karl said, putting his hand on his chair to stand. "Shall we?"

Narcissism had nine bedrooms split between the remainder of the first floor and on the second floor. They would all be in full use by the end of the night.

SIX

Braddock was surprised at the tone in detective Jason Fisher's voice as Fisher requested that he come into the Delray Police station for an interview. It sounded much different than two days earlier, when it had been patronizing, haughty even. They set a time for two in the afternoon.

Fisher and his partner, Tambor Malmstrom, met Braddock in the reception area of the police station on West Atlantic, and Fisher led them over to a far corner. Fisher, who Braddock pegged as being in his late thirties, was a short, compact man with dark brown hair and eyes that constantly darted around, like he was wary of everyone in the immediate vicinity. Malmstrom was big, bulky and a year or two away from being completely bald. Braddock figured him to be around his age, mid-forties or so.

"It would be a little tight in my cubicle," Fisher explained to Braddock as they all sat down. "So, Mr. Braddock, I may have come off a little, ah, blunt with you the other day, and I apologize for that. I'll level with you: we need all the help we can get and would appreciate everything you can tell us about Mr. Carr."

"And also," Malmstrom added, "anything you can about someone who may have wanted to kill him. We'll take theories, hunches, anything ya got."

"Okay, so I guess nothing panned out when you talked to the residents in buildings 3 and 4?"

Fisher glanced at Malmstrom, then Braddock. "Yeah, I'd say that's pretty accurate. The one thing we heard more than once was that Carr was a—how should I put it?—a ladies' man."

"And we could use some details on that," Malmstrom added.

"Okay, I'll tell you what I know because Larry was, as I told you, a good friend of mine."

Fisher nodded.

"He was married, had three kids and a place up in Greenwich, Connecticut—I still can't get used to the past tense—and used to have a business headquartered in Stamford, Connecticut, which he sold last year or the year before."

"Mrs. Carr said it was a reinsurance business, right?" Fisher asked.

"Yes, exactly, he and his brother inherited it from their father, and Larry once told me it didn't end too well between them."

"He and his brother?" Malmstrom said.

Braddock nodded.

Fisher was taking notes on an iPad, while Malmstrom did the same on a black leather note pad that looked like something he had, also, inherited from his father.

"'Didn't end too well?'" Fisher repeated. "Like what happened?"

"Well, from what I understand, Larry, who ran the company, figured he should get a lot more than his brother got when it was sold. His brother, Neil, basically had a token job partly because he was in and out of rehab facilities."

"For drinking or what?" Malmstrom asked.

"Drinking, drugs, whatever he could get his hands on, apparently," Braddock said, raising a hand. "But you gotta remember, this was Larry doing the explaining. His brother might have a totally different story."

"Have you ever met Neil?" Fisher asked.

"Never have. Larry told me they didn't speak too much anymore. I didn't get the sense that they were totally estranged, but not that close either."

Fisher tapped the side of his chair. "Do you think we should put him on our list of possible suspects?"

"I thought about that." Braddock had thought about a lot of possibilities earlier in the day, as he watched the waves crash from his condominium. "But I'd tend to doubt it. First of all, if Neil ever thought he was getting screwed so badly that he wanted to kill his brother, wouldn't that have happened a while back? Instead of, whatever, a year and a half later? And, secondly, it strikes me that Larry's murder was almost…professional. I mean, done by someone who knew what he was doing. Someone who could shoot. But just so you know, Neil does have a house not far away."

"Whereabouts?" Fisher asked.

"Palm Beach."

Fisher leaned forward. "That's good information, Mr. Braddock. I'd say Neil's certainly someone we should talk to"—he glanced over at Malmstrom—"especially if he was down here at the time of his brother's murder."

Malmstrom nodded. "That's one more guy than we had on our list."

"Keep going, Mr. Braddock," Fisher said.

"I've got a suggestion," said Braddock. "How about if I'm Matt and you guys are Jason and..." He turned to Malmstrom. "Sorry, never caught your name?"

"Tambor."

"Okay," Braddock said with a nod. "Might make it easier."

"Okay, Matt, fair enough," Fisher said. "So I want to get into this subject of Mr. Carr 'liking the ladies' and being 'a ladies' man.'"

"I figured you would."

"Yeah, I mean, we've heard it at least three times," Malmstrom said.

"Can you give that as much detail as possible," Fisher said. "I mean, let's face it, it wouldn't be the first time a man was killed for having a relationship with a married woman."

"Or a woman who was another man's girlfriend," Malmstrom added.

"Yes, I know," Braddock said. "Probably one of the oldest motives in the book, right?"

"Right up there," said Fisher.

Braddock slouched back in his chair. "Well, I kind of hate to say it, but it's almost like...where do I start?"

"How 'bout when you first heard about him being a...ladies' man."

Braddock cleared his voice. "Or *man whore,* as a guy once called him."

Fisher laughed. "That's pretty strong."

Braddock nodded. "That's what I thought, too. So anyway, I met Larry on the golf course when I first moved down here. Guys would make little jibes out there like, 'Who's the latest, Larry?' Or 'You look like you had a long night.' It didn't take me long to figure out what they were talking about."

"A lot of that go on at the Island Club?" Malmstrom asked.

Fisher shot his partner a look like that was either an out-of-bounds question or not relevant.

"No, actually not," Braddock said. "Partly because most of the membership is pretty old. And partly because, well…it just isn't like that."

Which was mainly because the old folks were too fragile to take off their clothes and bed-wrestle, Braddock mused to himself.

Fisher and Malmstrom nodded.

"Anyway, yes, Larry was a…well, there's just no other way to say it, an inveterate womanizer. Usually, he was pretty subtle about it, but I knew. A lot of other people knew, too. I think sometimes he had affairs with two different women at the same time."

"Married women?" Fisher asked.

Braddock nodded. "Yes, at least in two cases, I remember."

"And you're probably not going to tell us, but I'll ask anyway… What were their names?" Fisher asked.

"I knew you'd get around to that."

Fisher nodded. "Well, of course, since their husbands or boyfriends are possible suspects."

"I get it," Braddock said. "I'll tell you about a few who aren't members of my club. One's name is Holly Gardiner. She's a member at the Gulf Stream T & B—"

"Which stands for what again?" Malmstrom asked.

"Tennis and Beach Club."

"Oh, right," Malmstrom said.

"I think it went on for quite a while with her," Braddock said. "Couple years or so. Then there was a woman at the Refuge, Sally, ah, can't remember her last name."

"But what about at your club?"

Braddock avoided Fisher's eyes. "I told you I wasn't going to name names, but let's just say, there were a fair number of rumors."

"Come on, Matt," Fisher said. "I know you're being protective of your Island Club members, but help us get to the bottom of this."

Braddock slowly shook his head. "And what would happen if you were to go to a woman, or her husband, or both, and say, 'So Mrs. X, we know you were having a raging affair with Larry Carr, tell us all about it.' And she'd go, 'Where in God's name did you hear that?' And you'd hem and haw, and she'd snap her fingers and go, 'Oh I know, it was Matt Braddock, wasn't it? I heard he's been poking around.'"

"Wait a minute," Fisher said, holding up his hands. "How would she make that leap?"

Braddock was silent for a few moments. "I don't know. Look, I've given you enough to work on. Let's just leave it there."

"Come on," Malmstrom said. "You might be leaving out the best suspect."

Braddock held up his hands. "Sorry, that's all you're going to get out of me. But by my count I've given you at least three possible suspects to look into."

"And we're grateful to you," Fisher said. "But how 'bout a fourth?"

"Nope," Braddock said, getting to his feet. "Gotta get going. I got things I need to do."

Fisher and Malmstrom got to their feet too. Fisher stuck out his hand. "Hey, thanks a lot, Matt. Appreciate your time."

Then Malmstrom shook hands with him. "Yes. We'll be in touch."

*****

Braddock hadn't thought of doing it before meeting with Fisher and Malmstrom, but decided, spur-of-the-moment, to give Larry Carr's brother, Neil, a call.

Then, just as quickly, he decided not to. Who the hell was he, Sam Spade? *Come on, man, stick to golf. Get that very expensive boat of yours out on the water.*

After a few minutes of internal debate, he overruled himself and decided he was going to contact Neil Carr after all. Something about feeding those detectives information, feeling a sort of kinship with them…it sudddenly seemed like heady stuff, and he was feeling caught up in the case. He better do it quick, though, he decided, before Fisher and Malmstrom got to Neil. So he did. First, he called Catherine Carr and asked if she had Neil's number.

"Yes, somewhere," Catherine said. "It's not a number that Larry called a lot anymore."

"You didn't talk to him after what happened?" Braddock said.

"No, 'cause he found out about it. Sent me an email right away saying how shocked and sorry he was. But we never talked. Which reminds me, I've got to email him and tell him when and where the funeral is… Oh, here it is." She read him a phone number.

"Thanks, Cath, I appreciate it."

"What are you going to talk to him about anyway?"

"I don't know. I just…I just really want whoever did it to be caught."

"You think Neil might have done it? Because of the business thing?"

"No, not really. Just a place to start, you know."

"Well, good luck. I'm sure Larry would be happy about what you're doing."

"I'm not really doing anything."

"I know…but…well, good luck anyway."

*****

He called Neil Carr that afternoon. Neil Carr was drunk.

"Whad ya say your name wass again?" Carr asked.

"Matt Braddock. Your brother and I were friends. My condolences, by the way."

"Well, thanks, but if you were a friend of Larry's, you probably know we weren't all that tight."

"He mentioned that. I'm down in Delray but I planned to be up in Palm Beach tomorrow and wondered if I could stop by."

"Stop by. What for?" Carr said.

Now that was a damn good question. *'Cause all my life I've secretly yearned to be a gumshoe?* He couldn't come up with a good answer. Fortunately, Neil plowed ahead.

"Wait a minute. Matt Braddock, I know that name. Are you the guy at Blackstone?"

"*Was* at Blackstone."

"Oh, yeah, I read about you. Some big pharma deal or something. And that tech start-up the Facebook guy paid billions for. I was in the reinsurance business."

"I know. So, any time tomorrow work?"

"Yeah, sure. Drop by for lunch why don'tcha? Twelve thirty." And Neil gave him his address.

"Okay, great, see you then."

Braddock hung up and asked himself what the hell he planned to accomplish going to a drunk's house for lunch when he could have been out on the ocean hauling in a nice billfish.

SEVEN

Hunter Snow was not his real name. But Cyrus Dalyrimple, the name he was born with, was not only lame, but also had way too many syllables. And *Hunter*? Well, how appropriate was that?

He was with Rainey—not her real name either—stretched out in two chaise lounges at the exclusive Vicenza condominium building in Palm Beach. Hunter, who had done a fair amount of traveling in his thirty-two years, wondered why it was that just about every city of any consequence in Italy had a condo named after it in Florida. He was going down the list in his head—Milano, Positano, Portofino, actually two in West Palm alone, Verona, Livorno, Padua, the list went on—when he spotted a man in his seventies or eighties with a big gut and a flashy wristwatch shuffling toward a chaise. He recognized the bathing suit as a Vilebrequin, which he knew started at around $250. All good signs.

He gave Rainey a little poke with his toe, then flicked his head in the direction of the man.

Rainey shaded her eyes, looked over at the man, then back to Hunter. "Perfect."

"I thought so too," Hunter said.

"Make it happen, maestro," Rainey said, watching the man stretch out in the chaise.

Hunter just smiled and nodded. *Child's play*.

He mulled over his approach for the next few minutes, then got up.

He walked over to the man. "Excuse me, sir," he said. "I've been admiring your bathing suit. Is that a Vilebrequin, by any chance?"

The man looked up at him and shaded his eyes. "Sure is. Just got it a couple of days ago."

"I love their suits. Is there a store around here that sells 'em?" Hunter asked, sitting down in a chaise next to the man.

"Yeah, there is. On Worth Avenue."

"I should have figured there'd be one there," Hunter said. "It's French, right?"

"Yeah, I guess so," the man said, rubbing his chin and smiling. "Cost me a goddamn arm and a leg."

"Yeah, but they're the best," Hunter said, putting out his hand. "I'm Hunter, by the way."

"Sam. Sam Camposi."

"Hey, Sam. You live here at the Vicenza?"

"Yeah, well in the winter. Up in Cleveland the rest of the time."

"Oh, really," Hunter said. "I've got a friend up in Gates Mills."

"Nice place," Sam said. "I'm from Chagrin Falls."

Hunter laughed. "Chagrin Falls…Gates Mills, how can you keep 'em straight?"

Sam laughed. "Never thought of that," he said. "How 'bout you? You live in the building?"

"Nah, my uncle's got a place here. I come over and mooch lunch off him occasionally."

Sam nodded. "How come you're not working?"

I am, Hunter didn't say. "On vacation. I work at Goldman Sachs."

Sam nodded. "Oh, over at Phillips Point?"

"Yup," Hunter said, not wanting to field too many questions on a subject he knew next to nothing about. He could only bullshit so far. "How 'bout you, you retired or what?"

Sam nodded. "Yeah, after fifty years in the muffler business"—he shot Hunter a thumbs-up—"but it was very good to me."

Hunter slapped Sam on the knee. "Cars gotta have mufflers, right?"

"Except electric ones."

Hunter glanced over at Rainey and gave her an imperceptible nod.

Hunter glanced down at Sam's wedding ring. "So where's Mrs. Camposi?"

Sam shook his head. "Speaking of fifty years."

"You've been married fifty years?"

"Almost. Forty-eight, actually."

"Congratulations."

"It ain't all roses and caviar, my friend," Sam lamented.

"Hey, Hunter," Rainey said, looming above the two men. All tanned, curvy and firm-breasted. "Introduce me to your friend."

Sam shaded his eyes and smiled ear to ear, clearly liking what he was seeing.

"Oh, hey," Hunter said. "This is Sam. Sam, meet my cousin, Rainey."

"How's it goin', Rainey?" Sam said, his smile broadening. "Pull up a chair. Any cousin of Hunter's is a friend of mine."

Rainey laughed a little harder than Sam's quip deserved and sat down in another chaise as Sam did his best to suck in his gut.

"So, I know a little about Hunter," Sam said. "Tell me all about you."

"Well, there's not that much to tell. I'm a real estate agent, I live in West Palm and...Hunter's been my cousin...all my life."

The West Palm part was true.

Sam laughed. "Which one?"

"Which one what?" Rainey said, bending forward slightly and giving Sam a visual treat.

"Which real estate company?" Sam asked.

"Oh, ah, Coldwell," she said, not remembering the rest of the name.

It didn't matter because all Sam was thinking about was her substantial breasts.

"Well, you guys," Hunter said, "I'm gonna excuse myself." Then, to Sam, "Gotta hit the head."

Sam nodded. It was clear he was thinking something along the lines of, *No need to hurry back, pal,* as Rainey gave Hunter a little wave and he walked away.

"So back to you, Sam," Rainey said. "What do you like to do in your spare time?"

"Well," Sam said, raising his head so his turkey neck would be less pronounced. "Fact of the matter is, spare time's all I have. I'm not a golfer or a boater or anything like that. I like some of the shows at the Kravis Center, go to the Four Arts every once in a while..."

"You're married, right?"

"Well, yeah, but..."

Rainey laughed and ran her hand through her bleached blond hair. "'But?' What do you mean 'but'?"

"Well, I..."

"Might have some of that spare time"—she curled a finger seductively at Sam—"for me?"

Sam nodded nervously.

Clearly, it had been a long, long time since a woman like Rainey had paid any attention to Sam.

Probably, never.

EIGHT

Larry Carr's brother Neil's drink of choice seemed to be red wine. But then, after knocking back a bottle of Chateau La...something, he switched over to the hard stuff: George Dickel.

Bourbon in the middle of the day... *Ugh*, thought Braddock.

"So, you retired. How old were you?" Neil asked him.

"Forty-six."

"My company got bought out when I was fifty-five," Neil said, "and big brother was fifty-eight."

Braddock wondered how Larry Carr would feel about his brother calling it, "my company."

They were sitting at a mahogany table in the penthouse of a twenty-story condo building in Palm Beach overlooking the ocean. Carr had given Braddock a quick tour, and Braddock had decided that he preferred his ocean view from the second story. He could see people and surfers and boats, whereas on the twentieth floor, the people and surfers were more like specks, and the boats looked like something you'd find bobbing in a kid's bathtub.

"What did you do after you got bought out?" Braddock asked.

"A lot of this," Neil said, hefting his George Dickel. "Too damn much, in fact. Then I was kind of a consultant on the side, but that didn't last long. So I guess you could say I didn't do shit."

"Yeah, I guess I could say the same thing," Braddock said, wiping his mouth with a white cloth napkin.

After they had been sitting for a few minutes, a Hispanic woman in a light blue uniform brought out two plates which featured cold salmon.

"Oh, this is Valeria," Neil said, then to Valeria. "Mr. Braddock."

Braddock smiled and nodded. "Hi, Valeria, it looks delicious."

"Thank you, sir," she said, doing a kind of curtsy, then walked away.

Braddock took a bite of his salmon.

"But not big brother," Neil said.

Braddock wasn't sure what he was referring to. "Excuse me?"

"Larry. Larry didn't rest on his laurels," Carr said. "Hooked up with a guy from around here. Invested in the guy's business, actually had some input in it, as I understand it."

Larry Carr had never mentioned this to Braddock.

"What kind of business was it?"

Carr took a long pull on his George Dickel and winced a little. "I kept trying to get Larry to tell me more, back in the days when we were speaking a little, but he never really did. It had to do with those of the distaff persuasion."

"You mean women?" Braddock said, putting his fork down.

"Yeah, why? You surprised?" Neil's head was weaving, like it was not that solidly attached to his neck. A drunk's tell.

"Larry never said a word about it. At least not to me."

Neil took a pull on his Dickel and downed it. "Well, I don't know that much. From what I could piece together, it was like this online dating company. Like that one, Operation Match, I think they call it."

Braddock nodded his head. "I think it's just Match."

"Yeah, whatever, but the guy Larry invested with had a bunch of real estate holdings, too, and s'posedly some nightclub."

This was getting interesting.

"So the online dating thing...I'm guessing they had a website where you could go and find...dates."

"Yeah, I think they called 'em 'companions,' which, when you think about it, was right in Larry's wheelhouse. You know, women looking for love, Larry...looking for action."

"You remember the name of it?"

Neil nodded. "He told me once... dreammates.com."

"Do you have any idea how much Larry invested in it?"

"He told me two tranches of a million and a half."

"So, three million total. You know what his ownership share was?"

"That I don't know," Neil said, pointing at Braddock's plate. "Hey, eat your salmon, it's good."

Braddock took a bite. "Damn good. Thanks for having me over, by the way."

Neil raised his empty glass. "Yeah, sure. I actually recognized your name when you called. I had no idea you were a friend of Larry's." He looked at his glass and shouted, "Valeria! More booze."

A few moments later Valeria came scurrying out with another bourbon and ice.

Neil looked down at Braddock's almost-empty wine glass. "How about you, another white wine?"

"No, thanks," Braddock said. "I have two glasses during the day and I've gotta take a little siesta."

Neil laughed. "Which in my case is called passing out."

Braddock raised his wine glass. "So I'm intrigued about…Larry's investment. Do you know how he got into it?"

"Sorry, can't help you there. He told me once it was the best investment he ever made. Monetarily and *otherwise*."

"What did he mean by that?"

"Well, I think it's pretty obvious. But I asked him anyway and he just smiled that little shit-eating grin of his and said, 'That's all I'm gonna say on the subject.'"

Braddock nodded. "You know anyone else who might know about it?"

"Um, not that I can think of off the top of my head," he said. "Maybe Catherine."

Braddock tapped the glass tabletop. "I'll ask her. You got me dying of curiosity."

Neil shrugged. "She may know nothing; she may know everything."

"So how 'bout you," Braddock said. "What do you do to keep busy?"

"You're lookin' at it," Neil said. "Fell off the wagon three months ago. But I also play a little tennis, go to an occasional concert at the Kravis, chase women—ineffectively, I might add. Never had Larry's touch."

Braddock glanced at Neil's gold wedding band.

Neil intercepted his look. "Oh, that. My wife died about six months ago and I've just never gotten around to taking it off."

Braddock nodded. "Sorry to hear that."

"Yeah, cancer."

Braddock nodded and waited a few respectful moments before plunging back in. "So I'm sure you've thought about it... Who do you think might have killed Larry?"

Neil stared off into the distance. "Yeah, I have thought about it, quite a bit actually, but I just really don't have a clue. I mean, there's always the pissed-off husband angle."

"Mm-hmm. Maybe several."

"So, what do you think? And why are you so interested in the whole thing?"

"Like you I have no idea at this point. And why am I so interested? That's a question I've been asking myself. I mean, Larry and I were friends, but not best friends... I guess maybe I just like to find answers to things. Fix things, figure 'em out, that's basically what I did for twenty-five years at Blackstone. I guess I miss doin' it," Braddock took a last sip of wine and continued. "But also, I was there when he was shot. I saw him lying there on the ground. Taking his last breaths. I feel...I feel, I don't know, that somehow, I owe Larry."

Neil nodded. "I understand. I totally get it," he said. "And you're not alone at missing stuff. I have some friends who are retired and bored as hell. Not all of 'em, but enough. I mean, they're on boards, get into philanthropic shit, play a lot of golf, but you ask 'em after a couple of pops, they'll tell you they're bored out of their minds."

"Yeah, and if I'm being straight with you, I'm a little bored myself."

Neil smiled broadly. "So you thought a little Sherlock Holmes mystery solving might change that?"

Braddock wondered why the hell he was opening up to a self-confessed drunk. He shrugged and nodded.

"Well," Neil said, "get out there with your pipe and goofy deerstalker hat and solve the sucker! Even though we had our issues, I really hope the guy who did it gets caught. I'm also curious as hell to know what his motive was."

"Yes, me too." Braddock had finished his salmon and wine. "Well, thank you so much for the delicious lunch and the wine, now I'm going to go put on the goofy deerstalker hat and solve this sucker."

Neil smiled and shot him a thumbs-up.

Braddock got to his feet. Neil did too, but much more unsteadily. "All right. Well, good to have met such a legend in high finance. Keep me up to speed, and if I have any thoughts that I think might be useful, I'll give you a call."

"Please do," Braddock said, putting out his hand.

They shook and Braddock walked through the house and out the front door.

He knew a lot more now than when he walked through the door an hour earlier.

NINE

Braddock decided when he got home to call Chris Coolidge and Jack Vandevere, the other two in the ill-fated foursome. He wanted to pick their brains about the moment it took place. For Braddock, it was all a blur, since he'd been solely focused on helping Carr.

He asked if he could come by the other men's houses as soon as possible and arranged to meet with Vandevere at 5:00 p.m. and Coolidge at nine the next morning.

Vandevere wasn't that helpful, though he did remind Braddock about seeing the white boat with the black hull—one minute it was there, the next it was gone.

"And did you see anyone on it?" Braddock asked.

"Not that I remember. I just saw it for a split second, then I turned back to Larry. Next time I looked it was gone."

"Did you get a sense how big it was? How many feet long?"

"Um, I would say not as long as yours, maybe ten feet shorter."

Braddock had a forty-five-foot Viking sport fishing boat.

Aside from that, all Vandevere remembered was hearing a "groan," then looking down at Carr on the ground. He described it as being "unimaginable," his friend lying there with a widening patch of blood on his chest. When Braddock asked him if he saw or heard anything around them that might have been related to where the shot had come from, he shook his head and said "no." His first instinct, he said, had been to run, thinking his own life might be in danger. Braddock figured that was logical, though he hadn't experienced that reaction.

That was it. After a bit of small talk, Braddock left Vandevere's house at 5:35 p.m.

*****

Meeting with Chris Coolidge the next morning was more productive. Coolidge fixed them up with mugs of coffee, and they sat in his living room. Braddock told him that Jack Vandevere's first reaction had been to bolt when Larry Carr got shot.

That started Coolidge nodding. "Mine was similar. I was off to the left of you guys and my first instinct was to stay there, that it was safer there, but something made me run over to you guys. I remembered, as I was running, to cover my head with my arms." Coolidge laughed. "A lot of good that would have done."

"Did you look around at all? Try to figure out where the shot came from?"

"Yeah, I did actually. I looked at the condo building to the south first, then out at buildings on the other side of the Intracoastal."

That was something that Braddock had never considered—buildings across the Intracoastal.

"Did you see anything? Any movement?"

"No, nothing."

"And you never saw that boat that Jack mentioned?"

"With the black hull? No, I never did," Coolidge said. "You know if the detectives have come up with anything yet?"

Braddock shrugged. "I don't think much. They canvassed those condo buildings and got nothing."

Coolidge, coffee mug in hand, leaned back in the sofa he was sitting in. "I've got a question for you, Matt."

"Shoot."

"Why are you so interested in this?"

That question again.

He certainly understood why everyone was asking it.

"I don't know, man, I just…I don't know. I guess it may be as basic as I don't want someone getting away with murder. Particularly, my friend."

He could have done better but that was all he could come up with at the moment.

"Why don't you just let the cops handle it? It's their job, you know…what they were trained for."

It was obvious and true.

"Well, goes without saying I want them to solve it. But maybe I can help somehow."

"Or maybe you'll just get in the way. It's not like you have a lot of experience in solving murders that I'm aware of."

"True. The way I see it is maybe I can dig up some stuff that the detectives can't. Because I'm an insider and they're outsiders. Maybe find stuff they can't."

Coolidge shrugged. "Maybe."

But it was clear he wasn't convinced.

"Well, listen," Braddock said. "I appreciate it. You were helpful. Thanks for letting me come over and for the coffee."

"You got it. You want to play tomorrow?" Coolidge asked, referring to golf.

"Um, maybe later in the week. I'm going to take my boat out."

Coolidge smiled. "Well, if you see a white boat with a black hull, call the cops."

*****

Braddock actually had had no intention of taking his boat out until Jack Vandevere reminded him about the thirty-foot boat with the black hull. He laughed at himself, it was like all of a sudden, he was playing Harrison Ford in *The Fugitive,* searching for the one-armed man. After he left Coolidge's house, he phoned his boat captain. He paid Chuck Day a yearly salary to run his boat and lately hadn't been getting his money's worth.

Day sounded excited to hear from Braddock, as if he was thinking his boss might be losing interest in bouncing around on the Atlantic.

"Want me to get a mate?" Day asked.

"Nah, not necessary, 'cause we're not going fishing."

"We're not," Day said, sounding surprised. "Well, what are we doing?"

"Exploring."

"Okay, I'm a good explorer."

After he hung up with Day, he walked down to the golf course. His condominium overlooked the ocean and the Island Club's golf course was on the other side of North Ocean Boulevard, between North Ocean Boulevard and the Intracoastal. He walked across the road and onto club property, waved at Darlene, the woman at the guard house, and walked up to the northern end of the club's property, which was where the golf course ended. He cut in behind the tee on the seventh hole of the course and headed toward the fifth hole, which ran along the Intracoastal, north to south.

As he walked along the side of the sixth hole, he saw a two-some up ahead. He knew both men. One of them spotted him.

"Hey, Matt, whatcha doin'?" the man asked quizzically. "You're going in the wrong direction."

Braddock had not prepared an answer. "Just taking a little walk. Keeping an eye out for lost balls."

Both men looked at him askance. One of them reached into his golf bag and pulled out a sleeve of new balls. "Well, here you go, this ought to tide you over for a while."

The other man laughed.

"Thanks, but you keep 'em, Bennie," Braddock said. "I like ones with a little more wear and tear on 'em. Have a good round, boys."

He started walking.

He heard the men laugh behind him as he approached the sixth tee and the fifth green.

Then something suddenly dawned on him as he glanced to his right and through some trees, where he could make out a row of metal trailers. *Whispering Pines* was a massive trailer park that bordered the Island Club on the north and ran from the ocean to the Intracoastal. Someone had once told Braddock that it actually had been incorporated as a town back in the sixties and had close to five hundred trailers on separate lots with six hundred feet of ocean and Intracoastal frontage. He also remembered hearing that twenty years ago a developer had come along and offered $500 million to buy the hamlet and all its trailers. He knew the deal had fallen through, somehow, but didn't remember why.

He walked farther to his right and parted the branches of a tree.

There were at least five trailers that had unobstructed views of where Larry Carr had been shot.

TEN

As he turned back and walked down the fifth fairway, he saw a golfer up ahead. It was a woman wearing sunglasses and pushing a golf cart. As she got closer, he realized that he didn't recognize her, which was odd because he knew almost all Island Club members by sight.

"You're going the wrong way," she said with a smile as she approached him.

"You're the second person to point that out," Braddock said, taking off his golf cap. "I'm Matt Braddock, just out for a little stroll."

"And I'm Leah Bliss, just out drowning a few golf balls."

"Are you a new member?" he asked looking at her ring finger. Nothing there.

"Yes, just joined a few weeks ago," she said.

He guessed she was in her mid-thirties. She had long blond hair, a spray of youthful-looking freckles, cobalt blue eyes, and the figure of a woman who was a gym regular.

"Well, if I'm not being too forward, can I buy you a 'welcome to the club' cocktail?" he asked, having decided some time ago that being too quick on the trigger was better than being too slow, then regretting it afterward.

She smiled a dazzling smile. "Sure. That would be nice. When were you thinking?"

"Well, let's see, I've got nothing going on tonight, tomorrow, the next night…"

"Are you unpopular or something, Matt?" she joked.

"No, just single in a couples world," Braddock said. "I am doing something on Saturday, though."

She smiled that smile again. "Oh, well, good…so let's do tonight then. Where were you thinking?"

"The bar at the club. Can I pick you up?"

She shook her head. "No need. I live right over there." She turned and pointed at one of the club's buildings. "Probably about a hundred steps to the bar."

"Sounds good," he said. "Well, I'll let you get back to your game. Is six o'clock good?"

"Perfect," she said. "That's a record, by the way."

"What do you mean?"

"The shortest time between meeting someone and having been asked out."

He laughed. "For me too."

"Bye, Matt."

"Bye Leah. Hit 'em straight and keep 'em dry."

It was then that he realized they were standing on the exact spot where Larry Carr had been murdered. He glanced where he had knelt down to help Carr and saw a discolored patch of grass. He shuddered, knowing exactly what it was.

ELEVEN

He went directly from the golf course to see Catherine Carr at her condominium. He had called her the night before and asked if he could talk to her in person and she had agreed. The Carrs lived in a large three-bedroom condo across from his condo which was also on the ocean side.

He walked up to her front door and saw a huge bouquet of flowers in front of it. Apparently, whoever had left them was more comfortable dropping them off than seeing Catherine face to face.

He pressed the buzzer, and a few moments later Catherine opened the door. She smiled at him and the flowers in his hands that he could barely see over.

"They're not from me," he said. "Someone left them. Maybe a delivery guy."

"They're beautiful," she said. "Come on in. Can I get you any-thing?"

"No, thanks. I'm good," he said, as she took the flowers from him and set them down on the kitchen counter.

She waved her arm. "Let's go sit out on the balcony. You're pretty familiar with the view."

"Yours is actually better than mine," Braddock said. She had the end unit. Right on the ocean too.

They sat down in two lounge chairs that swiveled.

"So," Braddock said, "how are you doing?"

"Oh, God, Matt," she said, "keeping busy with a million things. What I fear the most is when all this…having friends calling all the time and organizing and taking care of everything is over and it's just me, all alone, the widow Catherine."

He reached over and patted her arm. "I'm not worried about you. First of all, you've got a ton of friends. Plus, you're active as hell with your tennis and golf and whatever else you do...yoga maybe?"

"Pilates, actually, and who can forget croquet?"

"There you go," Braddock said. "I think the key is definitely to keep busy."

"So everyone says," she said. "Course I have a whole gang of unpaid advisors all of a sudden."

"I'm sure," Braddock said. "So, I wondered if I could ask you a few questions."

Catherine curled a strand of hair with her fingers. "Ask away."

"Okay, well first, I need to explain something. If it seems like I'm overly interested in what happened to Larry, I guess I'm guilty. I just want to do whatever I can to make sure his killer is caught."

She nodded. "That makes two of us, of course."

"Of course, but I've already gotten pretty involved. And you wouldn't be alone if you asked me why."

"Okay then, why?"

Braddock glanced out at a tanker far off in the distance.

"Well, it's kinda hard to explain. I tried explaining it to Chris Coolidge and Neil Carr—"

"Wait, you spoke to Neil?"

"Yes, I actually had lunch with him. By the way, and I know I don't need to tell you this, but he can really put away the booze."

She nodded and rolled her eyes.

"Anyway, he told me about something that Larry invested in after he sold his company—"

"Oh God, I know what you're going to say."

"Dreammates.com."

"Yup. I thought it was really weird when Larry told me about it. I mean why not just invest in stocks and bonds or real estate like he did with most of the other money from the sale."

"And what did he say? Why did he?"

"He said it was a business he could...what was it...oh yes, I remember now, 'add value to.' Which I thought was odd, because what did he know about a dating website?"

Braddock nodded. "So question is how did he get involved with it in the first place?"

"What he told me was that he met this man Frank some-thing…and I can't even remember how or where. Maybe the golf course, maybe through a business friend, I just don't remember."

"Do you remember Frank's last name by any chance?"

"No, sorry, but I would think you could just Google dreamdates.com and find out."

"Yes, I was going to do that. Haven't had a chance yet," Braddock said. "So did Larry have any other investments like this?"

Catherine shook her head. "No, isn't one enough?"

"So as far as 'adding value,' I guess you just don't know what he was referring to."

"No clue. I just know that he met with this man Frank a num-ber of times in Palm Beach. Presumably to talk to him about the busi-ness. I mean, what else could it have been?"

Braddock looked out on the horizon for the tanker, but it had disappeared. "So it's been a few days since I saw you last, have you thought any more about who might have killed Larry?" he asked, then winced. "I'm sorry, it seems so strange that I'm even asking you this, like what happened is something that only happens to other people or in the movies."

Catherine reached out and patted the back of his hand. "I know what you mean, but don't be sorry, it's an understandable thing to ask and wonder about. But I really have no idea, and I've had plenty of time to think about it."

He thought for a second. "Well…is there anything you need? Anything I can get you?"

"No, thanks. My women friends have been kind of smothering me with everything under the sun. Sweet but a little overwhelming."

Braddock put his hands on his knees and pushed himself up. "Okay, well, I'm going to hit the road then. If I can do anything for you, just let me know."

She got to her feet. "You can keep doing what you're doing. Find Larry's killer."

He was relieved to hear someone thought it was a good cause.

They walked to the front door.

"Thanks for coming," Catherine said.

"Of course," Braddock said, and he leaned forward to give her a kiss on the cheek.

But she suddenly turned and kissed him on the lips. Braddock could tell she seemed ready to prolong it, but he quickly turned away and opened the door, leaving her looking embarrassed, flustered, and frustrated.

TWELVE

Braddock was stunned and stupefied.

What had brought that on? Nothing he could think of in any of his actions. It was going to make his future dealings with her at least a little awkward. The best course, he decided, was to steer clear of her for a while. Talk on the phone if need be. But this was going to make his investigation—if he could use that word—more difficult.

He walked back to his condominium, went to his balcony, where he knew Catherine couldn't see him, and looked out over the ocean. The tanker was back. Or maybe it was another one.

He turned on his MacBook Air and Googled dreammates.com. The landing page included various pitches about how, if you joined the site, you'd find the man or woman of your dreams. There was nothing detailing any of the personnel of the company or even a number where you could contact someone. It was all about signing you up and nothing more.

Then he went back to Google and again typed in dreammates.com, scrolled to the bottom of page one, clicked on the dreammates.com Wikipedia entry, and hit the information jackpot.

"Dreammates.com is an online dating website launched in 2015, based in Palm Beach, Florida, and owned by DiCa e-commerce"—he read on—"a joint venture of Diehl Epic LLC and Carr Capital."

It went on to say, "Dreammates.com was founded by Frank J. Diehl, a Florida-based venture capitalist. In 2020, a capital infusion of $3 million was provided by Carr Capital, which then became a fifty percent partner with Diehl Epic. Like other similar companies, dreammates.com is an algorithm-based dating site. Between 2015-2020, approximately 2 million members were active users of the site. From 2020 to today, the number of users has increased to 3.5 million members."

There it was. Larry Carr somehow adding value to the company.

He looked up again and saw that the tanker had gone about an inch across the distant horizon.

He sat and pondered for a few minutes. Why had Larry Carr never told him about dreammates.com? With the exception of golf and sports in general, business was what they had talked about the most. Their own former businesses, articles they had recently read in the *Wall Street Journal* and the *Financial Times*, what they had just heard on CNBC, Bloomberg and Squawk Box… It seemed inconceivable that this significant venture had never come up.

So, Braddock's first conclusion was that there was something about dreammates.com that Carr didn't want to talk about. Didn't want people to know about. What else could it be? Was it that he felt his friends might think it was a business that was somehow beneath him, like owning a strip club or something? Maybe. But if Braddock owned a business that had increased its paying membership by 1.5 million in a few years, he sure as hell would have crowed about it to friends.

So it had to be something more. Something Larry wanted to hide or not let anybody—including his wife—know about.

He turned off his MacBook Air. It was time for a little recreation. He decided to go to the Island Club driving range and bang out a few buckets of balls.

*****

After finishing on the range, then showering, he changed into white pants and a crisp blue and white shirt, and was feeling natty. He got to the Island Club's bar a few minutes before Leah Bliss, who walked in looking far nattier.

"Well, don't you look nice," Leah said.

"Well, thank you. But you," he said, doing a quick top-to-bottom. "You look like…a million bucks."

"And I'll take that," she said sitting next to him. "Even though everything today is a billion. A million is chicken feed these days."

He laughed and nodded.

She was wearing a pink silk top with a slightly revealing neckline but nowhere close to daring, and a short skirt which highlighted her long, tanned legs.

"What can I get you?" he asked.

"Um, how about a rosé?"

Braddock tapped the marble bar top. "That's exactly what I thought you'd want."

"Well, I almost said a shot of tequila."

Braddock raised a hand to the bartender. "One rosé and a shot of tequila, please."

"Aha," Leah said. "Trying to get me drunk. Gotta look out for guys like you."

"You can just nurse them."

She pointed at his drink. "What's that you're having?"

"Myers's dark, orange juice, and a wedge of lime."

"Um, yummy."

"So how was your golf?" he asked.

"I got three pars and the rest double-bogeys."

He nodded and smiled. "Well then, we'd be competitive."

"It's just such a frustrating sport."

"No kidding."

Her drinks showed up.

"Eeny, meeny, miny," she said, then reached for the shot of tequila. "I don't knock these things back in one gulp anymore. Those days are gone."

She took a dainty sip of the tequila.

"So how is it that a man like you isn't married?" she said. "By the way, the first thing I noticed about you on the course today is that your eyes went right to my ring finger."

"Not too subtle, huh?"

"No, but I gotta admit, I kinda liked it."

"Good to hear," he said. "So, in answer to your question, I was married. It had a pretty good run…but I got divorced three years ago."

She nodded. "Kids?"

"Two. Well, one actually," he lowered his voice, and his eyes sank. "My son, Connor, died."

She touched his hand. "Oh, Matt, I am so sorry."

He suddenly felt a need to unburden himself about Connor and knew she'd be a sympathetic audience.

"Thank you," he said somberly. "He was killed in a car accident. A drunk driver hit his friend's car head-on."

She put her hand on his arm. "Oh my God, I am just so, so sorry. What an awful thing."

He felt close to tears and fought it hard. "Eighteen years old. He was in the passenger seat. His best friend, the driver, was killed too."

She patted his arm. "I just don't know what to say."

"There isn't anything *to* say."

"And what about your other child?"

"My daughter was his twin."

By the sudden look on Leah's face, he could tell she was sorry she had asked.

"She's in her junior year at Stanford now. Her name's Nell," Braddock said. "I don't see her nearly enough, but I'm going out there next month. I'm really looking forward to seeing her."

"I'll bet."

"Enough about that," he said. "Tell me about you."

"I was married once. It was fine for a while…then, it wasn't. No kids. After that I lived with a man for six years. It ended a little while ago."

He nodded.

"So, enough on that subject," she said. "I heard you were good friends with that man who got shot. Larry Carr."

"Who told you that?"

"Do you know Wendy Callan?"

"Sure."

"Well, she asked me if I wanted to join Peter and her for dinner and I said, sorry, I have a date. She asked who and I told her. She said, 'Oh, lucky you. Not only a date but a *hot* date. Island's most eligible bachelor.'"

"She said *that*? Never been called a *hot date* before."

"How would you know?" Leah said. "By the way, I still find it hard to believe your friend was shot here, of all places."

"Yeah, me too. It's really hard to process."

"What was he like anyway?" Leah asked.

"I'll tell you, but how about we order first?" Braddock said. "You okay eating at the bar or would you prefer a table."

"No, this is fine here. I've gotten pretty comfortable."

Braddock raised his hand to the bartender, and they ordered.

"So, about Larry"—Braddock made a spur-of-the-moment decision to skip any reference to Carr's womanizing—"if you'd asked around about him when he was alive, you'd have found he got mixed reviews. Very smart, very loyal, good sense of humor but almost too opinionated."

"What do you mean by that?"

Braddock thought for a second. "Well, he'd size up people really quickly and you'd know immediately where you stood with him."

"Why is that a bad thing?"

"Because sometimes he was just too blunt and totally lacking in tact. The man had no time at all for tact. See, to me it was kind of refreshing because there was no…pretense about him. No—you'll excuse the word—bullshit."

Leah laughed. "It's a very descriptive word," she said. "Sounds like a man who didn't suffer fools gladly?"

"Exactly. I was just thinking that right after he got killed. That phrase was custom made for Larry," Braddock said. "By the way, he would have liked you."

The food came and they ate and drifted away from the subject of Larry Carr.

"So, how'd you end up here?" Braddock asked. "I don't mean sitting on this barstool at this very moment, I mean joining the Island Club and living here."

"Well, it was kind of a toss-up between Palm Beach and here. I have a lot of friends up there. But I just decided, I don't know, it's a little lower key down here, which I like. A little less—I don't quite know how to put it—socially competitive maybe, if that makes sense?"

Braddock laughed. "It makes complete sense."

They finished up dinner and Braddock walked Leah back to her condominium.

She turned to him when they got there "Well, it's been fun, Matt. Thank you for dinner. Next time it's on me."

"You're welcome, it was a lot of fun," he said, happy to hear she wanted there to be a next time.

THIRTEEN

Six months ago...

There were four couples at the table at Narcissism. All four had already "gone upstairs" which was code, then had come back for another round.

"So, you and Rick live up in Jupiter?" a man named Sully asked a woman named Carol.

"Yes, a place called Admiral's Cove. We go out to the Hamptons in the summer," Carol said. "What about you?"

"We live on the island year-round," Sully said.

"Which island? There's Palm Beach, Singer Island, Jupiter Island—"

"Palm Beach. I wouldn't be caught dead on Jupiter Island."

"Why?"

"Too rich and stodgy for my blood."

"But don't you own some company?"

"Yeah, I do, but Jupiter Island people would never allow a guy who owns an auto parts company to set foot on their precious little island."

Carol laughed. "But Palm Beach did?"

He nodded. "They're a little more democratic there."

Carol nodded, bored with geography.

"Let me ask you a question, Sully?"

"Sure. Anything."

"Does this place and what goes on here ever seem like a throwback to the seventies."

"What do you know about the seventies?" Sully asked.

"Well, you know, Studio 54, Plato's Retreat, Free Love and all that?"

"You got a problem with…*all that?*"

"No, no, not at all, just saying this place could have been around back then."

She could tell she was losing Sully's attention but didn't much care. She turned to the man on her right.

"So it's Mark, right?" she said.

The man nodded.

"Hi, I'm Carol."

"I know," said Mark, giving her the quick once-over. "Carol with the most awesome body in the room."

"Well, thank you. You don't look too bad yourself."

Mark smiled. "Guess you'll find out."

Carol smiled back. "Guess I will."

Across the table was Tony, sitting between Josie and Donna.

None of the women was too thrilled to be stuck next to Tony, who was fat, bald and bowlegged. However, he was rich.

But so what? They all were.

Josie seemed resigned to have "Tony duty." "How's the boat?" she asked.

"Good," said Tony, known for monosyllables. "It's a yacht."

Word was that Tony had paid upwards of fifteen million dollars for it.

"How big is it?"

Tony laughed. "The yacht or—"

"Stop it," Josie said, rolling her eyes and cuffing him playfully. "Yes, the yacht."

"One fifty."

"Nice."

Tony locked onto her eyes. "It's a Feadship. Need I say more."

"I don't know what a Feadship is."

"A Feadship is a Feadship."

"Yeah, but—"

Tony put his arm around Josie's shoulder. "Hey, 'nough talk. Wanna go upstairs?"

"Not yet," Josie said, and turned to the man next to her, who was a step up from Tony.

"Man's sometimes a little hard to take," Josie said, lowering her voice.

"Tony?"

Josie nodded.

"He tell you about his boat?"

"It's a yacht. A Feadship."

The man nodded and smiled. "Whatever that is, right?"

One man at the table was sitting right across the table from his wife. She was talking to J.P., who she kind of liked. He was tall, in good shape, and had a full head of dirty blond hair. She guessed he was around fifty but didn't know for sure so she decided to ask.

She just came right out with it. "So how old are you, J.P.?"

J.P. leaned closer and put his arm around her. "A young fifty-four."

"I can tell," she said.

"Want to find out?"

She got to her feet and grabbed his hand. "Come on, lover boy."

J.P. didn't tarry.

"Have fun, Cath," the woman's husband said, giving her a little wave.

FOURTEEN

The first thing on Braddock's to-do list the next morning was to track down Frank J. Diehl, dreammates.com founder and former partner of Larry Carr. He went out on his balcony with his MacBook Air and watched six women and a man do yoga on the beach.

He tried good, old-fashioned directory assistance but found Frank J. Diehl had an unlisted number. Then he Googled him: *Frank J. Diehl Palm Beach*. He had tried this before with an old college friend and had gotten a list of four numbers, three of which were old, disconnected numbers, but when he tried the fourth one, he reached him.

It looked like a similar situation when he found Frank J. Diehl, with an address at 219 Barton Avenue, and five listed numbers. He tried the first one and, sure enough, it had been disconnected. But on the second one, he lucked out.

"Hello?"

"Is this Frank?"

"Who's this?"

"Hi Frank, you don't know me, but I'm a friend of Larry Carr. My name's Matt Braddock."

Long pause. "Your name is familiar, why is that?" Diehl asked.

"I don't know, maybe Larry mentioned me?"

"Nah, I don't think so," Diehl said. "Anyway, a real shame about Larry." Then he turned all business. "What can I do for you?"

"I wondered if we could meet up. I wanted to ask a few questions about Larry. I'm down in Delray."

"Well, I tell you, Matt. I'm pretty busy at the moment. What's this all about?"

"I just wanted to ask you some questions. I'm looking into Larry's murder and—"

"*You're* looking into Larry's murder? Isn't that the job of the police?"

That reaction again.

"Yeah, it is. I'm just trying to help out because Larry and I—"

"Can't help you, my friend. I gotta go."

Click.

Not exactly the desired outcome, Braddock thought, as he watched a man catch a wave on a boogie board.

*****

Braddock kept his boat at a marina on George Bush Boulevard, which was owned by the son of a man who had run JP Morgan. Braddock had known him back in his Blackstone days. He arrived at ten o'clock and his captain was waiting for him.

"Morning, boss," said Chuck Day cheerily. "Nice day for a boat ride."

"Sure is. But like I told you, we're just gonna stay on the Waterway." Braddock said, using the alternate name for the Intracoastal that Day often used.

"Whatever you say," Day said with a smile.

They boarded the boat and as they did, Braddock noticed several CCTV cameras mounted above them.

He pointed at one. "I've never seen those cameras before."

"Yeah, they're new," Day said. "Bob told me they had some robberies here"—Bob was the owner of the marina—"expensive nav systems and stuff like that. Bob figured the guy climbed over the fence"—Day pointed—"maybe a couple of guys."

"That camera"—Braddock pointed—"is looking out at the Waterway."

"I know. So fill me in. What's our mission today?"

Braddock didn't feel he needed to fill him in too much.

"Remember that old TV show—maybe you saw it in reruns—called *The Fugitive*?"

"Sure. Harrison Ford."

"Yeah, there also was a TV series with a guy named David Janssen. So anyway, he was on the run and at the same time trying to track down a one-armed man."

"I remember."

"So instead of a one-armed man we're looking for a black-hulled boat. About a thirty- or thirty-five-footer. You ever seen one like that around here?"

"I've seen a few black hulled boats but usually much bigger."

"Okay, so that's what we're after. Let's go up to the bridge on Ocean Avenue and down to, say, Linton Boulevard."

"You got it," Day said starting up the engine. "Which way first, you have a preference?"

"Um, why don't we go north."

Day nodded.

*****

It only took them about twenty minutes to get to the scene of Larry Carr's murder at the fifth hole of the Island Club and, so far, no black-hulled boats.

"Slow down here," Braddock said, looking out at the hole on the golf course.

Day throttled back the engine.

"That's where my friend was shot," Braddock said, pointing.

Day shook his head. "I still can't believe that whole thing. You were playing with him when it went down, right?"

Braddock nodded. "Right there," he said, pointing to the spot.

"I get it now," Day said. "You're thinking maybe this black-hulled boat might have had something to do with it?"

"Yeah, just a theory at this point," Braddock said, looking over at the other side of the Intracoastal. "But now that I look around, the shot could have come from any number of places."

He pointed at a condominium building on the Boynton Beach side of the Intracoastal. "Plenty of vantage points from that one," Braddock said, then pointing at another complex farther north. "Or even that one. It's called Tuscany—a friend of mine lives there."

"But isn't the most obvious location to take the shot from"— Day pointed—"one of those buildings on the course?"

"Yeah, you're right. But there are plenty of others that I never considered before. But you gotta be a hell of a good shot from wherever it came from, because none of them are exactly close. The detectives handling the case have gone through the two buildings on the course talking to the owners. I don't know where else they've done that."

Day shook his head. "It still just amazes me something like that could happen. I'm really sorry about your friend."

"Thanks," Braddock said. "All right, let's just go up to Ocean, then U-turn it."

*****

The bridge at Linton Boulevard was about eight miles south of the Ocean Avenue bridge. Day and Braddock took their time as Braddock told his captain he wanted to not only check marinas for black-hulled boats, but also private docks along the way.

As they headed back to the marina at George Bush Boulevard, having spotted a grand total of zero black-hulled vessels, Day turned to Braddock, "You don't feel like going out to the ocean and throwing out a line, do you? It's a perfect day for bills."

"Thanks, Chuck, but I've got my hands full at the moment. Maybe after I'm done with it."

Day shrugged. "Hey, whatever you want, you're the boss."

FIFTEEN

Braddock took a shower to cool off and clean up after he got back from the boat ride, then placed a call to Neil Carr. He got Neil's voicemail, left a message, then made a tomato sandwich. Big slices of tomato, heavy on the Hellmann's.

Just as he finished it off, he got a call back from Neil.

"Hey, Matt, how's it going?"

"Good, Neil. I found out that the last name of Larry's partner at the dating site is Diehl. Frank Diehl. I had a conversation with him. Short, but not sweet. When I asked him if I could meet with him and ask him some questions about Larry, let's just say, he demurred."

"Hung up on you?"

"No, just clearly didn't want to talk about Larry."

"Hmm. Wonder why?"

"No clue."

"I actually was about to call you," Neil said. "I thought of something that might be helpful."

Braddock wasn't hearing any slurs or any other signs of a boozy lunch, which he had come to expect to be Neil's normal state.

"Tell me. I could use some help."

"Well, so as we both know, Larry wasn't exactly a faithfully committed husband."

"No kidding."

"Well, at one point, about two years ago, he got into a hot-and-heavy relationship with a woman named Faye."

"That's ironic."

"What do you mean?"

"Faye means loyal."

"Unlike Larry, you mean."

"Exactly," Braddock said. "But my question is how the hell is it possible to get into a 'hot-and-heavy' relationship when you're married?"

"That's a good question, but, trust me, it was. I mean, a real raging affair."

"Amazing."

"What?"

"Well, that I never knew anything about it. Which I guess just means you can have a raging affair and keep it under wraps."

"There you go," Neil said. "Anyway, I think she's someone you should definitely talk to. Just because I bet she can shed some light on Larry's life."

Braddock sighed. "So, according to the grapevine here at the Island Club, he was also having an affair with a woman named Maisie at the time he died."

"What can I tell you? The man was a master at juggling two at a time. Well, three including Catherine—" Neil paused. "Oh, and by the way, Larry mentioned that Catherine might just have had something going on the side too."

Braddock's head jerked back. "Come on, really? Catherine?" he said, but then he remembered the kiss on the lips.

"Can you blame her?"

"No, I guess not."

"Give her a call. Faye, I mean. Something tells me that she might know where the bodies are buried." Neil groaned. "Uh, maybe that's not the best way to phrase it. By the way, Larry told me once he was even thinking of leaving Catherine."

"Really?"

"Yup."

"I'll be damned," Braddock said.

"Kind of a bad soap opera, huh?"

"Sure seems it. So Faye… What's her last name and where does she live?"

"I can do better than that. I can give you her phone number."

"Why do you have that?"

"Because one time Larry called me from her phone and left a message to call him back on it. Said he'd just dropped his phone in the pool."

"Gotcha, so what is it?"

Neil gave him the number and said her last name was Mayhew.

"Thanks. I'm going to give her a call. Where's she live?"

"Down near you. Gulf Stream or Delray."

"That's good info, Neil. I appreciate it."

Braddock had gotten a text from the Delray detective, Jason Fisher, that said simply, "Call me." But he was itching to speak to Faye Mayhew. He decided to call her first.

He dialed her and she picked up after the second ring.

"Matt Braddock?" she said. "I've heard of you, but I don't believe we've met."

"No, we haven't. Neil Carr gave me your number and said you were a friend of his brother, Larry."

"You could say that," she said. "Oh, now I remember, Larry mentioned you a couple of times. You played golf together, right, and were friends?"

"We did and we were. So, first of all, I just want to say how sorry I am about what happened to Larry."

"Yes, thank you, it was just terrible," she said somberly, and he could hear her inhale deeply.

"I was wondering if I could come speak to you. Ask you some questions about Larry."

Silence for a moment. "Ah sure, I guess so. Like…what do you want to know?"

"Well, I'm specifically interested in Larry's investment in something called dreammates.com. Plus a few other things."

Another pause. "I guess my question is *why* do you want to know these things?"

He hated the explanation question but by now was getting used to it. "I'll be as honest as possible with you. I want to help the police find Larry's killer or killers."

"Why…are you like some kind of vigilante?"

Braddock laughed. "That seems to be what a lot of people are beginning to think. Fact is, I was right next to him when it happened. I watched the poor man die. I guess I feel I owe him. I just don't want his murder to go unsolved. I know it's unusual but…"

That was the best he could do. He thought he was getting a little better answering the question everyone asked.

"I've got bridge this afternoon. How about after that, say five o'clock."

"Sure, that would be great. Thank you so much."

"No problem. See you then."

Jason Fisher was next.

He dialed his number and Fisher picked up right away. "We need to talk," Fisher said.

"Okay, let's talk."

"I'm hearing you're going around asking a lot of people a lot of questions. We need to have an understanding here."

"About what?"

"Boundaries. Which, from everything I hear, you've already crossed."

"I'm sorry you see it that way," Braddock said. "I'm really just trying to help. I figure that because I know a lot of people here maybe I can find out things, hear things, that you might not."

"Okay, look, I can't stop you. I've been doing this a long time without any help from John Q. Citizen," Fisher said, then he sighed and changed his tune slightly. "Do you have anything useful at this point?"

The man was a veritable dichotomy of scolding and inquiring.

"Not much. I'm still trying to figure out where the shot came from. A guy who was with me when it happened said he saw a boat with a black hull not far away in the Intracoastal. Also, I don't know whether you've noticed, but a couple of trailers at Whispering Pines have straight shots at the site where Larry got shot."

"We're all over that black-hulled boat."

"Have you found it?"

"Not yet."

"What about the Whispering Pines trailers?"

"I'll look into that," Fisher said, dismissively.

"I also spoke to Carr's brother in Palm Beach, Neil. I figured it wouldn't hurt to see if he could shed some light on things."

"Did he?"

"Well, tell you the truth, it remains to be seen if anything he told me leads anywhere. But he did come up with a few interesting things. Have you spoken to him?"

"He's on my list," Fisher said.

"'Cause if you had talked to him, you'd find out that Larry invested in a business owned by a guy who strikes me as kind of a shady character."

"Keep going."

"No, Jason, that's all you're getting out of me except his name is Frank Diehl. You do your own homework."

"All right, fine. Just stay on your side of the line, will ya. Someone even said you were impersonating a police officer."

"That's total bullshit. Not even close. Who said that?"

"I forget. Look, I don't want to have an adversarial relationship with you. We'll talk again."

And he clicked off.

One thing that was really bothering him was Catherine Carr. In the fairly short time he had known her he had always seen her as a nice-looking, sociable, athletic woman who was a loyal, loving wife. But now there was the kiss that could have gone further if he let it, and Neil Carr's mention of her possibly having some action on the side. That didn't jibe with his impression of her, and he wondered if Neil might simply be wrong.

He was also worried about something else. The Island Club was one of those places where most of its members lived within a stone's throw of each other. So it was inevitable that word would get around pretty fast. "Did you hear about Matt Braddock? He's going around playing Dick Tracy, trying to catch Larry Carr's murderer." But it seemed it had gone beyond that: someone complaining that he was impersonating a police officer. That was bad. And inaccurate. Or was Jason Fisher just making it up in an attempt to get him to scale back?

Speaking of Fisher, Braddock had serious concerns about Fisher's investigation. The fact that he hadn't even looked at the Whispering Pines trailers, which directly faced the fifth hole, as possibly being the sniper's nest. And the fact that he wouldn't consider speaking to Neil Carr a top priority—also disturbing. He wondered exactly what Fisher and his partner were doing.

Not slapping handcuffs on a killer, that was for damn sure.

SIXTEEN

Many years ago in Los Angeles…

Caleb Jensen never knew who his father was, and his mother was, at best, a part-time mom. Part-time because she was hustling to get parts in movies—B movies, because she wasn't good enough for the plum roles and was starting to be regarded as over-the-hill at age thirty-eight. She did hundreds of *go-sees*—or so it seemed—simply to get one walk-on role that maybe…*maybe* paid a hundred dollars.

She had gotten knocked up by a gaffer who told her his brother was a director who could get her good parts. That was bullshit and after the one-night stand she never saw him again. Then, nine months later, along came Caleb.

At age twenty, Caleb, who had never listened to a word his mother said, tried to become an actor himself. He didn't have much more luck than she did, but because he had a gregarious, affable nature and was handsome he made a lot of friends, particularly women.

One woman, older than he was by ten years, and wiser, was instrumental in helping him concoct a plan that ended up being far more profitable than if he'd muddled along as a struggling actor.

Caleb and the woman, Mona, were in a West Hollywood dive and had had a lot to drink. They were sitting in a booth, and Mona, who wore the clothes of a well-endowed Goth years before Goths were a thing, was doing most of the talking. She was drinking Jägermeister, and Caleb was drinking Schlitz, and Caleb had a grand total of nine dollars in his paper-thin wallet.

"So, how's this acting thing working out for you?" Mona asked.

Caleb reached down for his wallet, opened it up and smiled at Mona. "What's this tell you?" he said. "Nine bucks."

Mona laughed. "Well, looks like we're gonna have to bolt this joint, 'cause nine bucks ain't gonna cover the tab."

"Won't be the first time," Caleb said.

"But first I'm gonna run something by you," Mona said.

Caleb nodded.

"I'd be just as poor as you," Mona said, "except for one thing."

"What's that?"

"A four-letter word that rhymes with horn and starts with a *P*."

He put down his drink and pushed closer to her. "You're kidding? You?"

"How do you think I can afford this Balenciaga," she said, pinching the top of her dress that looked like something Morticia of the Addams family would wear.

"What's a Balenciaga?"

"That was a joke that I shoulda figured would go right over your head," said Mona. "You should give some thought to that particular four-letter word I just mentioned."

He actually had thought about it one time when he'd had even more to drink.

"How did you get into it?" Caleb asked like he wasn't sure he wanted to hear the answer.

"Simple. It was either starve or fuck."

It was like cold water being splashed in his face. "But you seem so—"

"What?"

He put his hands up. "I don't know…um, wholesome, maybe?"

"Well, thank you, Caleb," she said sarcastically. "What? You think we all look like three-dollar hookers down on Figueroa Street?"

"No, I just—"

"Here I'm trying to help, and you insult me."

He took a pull on his Schlitz and looked up at her. "I wasn't insulting you. It actually was a compliment. So how long have you been doing it?"

Mona laughed. "*Doing it*, you mean as in…*doing it?*"

Caleb's face turned beet red. "I meant—"

Mona patted his arm. "I know what you meant. The answer is three and a half years."

He shook his head. "Man, you'd never know."

Mona shook her head in response. "You just can't get it into your head, can you? Just think of it as being, I don't know…like a tri-athlete or something. You know, lots of exercise and, um, physical exertion."

Caleb laughed. "If you say so… So how would I even go about it?"

"That's the easy part," Mona said. "There's actually going to be a casting call next Thursday. I can get you in."

"So what's the description? What's the role that's being cast?"

"Young stud with attitude. You're a shoo-in."

Caleb laughed. "You think I've got attitude?"

She shrugged. "Not really, but you've got six days to come up with it."

SEVENTEEN

B raddock could certainly see what Larry Carr saw in Faye Mayhew, though he still thought that Catherine was better looking.

Faye lived at the Maidstone building in Delray Beach and was not a member of the Island Club but rather the Gulf Stream Tennis and Beach Club—the T & B, as it was called—which was located farther south on North Ocean Boulevard.

She was average height but way above average in every other department. She had flaming red hair, brilliant blue eyes, and a body that was no doubt the envy of all female beachgoers.

She met him at the door of her condominium, which overlooked the Intracoastal.

"Thanks for letting me come over," Braddock said. "I really appreciate it."

"Happy to help…if I can," she said and ushered him in.

She asked him if she could get him anything to drink and he thanked her but said no, then she led him out to a balcony that had a wide view of the Intracoastal.

"Wow, what a view," he said, thinking this would be a great vantage point to spot the black-hulled boat. "I live on the ocean, but I prefer this; there's so much more going on."

"True," she said. "The only problem is the afternoon light facing west can be brutal."

"Never thought about that," he said. "So, if I could, can I ask you a few questions about Larry."

"Sure, that's what you came for, not the view. Fire away."

So far it hadn't seemed awkward that he was going to ask her questions about her married, murdered lover. He was thinking that he might have to tiptoe around it a little.

"Well, I know you and Larry were friends—"

"Please, Matt. 'Friends?' Come on."

"Okay, you had a relationship then, is that better?" He was not keen on referring to her as his friend's "lover" or "lady friend" or "mistress" or "paramour" or any of the other hundreds of words for it. "And you probably know a lot about him."

"More than Catherine, I bet," she said with a hard-to-read smile. "I'm sorry, it's just—well, I'm just going to come right out and say it—Larry was the love of my life, and he almost divorced his wife and married me. So yes, you could say I knew a lot about him, and I miss the man dearly. Even though he cheated on me, same as he did with Catherine."

"I certainly understand that. And though our relationships were obviously far different, I miss him too."

Faye nodded. "Go ahead, ask away. What do you want to know?"

"Well, as I mentioned, I'm very interested in Larry's investment in dreammates.com and how that even came about."

Faye leaned back in the sofa. "Oh, that's an easy one," she said. "Catherine introduced Larry to the owner."

Braddock's mouth dropped. "Wait, what? *Catherine?*"

"Yup, she introduced Larry to Frank Diehl. That's the name of the man who started dreammates?"

"I know. I spoke to him…briefly."

"Meaning he didn't want to talk to you?"

"Exactly."

"That doesn't surprise me."

"Hang on a second—how did Catherine know Diehl?"

"She met him at Narcissism."

"Which is what?"

"Oh, sorry, I thought Neil filled you in on the whole thing."

Neil had maybe forgotten a thing or two…the booze probably. Or had held back. Or never knew.

"All I know about Frank Diehl," Braddock said, "is that Larry invested three million dollars in dreammates and became a partner. What else is there?"

"There's definitely more, though Larry probably didn't tell me everything. So, there's the website and Narcissism, which is…I guess you could call it a nightclub, on Narcissus Avenue in West Palm."

"Which is where?"

"You know the Ben Hotel in West Palm?"

"Yeah?"

"Not far from there."

"Okay, so that three million dollars bought Larry part of this Narcissism nightclub too?"

"Half of dreammates and half of Narcissism."

"Anything else?"

"That's it. But as I remember, Frank also owns a bunch of other buildings in West Palm and up in Jupiter that Larry had nothing to do with."

"Okay, so can we go back to Catherine introducing Larry to Diehl?"

Faye smiled and pushed back her long red hair from her forehead. "I thought you might want to. But first I need to know this will never go outside of this room."

Braddock put up a hand. "Oh, absolutely. I was just going to say the same."

"Not a word, right?"

"Not a word."

"Okay, so maybe as an act of retaliation, Catherine started—what's that cute euphemism?—'steppin' out.' She met a man who lived in Palm Beach and, as Larry explained it, they ended up at Narcissism one night where the guy with Catherine somehow knew Frank. And I think what happened later is Catherine took Larry to Narcissism one night, where he met Frank."

"Wow, this gets complicated. I need a playbook."

"Yes, I know. So anyway, Larry met Frank and one thing led to another and—boom!—Larry writes a big check, and they end up partners. I'm giving you the abbreviated version of the whole thing because it didn't just happen overnight. This happened right after Larry told me he almost invested in another company but pulled out at the last minute, which didn't make the people in that other company too happy."

Braddock remembered Catherine Carr mentioned something about Larry reneging on the purchase of something.

"Gotcha. You know what amazes me is that the Island Club is such a little fishbowl and none of this ever got out. I mean, I never heard a thing."

"Well, of course. That's 'cause Larry and Catherine were discreet as hell." She patted Braddock's arm. "I mean, you never heard about me and Larry, right? Never even knew my name, I bet?"

"Never did."

"That's just the way I like it. Being that 'nice Faye who plays a mean game of bridge' and nothing more is exactly how I want to keep it."

Braddock smiled. "This is like...one question leads to ten more."

"I hear you. So ask away."

"You mentioned there might have been more to Larry and Diehl's partnership?"

"I'd tell you if I knew, but I don't. I'm just guessing there was more than just dreammates and Narcissism. But I really don't know."

"So I wouldn't be doing my job as a self-appointed vigilante if I didn't ask the big question—"

"Who do I think killed Larry?"

"Exactly."

"This will sound strange. But my theory is that Larry killed Larry."

Braddock frowned. "What do you mean?"

"Went somewhere where he shouldn't have. Or got into something he shouldn't."

Braddock cocked his head. "You mean with a woman...or a business situation...what?"

She tugged at a lock of hair. "I know I keep saying this, but I really don't know exactly."

Braddock raised his arms in surprise. "But Larry...the mild-mannered corporate reinsurance man?"

"Don't kid yourself. Larry had a wild side. Underneath all the conventional, handsome, pink pants WASP-iness, was a bad boy just dying to get out. And...sometimes he did."

She was, of course, right. The bad boy did "get out" as far as chasing women went. So, it shouldn't have been such a big stretch to believe that he got out somewhere else too.

"But as far as someone specific who you think might have been behind his murder, you don't have anyone in mind?"

She shook her head. "Sorry."

"Well, I've clearly got my work cut out for me."

"Or you might want to just think about dropping it at this point."

"As in, it might get dangerous, you mean?"

"Yes, Matt, that's exactly what I mean."

EIGHTEEN

Catherine Carr seemed to have gone from a bouncy, athletic, genial woman to...all that and so much more. Braddock was starting to doubt his powers of observation, but then he realized that Larry and Catherine Carr, as Faye Mayhew had said, had just done a masterful job of disguising what they did when they were not on the tennis court or golf course.

He thought back to the last dinner he'd had with them at the Island Club.

It was Catherine and Larry, and another couple, and Braddock and a woman Catherine was "fixing him up with." The fix did not take but there were a lot of bottles of wine, followed by some spirited dancing, followed by a nightcap at the Carrs'. Braddock got home at eleven which was probably two hours later than most of the other Island Club diners knocked off for the night. Most nights, there was something called a "prison break," when the older members exited the club after dinner between 7:45 and 8:15 p.m.

Braddock replayed his conversation with Faye Mayhew. On one hand, it was unimaginably eye-opening, on the other somewhat menacing and ominous just beneath the surface. If he was to guess who the murderer was at this point, he'd have absolutely no idea; but his gut told him it had something to do with the whole dreammates.com, Narcissism, Frank Diehl tangle.

That seemed to be affirmed by Faye Mayhew's parting words that it might be wise for him to drop the whole investigation and go back to his comfortable, safe life.

His cell phone rang. He looked down and the display said. "Leah Bliss." He needed a nice diversion and was game for just about anything she might come up with.

"Hello, Leah."

"Hey, Matt. So let's pretend it's Sadie Hawkins day."

"Okay."

"And I'm taking you out to dinner. I was thinking Prime Catch. Away from the gossiping lips of the Island Club."

"I accept."

"Wow, you're easy. So I already called and the only reservation I could get was at seven."

"What's wrong with that?"

"It's kinda early for young pups like us."

"Nah, that's fine. So I'll swing by and pick you up a little before seven?"

"That would be great."

Prime Catch, as the name implied, specialized in fish dishes and seafood and was located just across the bridge in Boynton Beach. It was a go-to for Braddock when he wanted a break from the convenience of the more limited menu of the Island Club. The Island Club had good food and good service, but fewer choices than Prime Catch.

*****

Braddock picked up Leah at a few minutes before seven, and they pulled up to the valet at Prime Catch right at seven. They went inside and were promptly seated at a table overlooking the Intracoastal. Braddock's first thought was that it was yet another good vantage point from which to spot the black-hulled boat.

"Tell me, what have you been up to today? Didn't see you on the links," Leah asked.

"Yeah. Took a day off. Caught up on some business stuff."

"I've been meaning to ask you," Leah said. "How do you like being retired?"

He patted her arm. "The real answer or the 'oh it's just great' answer?"

"The real one."

"Okay. Golf and fishing aren't enough," he said. "I mean, I'm on a few boards that I spend some time on, but it's still not enough. So, to kill a little time, I've ended up taking a nap every day."

"Oh, Matt, you're way too young to be taking naps. You gotta be at least sixty for that."

"I know."

"And what do you miss most about work?"

"Um, well first, I miss the camaraderie. A bunch of people in an office all trying to figure it out."

"I like that—'figure it out'—but what exactly were you figuring out?"

"Well, in our case, companies to invest in, or buy. Sometimes ones that looked good at first, but the more you looked the more you thought, 'stay away.' I always got huge satisfaction from making a deal. The endorphins flying…it's a real rush. I miss all that."

"I get it," Leah said. "I get the same thing decorating houses, the satisfaction thing. Where I'll look at a place, the finished product, and say, 'Man, we really nailed it.' Or I'll look at the face of a client and see how much they love it. Of course, that's not always the case."

"Hey, there're winners and losers with everything, right?"

"Amen."

"What I don't get is the whole remote thing. People working at home or wherever. I mean, I can't see working unless you're with other people. The feedback. The collaboration. The back-and-forth."

"I know what you mean," Leah said, taking a bite of her sword-fish.

A half hour later they had finished up, and Braddock was down to the last of his red wine.

"So, I've got an idea I want to run by you," he said.

She raised her glass of white wine. "Run it."

"Okay, the night is still young"—it was only eight fifteen—"and there's a club up in West Palm that a friend told me about. S'posed to be kind of a fun spot. Want to check it out?"

"Sure. What's it called?"

"Narcissism."

"Okay. I got a little of that in me."

"You disguise it well."

*****

Leah had Googled the location of Narcissism on the way up. It was less than a half hour drive and Braddock parked in a nearby parking garage.

They walked into the building on Narcissus Avenue that Google had given as the address of the club. There was no sign out front but there was a hostess standing behind a lectern inside the front door.

"Good evening," she said. She was a statuesque Asian woman with a stunning figure and dark almond eyes.

"Hello," Braddock said. "Can you seat us? I didn't call ahead."

The hostess was hesitant. "Are you members?"

"Ah no, we're not."

"I'm sorry, but it's strictly members only, or friends of a member."

"Oh yes, well, Faye Mayhew suggested we come. She's a friend of Larry Carr."

The woman's gaze went from dark to light.

"Oh, sure, Ms. Mayhew. In that case, let me seat you."

They followed her to an eight-person table that had three other couples at it.

"No tables just for two?" Braddock asked, lowering his voice, as the six others at the table looked up at them.

"Oh, no, sir, we just have large tables here."

Odd, thought Braddock, shooting a glance at Leah. She just smiled as she sat down between two men and directly across from Braddock.

The men introduced themselves to Leah, and Braddock introduced himself to the two women on either side of him. They were young, buxom and showed off their impressive physiques with immodestly plunging necklines. It was hard not to stare, even for Leah. The whole situation felt somewhat awkward.

Leah looked across at him and shrugged. "Well, here we are."

He leaned toward her and whispered. "I need a drink."

"Me, too."

Braddock raised his hand to a nearby waiter and they both ordered. Braddock made his a double.

"Guess I'm driving," Leah said.

"So, tell me about yourself, Leah," a man named Wayne seated next to her asked.

"Well, it's not that interesting," she said.

Wayne gave her a long look from top to bottom. "Oh, I bet it is," he said. "Leave out the boring things. Just give me the spicy stuff."

Leah looked up at Braddock in alarm, but he had fallen into a conversation with a woman named Laura.

Their drinks came and they both came close to guzzling them.

Wayne told Leah that he owned a chain of nursing homes in New York and Pennsylvania, and she said, "Oh, that's nice." Then she turned to the man on her left, who she thought had introduced himself as Fripp.

"So…it's, ah, Fripp, right?"

He nodded.

"First or last name?"

"First."

"I don't believe I've ever met a Fripp before."

He beamed. "Well, here I am… So have you and Pat been going out for long?"

"It's actually Matt," Leah said. "And no, this is only our second date."

Fripp gave her a light punch on the shoulder. "Well, it's definitely gonna be one you'll never forget."

Leah looked afraid to ask what he meant as she looked across at Braddock.

But he was now talking to the woman on the other side of him.

After another half an hour a man at the end of the table stood and raised his highball glass.

"Well, shall we?"

Fripp leered at Leah.

"Shall we what?" Leah asked Fripp in close to a panic.

"Playing coy, huh?" Fripp said, standing.

She shot a glance at Braddock who was looking wildly unnerved. Suddenly he put his hand to his temples and looked at her. "Ahh, damn. My migraine's just killing me, honey. I'm afraid we've got to go."

*****

They were driving out of the garage next to Narcissism.

Leah laughed. "Quick thinking. That migraine thing."

"Thanks."

"But that's supposed to be the woman's line. And, by the way, I did like the 'honey' you threw in. Nice touch."

He nodded and smiled.

"But you might just want to think about de-friending the woman who recommended that place," Leah said.

"Yeah, no kidding," Braddock said. "Actually, in her defense, she didn't exactly recommend it. She just mentioned it, got me kind of curious."

"And now…you know."

"Sure do."

"So just who was the enlightened woman who told you about the place. Faye Someone, you said, right?"

Braddock nodded. "Girlfriend of my friend, Larry."

"The married man."

"Yes."

"You know, you might *also* have thought about de-friending him, too. But, of course, it's too late now."

Braddock frowned and turned to her. "Why do you say that?"

"'Cause he was a philanderer and I'm not a big fan of philanderers. You weren't one when you were married, were you?"

He shook his head. "Nope, one-man dog."

"What does that mean?"

"You know…like loyal and true as a dog."

"Good boy."

"You know what I like about you?"

"What?" Leah asked.

"You've got a very good sense of humor."

"Well, gee, thanks," she said. "Know what I like about you?"

"What?"

"You drew the line back there. Date-swapping, wife-swapping, God knows the extent of it. I didn't know stuff like that was still around."

"Could you believe it?"

"By the way, I caught you sneaking a peak at Laura's boobs."

Braddock laughed. "How could I not?"

"Yeah, guess you're right. They were pretty hard to ignore."

NINETEEN

Caleb Jensen was at a respectable dive in West Hollywood with Mona, talking shop. It had been a year since she suggested he try "acting with no clothes on." He had taken her up on the suggestion.

"When I first started out, the director said I had to come up with a pseudonym. I like nodded but had no idea what a pseudonym even was. I went home and looked it up then racked my brain for a couple of days. My first two were Warren G. Hardon and Dwight D. Eisenhumper—"

Mona burst out laughing. "Funny but not very sexy. What was it with you and presidents?"

"I don't know. Think big, I guess," Caleb said.

"Well, I like what you ended up with," Mona said, "Pistol Pete."

Caleb shrugged. "I actually think it's kinda lame, but the director loved it. Some of the other ones I came up with were Ken Cannon and Peter Gunn."

"Gunn, like after that old TV series?"

"Exactly. Oh, and another one was Dickie Bang."

Mona gave him a thumbs-up. "I like that one too."

"Yeah, that was my second choice."

"You're pretty good at coming up with names."

"Well, thank you."

"So, you like the business?" Mona asked, taking a sip of her Jägermeister.

"To be honest," Caleb said, "not really. Because my true nature is kind of shy. I wouldn't mind being a director, though. I'm pretty creative. Bet I could come up with some new wrinkles."

"I'm sure you could."

"How about you, do you like it?" Caleb asked.

"Like I told you, I love the money," Mona said. "I wonder if we'll ever do one together."

Caleb put down his drink on the bar. He had traded up from Schlitz to Johnny Walker Black. "I hope not."

"Why not?" she asked. "I'm insulted."

"Don't be. I just think it's so much better keeping it platonic between us. You know, why spoil a good relationship with sex?"

*****

Two years later, at age twenty-three, Caleb got his break. A director with a major cocaine habit crashed his car on the way to the set after an all-nighter at the Viper Room and Caleb volunteered to step in. Fact was, he didn't have to do much. The plot was pretty thin, and it was all just a setup for the final lollapalooza of a sex scene, but he threw in a few spur-of-the-moment ad-libs that the actors and producer liked. He leveraged the opportunity into directing another film the following year and never worked in front of the camera again. He didn't miss it at all.

But then, two years later, he got into a side-hustle that got him into big trouble.

TWENTY

Caleb Jensen, who had become Pistol Pete, had to change his name yet again.

What happened was, though he was a respected director—if that word could be used for a director of porn flicks—he still wasn't making that much money. The ones who made real money were the companies that financed them. The studios. Companies like Adam & Eve and Elegant Angels and the one Caleb did most of his directing for, Holy Alliance.

Holy Alliance was ninety percent owned by a porn star named Jasmine Murtagh. Jasmine had been ahead of her time and established her own production company, much as Reese Witherspoon, Margot Robbie and Charlize Theron did years later. Why not keep the lion's share of the money for herself? she thought. And so she did. The other ten percent of the Holy Alliance was owned by her husband, Knightly Brimm. Jasmine had met Knightly at a mega church he was preaching at in Pasadena. Knightly was number two on the totem pole at the church behind a televangelist who took home more than a million dollars a year.

Knightly felt there was something inherently wrong with that, since he had gone to Yale Divinity School and the big-name televangelist had barely graduated from high school. But when Jasmine Murtagh came into Knightly's flock and fell under his oratorial spell, he saw a major opportunity in the bottle blonde with piled-up blond tresses and black stiletto heels and married her in Las Vegas six months later. A few weeks after that, Knightly retired from the church when Jasmine decided she was going to produce skin flicks instead of star in them.

And two years after that, Caleb Jensen was one of Holy Alliance's regular directors, making decent money, but not as much as he felt he deserved. Jasmine, despite what she now did for a living—

produce porn—and what she *had* done for a living—star in porn—was a born-again Christian who believed every word in the Bible was true, sex before marriage was immoral, and that one should never cheat on one's spouse.

Knightly, on the other hand, just believed in the first two. And that was where Caleb saw his opportunity, which was exactly what he approached his old friend Mona about.

"Knightly's being a real dick," Caleb said in the hotel bar. "He's trying to cut my salary by fifty percent. Says 'cause they give me so much work, it's only fair."

"What is he, like the business manager?" Mona asked.

"Yeah, claims he went to Harvard Business School and Yale Divinity School. Actually has their diplomas hanging on his walls. I think they're bogus."

"Not to mention, he's a total ass-grabber," Mona said.

Caleb's eyes got big. "He is?"

"Oh yeah, the worst," Mona said. "Always lookin' for a little side-action."

"Oh, man, perfect," Caleb said, seeing his opportunity as he raised his glass of Johnny Walker Black. "You just gave me a million-dollar idea and you get to play a starring role. You in?"

She shrugged. "I don't know. Tell me about it."

"Okay, so next time he grabs your ass, act like you're interested."

"You mean like in…*doing* him?"

"Yeah, exactly, so then he like…sets up a meeting at a bar or something, and after that takes you to a hotel. Meantime, I'm following along behind you. I dog you from the bar to the hotel, the two of you go up to the room and, oops, you forget to close the door."

"I love it, so you follow us in with your Nikon—"

"I'm actually thinking this little movie camera of mine."

"Perfect," Mona said. "So now you got leverage and he ends up paying you double for every directing gig you do. Something like that?"

Caleb nodded. "Even bigger," he said. "He pays me double *and* gives me twenty grand to keep it quiet from Jasmine. Of which you get half."

TWENTY-ONE

Only thing was, it didn't quite work out that way. No, Mona was dead, and Caleb was running for his life.

Everything went smoothly at first. Knightly Brimm had, in fact, propositioned Mona in an off-the-beaten-path bar, which led to them going to the Peninsula Hotel, with Caleb and his camera right behind them. Caleb got what he called the "money shot" without Knightly even knowing he had entered the hotel room. The next day Caleb had clandestinely approached Knightly and made his demand. Caleb was surprised how calmly Knightly had reacted to it and readily agreed to Caleb's terms: twenty thousand dollars to burn the film from the hotel room and double Caleb's director's salary for all upcoming movies scheduled with Holy Alliance Productions.

Caleb insisted that the twenty thousand be in cash, so Knightly said he would meet him at a remote location in Topanga Canyon and hand it over. In retrospect, Caleb felt he should have been a lot more wary about Knightly's quick capitulation. He arrived ten minutes late to the location in the mountains and kept the car running, but there was no other car at the appointed spot. He waited, getting increasingly more worried that Knightly was a no-show. He didn't have to wait too long, though, as within minutes five gunshots tore into his front windshield with one hitting him in the left wrist.

He stomped on the accelerator and got the hell out of there. He decided it was not safe to go back to his apartment in West Hollywood. So he checked into an obscure motel on Route 1 in Santa Monica, got to the room, and dialed Mona. She didn't answer so he left a terse message on her machine: "You're not safe. Go somewhere safe right away!"

It was too late. Her blood-stained body was discovered later that night when gunshots were reported by another tenant in her building. Caleb heard the grim news when he called a woman in the building who had become friends with Mona.

Now he not only had no future as a Holy Alliance porn director, but he also had no future in living if he stuck around Los Angeles. He didn't go back to his apartment in West Hollywood and instead drove the four and a half hours from L.A. to Las Vegas in just over three and a half hours. He spent the night there, got up early, and a little more than two days later was in New Orleans.

He thought he was probably safe by now but still decided he should at the very least change his identity. So Caleb Jensen and Pistol Pete vanished into thin air. As if they'd never existed.

TWENTY-TWO

Hunter Snow spotted the old man shuffling toward a row of unoccupied chaise lounges four days after they first met. He let Sam Camposi get settled on the chaise with a paperback he had brought with him, then he stood up and started walking toward Sam.

"Sammy, my man," Hunter said, approaching Camposi and giving him a thumbs-up. "How ya doin', bro?"

It might have been the first time the seventy-seven-year-old man had been called "bro," but he seemed to like it as he flipped an arthritic thumbs-up back at Hunter.

"Good," Sam said. "Everything's good."

Hunter looked down at Sam's paperback. "Whatcha reading there?"

Sam held it up. "It's called *Palm Beach Pretender* by an author I never heard of. Pretty good, though."

"I like the cover."

"Know what that is?" Sam said, pointing at the cover of the book.

Hunter shook his head.

"The entrance gate to Mar-a-Lago."

"No shit," Hunter said, looking closely. "Just down the road from here."

"Yup, exactly," Sam said. "So, ah, where's your cousin, Rainey?"

"Well, now that's exactly what I wanted to talk to you about," Hunter said, taking his iPhone out of his pocket. "See, I got these photos on my iPhone I wanna show you."

"Sure. What are they of?"

"Wait a sec. I'll show you," Hunter said, holding up the iPhone.

The first one was all Sam needed to see. It was a naked Rainey lying in a bed, the covers just above her waist, and the alabaster white, chubby body of Sam standing at the side of the bed. But just to make sure Sam got the message, Hunter clicked the iPhone, and the next photo was…well, a lot more graphic.

Sam's mouth dropped and his paperback tumbled out of his hands and fell on the chaise. He moved to snatch the iPhone, but Hunter pulled it back and smiled.

"Not so fast, my friend."

"You bastard," Sam growled. "How'd you get that."

"Simple," said Hunter. "Rainey left the door open."

Sam was piecing it all together. "What do you want?"

Hunter looked down at the paperback book's cover. "I guess you could call *me* a Palm Beach pretender, too. Pretend to be this nice, friendly guy, introduce you to my hot cousin…but here's the reality, Sam, I want you to go up to your condo and come back with a check for twenty large—that's twenty grand—made out to Cyrus Dalyrimple. Spelled C-y-r-u-s D-a-l-y-r-i-m-p-l-e. And if you even think about calling the cops, Mrs. Camposi's going to get the shock of her life when a FedEx envelope shows up with photos a hell of a lot more graphic than"—he held up his iPhone—"these bad boys."

TWENTY-THREE

Braddock got a call on his cell as he was finishing up breakfast. "Jason Fisher" said the display.

"Good morning, Detective."

"Hello, Matt," Detective Fisher said. "I was wondering if me and my partner could come by and talk to you."

"Right now, you mean?"

"Yes."

"Ah, sure, come on over," Braddock said, and he gave Fisher the condominium number.

A few minutes later Fisher and Tambor Malmstrom were at Braddock's door.

Braddock opened it. "You boys getting an early start today," he said. "Come on in, have a seat."

"Nice view," Fisher said as he sat down in a couch next to Malmstrom and opposite Braddock. "I thought maybe we should compare notes again."

Braddock cocked his head. "You know, Detective, you confuse me. One day you tell me it's not 'amateur hour' and discourage me from trying to help in solving my friend's murder; now you're saying we should compare notes?"

Fisher put his hands up. "Guilty…of being confusing. Tambor and I got talking and we agreed that having you help us out can't hurt. The thing about you knowing the community here and lots of people has merit and—"

"All right," Braddock said holding up his hands, "you don't have to say any more. So, you want me to go first or you?"

Fisher smiled, for the first time Braddock could remember. "We had a break on the black-hulled boat."

"You found it?"

Both detectives nodded. "Actually, the owner called us back after we saw it on a CCTV camera and called him. We went and met with him last night and he told us he had just cast his fishing rod off the golf course when he heard a gunshot. He looked up and saw a man fall to the ground, then a guy on the golf course."

"No kidding," Braddock said. "Then what?"

"He ran into the cabin, gunned the engine, and got the hell out of there. He was afraid the shooter might go after him next."

"That is unbelievable," Braddock said, slowly shaking his head. "So, the shooter was a lot closer than we were thinking."

Fisher nodded. "Tambor and I just spent the last half hour inspecting the area where the guy saw the shooter. Looking for shell casings or anything at all but didn't find anything but a bunch of golf balls. We're gonna get a couple crime-scene techs to inspect the scene too, but I'm not real optimistic they'll find anything. But you never know."

"I know exactly where those trees are. Right on the Intracoastal about halfway between the tee and the green," Braddock said as Fisher and Malmstrom both nodded. "I know 'cause I hit a lot of drives into those trees. So, the shooter had to know we were playing golf that morning, then went there and just waited."

"Gotta be," said Fisher with a nod. "And it's not like he had to be an expert marksman like we were thinking when we thought the shot came from a long way off."

"Sounds like maybe he wasn't a professional after all?"

Fisher nodded. "Correct. And we need you to dig around and also think about who would have known you were playing that morning."

"So that's why you called me?"

Fisher nodded.

Braddock smiled. "It's good to be needed."

"Also, like Jason said, you know the community here," Malmstrom said.

"Well, it can't be too many," Braddock said, "I mean, people who would know we were playing at nine that morning."

"How's it work?" Fisher asked. "Do you call up and say you want a tee time and tell 'em who's playing?"

"Yeah, that's basically it. In fact, I was the one who booked it. Called the pro two days before and set it up."

"So, it seems like it would just be you, the pro, and the two other guys who would know. Not including Carr obviously," said Fisher.

"Well yeah, and the two wives maybe," Braddock said.

"Gotta be someone else who found out," Fisher said. "But wait a minute—was that a regular game and a regular time? So folks'd know that was when you four always played?"

"No, it wasn't a regular time. And the four of us played with a lot of other guys too."

"Well then, like I said, someone else must have found out somehow," Fisher said. "So anyway, that's our little bombshell. What do *you* have?"

"I sure can't top that, but I do have a couple of things," Braddock said. "Specifically about a guy named Frank J. Diehl who Larry Carr invested three million dollars with after he sold his company."

"What about him?" Fisher said. "Why would he be a suspect?"

"I didn't say he was. Just something about him that makes me want to know more."

"Such as?" Malmstrom asked.

"Such as the fact that Carr bought into a company Diehl owned called dreammates.com, a dating website with three million subscribers, plus a nightclub he owns in West Palm called Narcissism. Such as...when I got him on the phone, Diehl didn't want to talk about Larry Carr and practically hung up on me. I'd say there's some smoke there but no fire...yet."

"But what's wrong with owning a dating website and a nightclub?" Fisher asked.

"I didn't say anything was wrong with it but it's just not something that a man who just sold a reinsurance company and typically invests in stocks and bonds would usually invest in."

"I hear you."

"Not to mention that the nightclub seems to be all about wife- and date-swapping."

Fisher glanced at Malmstrom and laughed. "No shit. How do you know that?"

Braddock looked away. "I just know."

"Okay," Fisher said. "I know a detective up in Palm Beach who can maybe look into this guy. What's his name again?"

Malmstrom had written it down. "Frank J. Diehl"—he turned to Braddock—"D-e-a-l or D-i-e-h-l?"

"D-i-e-h-l."

"I'll ask my guy up there if he knows anything about him," Fisher said. "Anything else?"

"Not really. I'm just finding that there's a lot more than meets the eye in my little club."

"Like what?"

Braddock didn't really want to go there. "Well, actually nothing that's really relevant to the case," he said. "How'd you find the black-hulled boat, by the way? CCTV, you said?"

Malmstrom fielded the question. "Yeah, I just went to every camera I could find that looked out onto the Intracoastal until I found it. It was a really boring job, let me tell you. Me and Jason flipped for it, and I lost."

"Yeah, but look where your hard work got us," Braddock said.

Fisher turned to Braddock. "*Us?*"

"Oh, I get it," Braddock said, shaking his head. "Now I'm out of the loop again?"

TWENTY-FOUR

After Fisher and Malmstrom left, Braddock decided it was time to talk to Catherine Carr again. He was nervous about calling her but felt that he had to know more about what she knew. Which, it was clear, was a lot more than she had previously let on.

She answered on the third ring. "Hi, Matt," she said. "I've almost called you a dozen times but chickened out."

"Chickened out? Why?"

"Well, that kiss...was maybe a little too, um—"

"Oh, stop, you're just going through a lot. Think nothing of it."

She blew out a heavy breath of air. "Phew," she said. "Thank you for understanding. So, what's up?"

"I was wondering if I could stop by. I'm still playing gumshoe and have a few questions."

"Sure. Do you think you're getting anywhere?"

Braddock hesitated to answer. "It's really hard to tell. I'm not sure I would have made much of a detective."

"Well, come on by whenever you want."

"How's one this afternoon?"

"Can you make it two?"

"Sure. I'll see you then."

He spent a while trying to figure how to frame his questions. It would be tricky.

As he watched a fishing boat—he thought it was an HCB Suenos fifty-three-footer named *Syrena* he had seen close up in the past—bounce along in the ocean a half a mile out, he racked his brain about who else knew that he, Carr, Coolidge and Vandevere were playing golf at nine o'clock the morning Carr was shot. The only thing he could come up with was that maybe someone had asked one of the other three if they were free to do something that morning and they mentioned that they had a golf game. But he wasn't sure that was likely to go anywhere.

*****

Catherine Carr came to the door wearing a white caftan with yellow stripes.

"Hello, Matt," she said with a welcoming smile. "Come on in."

"Thanks," he said, walking in. "How's everything going?"

She led him into the living room. "I'll be totally honest with you: I hate this widow shit."

Refreshing candor, it was. "Just like I hated that divorce shit."

She laughed. "Yeah, but you had a choice."

"Good point," he said, and they sat down facing each other.

"So, ask away. What do you need to know?"

"This man, Frank Diehl"—Catherine flinched a little—"has got my interest. I'm not sure exactly why, but probably because—as I said before—he seems like such an unlikely partner for Larry to have."

Catherine nodded. "And like I said before, why didn't Larry just put that three million into his Goldman account like he did the rest of the money?"

"And you have no idea why?"

"Um, no. It wasn't like he asked me for my opinion."

"I gotcha. So, I warn you, this is going to get a little delicate now."

Catherine frowned at that. "What do you mean?"

"I mean I'm going to get into something that you're probably not going to want to talk about."

Her frown hardened. "What in God's name are you referring to?"

Braddock sighed. "Please understand the only reason I'm bringing this up is to help find Larry's killer."

She threw up her hands. "Oh, for God's sakes, Matt, get on with it! Quit stalling and ask what you want to ask."

"Okay, I heard from a source I deem reliable that you had a relationship with a man that led to you meeting Frank Diehl at his nightclub."

There was sudden fury in her eyes. "For Chrissake, what are you talking..." But, just as quickly, she slumped forward a little and seemed to have completely run out of steam. She was motionless for a few long seconds.

Finally. "Matt, you of all people know about Larry."

"What do you mean?"

"I mean, you know, how he screwed around. I mean, he screwed around *a lot.*"

"You're right, I was aware of that," Braddock said, grim-faced. "Maybe not as much as I've found out in the last week or so."

Catherine was nodding. "Well, so did I. Yes, I admit it, I had an affair. Just once. My first instinct with you was just to deny, deny, deny, but I can't keep doing that. It wears me out."

"I understand and I appreciate your honesty. It will help me."

"I want to help you, I really do, but who told you about this, anyway?"

Braddock shook his head. "I can't say. I gave my word. It doesn't really matter anyway."

"But do a lot of people know about it?"

"No. I'm certain they don't."

Catherine's face tensed. "I know. It was that woman, Faye, wasn't it?"

Braddock put up his hands. "I'm sorry, I just can't tell you."

"It was, I can tell. So, what more do you want to know?"

"You met Diehl through this man at Narcissism, right?"

She nodded.

"What was your impression of him?"

"Frank Diehl?"

Matt nodded.

"Likable guy. Kind of slick even though I could tell he was from the wrong side of the tracks. It was how he dressed. Very contemporary, very expensive, but kind of flashy."

"So, another time you went to Narcissism, this time with Larry, and introduced him to Diehl, right?"

"Yes, they had a few drinks, seemed to like each other right off the bat. And I guess one thing led to another. I wasn't privy to everything because I think they met a few times after that first night. Larry told me it came down to Diehl needing the money and Larry thought it was a good investment. It was funny that he and Larry hit it off immediately."

"You mean because Larry's from the *right side* of the tracks?"

She nodded. "And, let's face it, was kind of a snob."

Braddock smiled "Oh yeah, that he was."

"So next thing I knew, Larry told me we were fifty-fifty partners in dreammates.com and Narcissism."

"What did you say to that?"

Catherine laughed. "I said, 'Great, maybe now I can find a more acceptable mate.' He laughed. Why, do you think Frank might have had something to do with what happened to Larry?"

Braddock thought for a second. "I have no reason to believe he did. He's just kind of a murky character. Maybe I'm basing that on the fact that he didn't want to talk to me. It got me suspicious."

"I hear you," Catherine said, pushing up a sleeve of her caftan.

"Did you ever hear from Diehl after what happened to Larry?"

"Oh, yes, I was just going to tell you. Do you remember that huge bouquet of flowers outside my door when you came to see me right after Larry was killed?"

"Sure. Was that from Diehl?"

"Yes, it was."

"Did he ever call?"

"No, but he emailed me. Said how sorry he was, then got right to business. How the fifty percent ownership would be transferred from me and Larry to just my name."

"Well, I gotta admit, that was pretty thoughtful."

She nodded. "That was my reaction, too. Is there anything more I can do to help?"

"Thanks for asking, but nothing I can think of at this point," Braddock said. "I can't tell you how appreciative I am about everything you just told me. I know it was hard. Especially about how it all came about between Larry and Diehl. I would really like to talk to that man."

Catherine smiled. "So…join Narcissism. Frank's there a lot. And, hey, look at it this way, it's for a good cause since fifty cents of every dollar goes into my pocket."

TWENTY-FIVE

J ason Fisher's contact at the Palm Beach Police Department was Charlie Crawford, a homicide detective there. Fisher called Detective Crawford immediately after his meeting with Braddock and Crawford got back to him the next day.

"So, about your guy, Frank Diehl," Crawford said to Fisher, "he's got a clean record as far as I can tell. No sheet or anything. Apparently, he owns, or is part-owner, of a lot of office and residential buildings in the area. West Palm and Jupiter, mainly. Plus, as you said, he's the owner and operator of that dating website, dreammates.com."

"Which, apparently, my vic, Larry Carr, had a stake in," Jason said. "Along with a nightclub in West Palm."

"I was just getting to that nightclub. Narcissism is the name. It's like this private club that you gotta pay big bucks to be a member of. Like Trump's place or another one in Palm Beach called Club Colette."

"You know anything about it? Narcissism, I mean?"

"Not much. I drove by it a while ago. Doesn't even have a sign on it," Crawford said. "But the interesting thing about Frank Diehl is, it's like he was born twelve years ago."

"What do you mean?"

"Well, I can't find out a damn thing about him pre-2011. Like he just dropped in from outer space."

"What do you think that's all about?"

"I don't know, I'm still digging."

"Well, thanks a hell of a lot, Charlie," Fisher said. "I figured if anybody could find out about the guy, it would be you. I appreciate the feedback."

"Hey, no problem," Crawford said. "If I dig up anything more, I'll get back to you. Guy's got me very curious. Not many guys bury the first three-quarters of their lives."

TWENTY-SIX

Braddock felt he needed a break from playing detective, so he asked Leah Bliss if she wanted to play golf. She accepted and they were on the fifth tee.

"This is where it happened, right?" Leah asked.

"Yup. I get kind of a knot in my stomach on this hole."

"I understand. I would too."

Braddock placed his ball on the tee and hunched over it. He took a practice swing, then a full cut at the ball with his seven-iron. He hooked it left.

"Damn," he said, "don't go in the water."

"I don't think it did," Leah said. "Pretty sure you're in the trees, though."

They walked off the men's tee together then Leah teed off on the ladies' tee. Her drive landed on the green and stopped ten feet from the pin.

"Hell of a shot," Braddock said. "Looks like another hole for you."

She smiled and shrugged. "Hey, I grew up with three brothers. Things got pretty competitive in the Bliss household."

"I bet," said Braddock, walking up to the stand of trees where he had driven his ball. He felt the pit in his stomach again and turned to Leah. "We figure this is where the guy shot Larry from."

"Really? How do you know?"

He pointed to the Intracoastal. "A guy from a fishing boat spotted a man here when it happened."

Leah shook her head. "I don't know…the whole thing strikes me as kind of surreal."

"Yeah, I agree," Braddock said, searching for his ball.

"There it is," Leah said, bending down. "A Callaway?"

"That's it." The ball was up against a tree, making it impossible to hit.

"I think I need to take an 'unplayable.'" He picked up the ball and placed it a club's length away. He was thinking about the shooter as he swung his wedge. He skulled it into another stand of trees, this time on the other side of the fairway.

He glanced over at Leah, smiled, and shook his head. "At the rate I'm going I'm gonna get a quadruple bogey and you're gonna get a par."

"No way," she said. "I'm going to get a birdie! Hey, you've got another thirteen more holes to make your comeback."

*****

Braddock and Leah were having lunch by the Island Club pool at an outside table.

"If we were playing for money, I'd be broke," Braddock said, putting his BLT down on his plate.

"You were a gracious loser," Leah said.

"What did you expect me to do? Start throwing my clubs?"

Leah laughed. "I've seen men do it."

"So have I. Into the water, even," Braddock said. "By the way, thanks for not asking me a bunch of questions."

"You mean, about your sleuthing activities?"

"Yes, exactly."

"Which doesn't mean I'm not dying of curiosity," she said, taking a bite of her salad.

"Tell you what, how 'bout we talk about our next dinner date instead," he said. "How about Saturday?"

She smiled and nodded. "I'd love to, as long as we don't go back to Narcissism. Once is more than enough."

TWENTY-SEVEN

The more he thought about Catherine Carr's facetious suggestion that he join Narcissism, the more he liked the idea. One of the reasons was because he had left several messages for Frank Diehl and Diehl had never called him back. He needed to speak to him and figured if he joined Narcissism, Diehl couldn't avoid him. So, he called up Catherine.

"I want to take you up on your suggestion."

"Which was?"

"To join Narcissism."

"You're kidding?"

"No. I'm getting nowhere trying to get Frank Diehl to talk to me. I figure if I'm a member of his club, he can't ignore me."

"Gotcha. Well, I guess you want to know what the procedure is? How to get in?"

"Yes, according to the person who told me about it, it's like getting accepted on some website called LAYA or GAYA or something."

"I think you mean RAYA."

"Yeah, where you gotta be super-rich and super-attractive to get on it and need to know someone super-rich and super-attractive who's a member to get you in. And that…would be you."

She laughed. "Yes, well, it might help that I own half of it."

"Okay, what do I need to do?"

"You don't need to do anything, you're in. I'll just call the woman who runs it for us," Catherine said. "But it'll cost ya."

"How much?"

"Three thousand a month. You can afford it."

"That's crazy. For what?"

"Um, you'll find out."

Braddock chuckled. "I already have a pretty damn good idea."
He didn't tell her how he knew.

*****

Catherine got back to him later that morning to say that it was a done deal, but he had to go on a night when an extra woman had signed up. He told her he wanted to go on Friday. She called him back later and said there were no extra women signed up for Friday, but there was one on Saturday. He agreed to go then, at which point Catherine gave him the woman's name and reminded him he needed to bring a check for the first month.

He shook his head after he hung up and wondered what his daughter would think if she knew what he was up to. *You're joining a what?*

Speaking of his daughter, it had been too long since they had spoken. He dialed her number but got her recording. *"Hi, it's Nell. I'll get back to you as soon as I'm done with this damn paper."* He chuckled. She liked to change her messages a lot.

"Hey, honey, it's Pop. Call me when you're done with that 'damn paper.' I love you."

Just a few hours after he spoke to Catherine Carr, he got a panicked call from her. He could hear extreme distress in her voice.

"I don't know what to do, Matt! I'm just in a total panic—"

"Whoa, whoa, slow down. What's the problem?"

She took a deep breath. "I just got a big, fat certified letter from a law firm in West Palm. The gist of it, according to a whole bunch of lawyer-speak, is that I am now only a one-third partner in dreammates and Narcissism."

"What? Why would that be? You and Larry were always fifty-fifty with Diehl."

"I know, but I've read through this paperwork three times now and there's some mumbo-jumbo about how if one of the managing partners—meaning Frank or Larry—dies, then their ownership percentage is reduced."

"That makes no sense. Why?"

"Something about because the partner who dies will no longer be a contributing partner in the operation and management of the company. And how the partnership was founded on the principle that both partners would have valuable input and the loss of one partner would result in the 'diminution' of the company and blah, blah, blah."

"I can't believe that Larry would ever agree to that."

"I doubt that he did. I don't know, Matt, I'm not a businessperson, can you please help me with this? It's gotten me crazy."

"Of course, I'll help you with it," Braddock said. "The timing is good since I'm going to Narcissism on Saturday. I can try to find out just what the hell Diehl is trying to pull."

"It's obvious what he's trying to pull. Cheat me out of almost seventeen percent of the business," Catherine said. "It's also, when you think about it, a motive for Frank wanting Larry dead."

"That just occurred to me too," Braddock said. "Although it seems pretty unlikely that with all the real estate Diehl owns, he'd kill for seventeen percent of dreammates and Narcissism."

"I don't know, the whole thing has gotten me very suspicious."

"I don't disagree with you there," Braddock said. "Tell you what, why don't I come by in a little while and take a look at that paperwork."

"Oh, would you?" Catherine said excitedly. "I would really appreciate it."

"Sure. I'll drop by…say around two."

"Great. Thank you so much, Matt."

"You're welcome. See you then."

He hung up and wondered what the hell had he gotten himself involved in. Life had been so simple just a few weeks ago—he'd wake up, have breakfast, read the papers, and look forward to a nice game of golf, or maybe hauling in a few yellow tails or king mackerels on his boat, then a relaxed dinner at the club while polishing off a few stiff rum drinks, then fall asleep while watching *Shark Tank*.

But that was then…this was now.

TWENTY-EIGHT

Braddock had decided he wanted to see Leah Bliss more than just occasionally and didn't want his burgeoning—he hoped— relationship with her to be taking a back seat to Larry Carr's murder. Both were important to him. He hoped he had his priorities straight—his love life came first.

They decided to go to a funky place, just over the Ocean Avenue bridge in Boynton Beach, called Two Georges. Braddock had been there once before when his daughter was in town. It was raucous and a little rowdy and had a happy hour that went on far too long. But the food was good and the band easy to dance to—though the last thing on Nell Braddock's mind had been dancing with her ancient father.

It turned out that Leah had been there once before too. She too had been a victim of the four-hour happy hour and said she didn't recall much after that.

Braddock picked her up at six, so they'd only be at the mercy of the happy hour for less than an hour. He asked for a table that was off the beaten path, and they were seated in a corner at the opposite end of where the band would play. They had a nice view of the Intracoastal and an array of docked boats.

"So, what did you do today?" Braddock asked as he held Leah's chair for her.

"Thank you, sir," she said as she sat down. "I worked on an abstract painting of...God knows what."

He cocked his head. "Wait, wait, you never told me you were a painter."

"You never asked."

"So, in addition to being an interior decorator?"

"Yup."

"Okay," he said and shrugged, "tell me all about it. You never know, I might be a buyer ready to write a big check. I do have a couple of bare walls in my condo."

She smiled. "In that case," she said, taking out her iPhone, "a picture's worth a thousand words. I've got a few of them here."

She clicked on Photos and handed him her phone. They were of odd shapes and sizes, but with wildly vivid colors. He clicked through about ten of them.

"Oh, my God, I love them."

"You do? Or are you just saying that?"

"I'm saying that *and* I do," he said. "Your colors are incredible. What size are they?"

"Big. Most of them are like five by seven, six by eight feet. I can barely fit them into my studio."

"You have a studio? Where?"

"Well, I call it a studio, but it's also known as the second bedroom of my condominium."

"Can I come see them?"

Leah laughed. "That's a little forward, don't you think. Matt? Asking a woman if you can come to her bedroom on the third date?"

He laughed "But it's a studio."

"Okay then, you can come, But I warn you, it's a mess."

"Aren't all studios? Paint all over the place, brushes and everything?"

"True."

Braddock went through the photos again. "Wow. I mean, I *really* like 'em."

"Well, gee, thanks."

"So, I guess I still don't know that much about you, even though we ended up in a swingers group on our second date."

She laughed. "I still can't believe that."

He decided it would be unwise to tell her he was going there the next night.

The waitress came and they ordered drinks.

"I have some questions for you while we're in the getting-to-know-you stage of our...friendship," Leah said.

"That's all it is, a friendship?"

"Well, yeah, so far," she said. "Why, what would you call it?"

He shrugged. "I guess friendship works."

"Okay, first question is," she said, "what newspaper or news-papers do you read?"

He nodded. "Oh, that's an easy one. *The New York Times*, *The Wall Street Journal*, occasionally the *Financial Times*—which is sort of left over from my old job—and 'The Shiny Sheet,' religiously."

"Wait, isn't 'The Shiny Sheet' that Palm Beach gossip rag?"

"Sure is. I love to read about what the rich and famous and lascivious are up to. Don't you?"

She paused then nodded. "In a perverse kind of way, I guess I do. You read any of those supermarket rags?"

"Nah, just the headlines," he said. "What about you?"

"I also read the *Times*, sometimes *The Washington Post*, sometimes the *Daily Mail* online."

"Oh, I like that one too."

"What about TV?"

"What about it?"

"News on TV, I mean?"

"Um. CNN, MSNBC, also that guy Shepard Smith."

"I guess I put you down as a flaming liberal?"

He shook his head emphatically. "No, not even close. I watch Fox for a little balance, but I just can't stand some of their guys."

"Like?"

"Oh, I forget their names. Doesn't matter. Just the seriously radical right-wing nut jobs."

"Okay."

"What about you?"

"Um, I'd say we're probably on the same team," she said.

The waitress came back, and they placed their dinner orders.

"This is fun. What else? What's your next question?" Braddock asked.

Just as she started to answer, Braddock noticed an older man lumbering toward them. He was a member of the Island Club named Atticus Oliver, and it was rumored that he was a victim of something like, but not exactly, Tourette's syndrome. But unlike Tourette's, characterized by tics, repeated blinking of the eyes, shrugging of the shoulders and blurting out four-letter words, Oliver had a reputation for just saying whatever came into his head. It was as if he had no filter. And it sometimes could be quite unnerving.

"Uh-oh," said Braddock, lowering his voice, "get ready for a crazy man heading right at us."

Braddock looked up at Oliver when he got to their table. "Hey, Atticus."

"Hey, Matt," Atticus said. He had long, stringy gray hair, a prominent nose, red, rosy cheeks and was dressed to the nines in white ducks, a pink linen shirt, and a blue blazer.

"Looking very dapper tonight," Braddock said, then opening his hand to Leah. "This is Leah Bliss, she's a new member at the club. Leah, this is Atticus Oliver."

"Hi, Atticus, nice to meet you," Leah said.

"Wow," said Atticus, looking her over, "where you been hiding, hon?"

"Ah, I just joined a few months ago."

"Aren't you going to ask me to join you?" Atticus asked Braddock, but before he could answer Oliver said, "Thanks. Don't mind if I do."

He pulled out a chair, sat down and turned to Leah. "So, you ever spend any time at the pool?"

"Not really," Leah said. "I'm not much of a swimmer."

"That's too bad," Atticus said. "'Cause I'd like to check you out in a bathing suit."

Leah frowned.

"Okay, Atticus," Braddock said, holding up a hand in a "whoa" gesture. "How 'bout we change the subject." Though he wasn't sure any subject was safe.

"Sorry, I didn't mean to offend you," Atticus said. "Just meant that as a compliment."

Leah gave him a faint smile.

"What's with that president of ours?" Atticus said.

"What?" said Braddock.

"Said you wanted to change the subject," Atticus said. "He's older than I am and twice as senile."

"A little early in the night for politics," Braddock said.

"I hate that Putin. Despicable little runt," Atticus said to Braddock. "Or is he off-limits too?"

"No offense, Atticus, but is there anything you do like?" Leah said, out of the blue. It made Braddock laugh.

"Well, like I said, girls in bathing suits," Atticus glanced over at a scowling Braddock, "but I'm not allowed to talk about that. And ice cream. My current favorite is Layered Dessert Caramel Apple Pie."

"That's an actual ice cream flavor?" Leah asked.

"Yup. Breyers."

"Good to know," Leah said. "I'll try it sometime."

The waitress showed up with their dinners.

"Well, I guess that's my cue to leave," Atticus said.

Neither Braddock nor Leah suggested he stick around.

Atticus stood. "Oh, hey, wait," he said, turning to Braddock, "did I tell you about my conversation with Lucy Mitchell?"

"Ah, no, I don't think you did," Braddock said warily, afraid of where this might go.

"Well, we were playing croquet—talk about a dumb sport, like watching paint dry—and she was telling me about having gone to her doctor." He turned to Leah—"That's about all we do at my age, talk about our ailments and doctors, it's called *organ recitals*"—then turned back to Braddock. "She went to see him because she had pains in her chest and was having a problem breathing, so the doctor did a bunch of tests, and finally said to her—very serious and all—'Mrs. Mitchell, here's what I've discovered, you have acute angina,' and she looked at him not quite knowing how to react and finally said, 'Well, thank you doctor, but how could you tell?'"

Leah burst out laughing and Braddock, after holding back at first, joined in.

Delighted by their response, Atticus's eyes lit up. "I've got more stories if you want."

"No, that's okay," Braddock said. "Thanks for that little anecdote but I think it's time you let us eat."

"Well, nice to have met you," Leah said.

"Backatcha, girl," Atticus said with a little wave. "See you 'round the campus, Matt."

"See ya, Atticus. Thanks for stopping by," Braddock said.

Atticus snickered. "Once more with conviction," he said and walked away.

"Wow," said Leah, picking up her fork. "Talk about a man who just dropped in from another planet."

"Sorry I didn't get a chance to warn you," Braddock said. "He can get pretty outrageous. A couple people at the club talked about trying to kick him out because of some of the things he came up with."

Leah shrugged. "He seems relatively harmless to me."

"Yeah, but some of the things he could get away with twenty years ago, you can't say now."

"Which is a good thing."

"I agree."

"Well, what happened? With those people who wanted to kick him out?"

"I can't remember exactly—oh yeah, now I remember. Somebody said he had a medical condition, and they couldn't kick him out for something that was medical. Which—right or wrong—I thought was good, because he spends half his life at the club and would really miss it. Plus, in spite of all the bombast, he's got a lot of friends there."

"I love that word—bombast."

"Onomatopoetic."

"Oh, listen to you with the fancy words," she said, cutting into her salmon.

*****

They were walking on the beach behind Braddock's condo at the Island Club. It was just past ten. The band at Two Georges had been too loud for them to talk.

"So, we never got back to the getting-to-know-you conversation," Leah said.

"You mean, before being rudely interrupted by Atticus?"

"He wasn't so bad," Leah said, reaching for Braddock's hand.

"I like that." Braddock squeezed hers, then turned to her and smiled.

"So do you have any deep, dark secrets that I should know about?"

"If they were dark, I'd probably keep them to myself," he said. "Okay, I've got one—no, two actually. The first thing I go to when I open my *New York Times* is the obituaries."

"Okay, that's kind of interesting. And the second?"

"I love to watch women's tennis on TV."

"Oh, now that's *very* interesting. What about men's tennis?"

"Not as much."

"So what is it you like about women's tennis. I mean, besides the short skirts?"

"Well yeah, there's definitely that, but I love how they're in such amazing shape and how they run—glide almost—around the court."

"Okay, so that hardly strikes me as dark."

He started laughing.

"What?" she said.

"I was just remembering something that happened a while back. I was on the phone talking to an old friend up in New York, and he asked me out of the blue, 'Are you watching porn on the tube or something?' I said, 'No, I never watch porn. Why?' He said, 'Because I keep hearing all this grunting and groaning in the background.' I laughed and said, 'No, dumbass, it's a tennis match.' It was one of Serena's last."

Leah laughed. "That's funny."

"What about you? Your turn."

She stopped walking and looked up at the full moon. "Um, let me think. Well, for one thing, I snore."

"That's not exactly dark."

"But, I mean, really loud," she said, then snapping her fingers. "But I give really good massages."

"Oh, now you're talking."

"Speaking of talking, I sometimes talk to myself."

He put his arm around her and pulled her close. "Time for the talking to stop."

He bent to kiss her, and she was more than ready for it.

TWENTY-NINE

It was Saturday morning and the knot in Braddock's stomach had re-emerged. It wasn't as intense as it was when he was standing at the cluster of trees on the fifth hole, from which it seemed certain the sniper had shot Larry Carr. He knew it was an uneasy anticipation of tonight's trip to Narcissism. It made him wonder if it really was such a good idea.

It was balanced nicely, though, when he thought about the night before. The first kiss with Leah had led to many more kisses until she had finally said she better go home, or she might lose control of her fragile state, which hardly seemed like a bad thing to Braddock. But he wasn't the type to push it, so he didn't. He walked her back to her condominium overlooking the Intracoastal and the kissing began all over again.

He almost said something dopey like, "Can I come up and see your etchings?" but caught himself at the last moment. Instead, he kissed her again. A good default.

When he started to leave, she asked him if they could get together on Saturday, but he just couldn't bring himself to say he was going to Narcissism. *Just research, you understand.* So, he simply said thanks but he couldn't, which didn't seem like the right answer either. He could tell by her reaction that she was a little...not exactly hurt but maybe curious as to why not.

*****

He parked in the same garage on Narcissus Avenue as he had the week before with Leah. He wished she was with him—despite their last trip there—and wondered again what the hell he was doing. Giving up a chance to be with a beautiful, funny, smart woman who seemed to like him so he could go to a swingers' club and try to track down the killer of a friend. Who maybe didn't really deserve all the time Braddock was spending on the pursuit. But he had come this far…

He made the spur-of-the-moment decision that if Frank Diehl wasn't at the club, he'd bail, give Leah a call, and ask to take another walk on the beach.

Girding himself, Braddock walked up to the Asian hostess, who greeted him like they were long lost friends.

"Mr. Braddock, so nice to see you again," she said pointing at a table. "Amber is waiting for you."

Amber looked pretty good from afar. "Oh, great. And, what about Mr. Diehl, is he here?"

"No, but he's expected. Should be here before too long."

"Okay, thanks," he said, walking toward the table and saying hello to his "date," Amber.

She looked ever better close up.

"Hi, I'm Matt," he said, "your, ah—"

"Oh hi, Matt. Amber," she said motioning to the chair next to him. "Have a seat."

He managed to size up her body as he slid into his chair. It was spectacular. But so what? He was spoken for? Wasn't he?

A waiter came up to them and they both ordered wine. Red for him, rosé for her.

"So, you're a new member, huh?" she asked. "I haven't seen you around."

"Yes, just joined. I've only been here once before. How about you?"

"Oh, I've been coming here for almost two years."

Okay, so where did he go from there? "Where do you live?"

"Out in Wellington. I live up in D.C. in the summer."

The waiter served their glasses of wine and handed them menus.

"Are you a rider?" Braddock asked.

She looked bemused. "A *rider*?"

"You know, horses?"

Wellington was known as a town where horseback riding and polo were common.

"No," Amber said, "but what's-his-name's daughter lives near me. She's a big horsewoman."

"What's-his-name" wasn't much of a clue, but Braddock gave it a shot anyway. "You mean, Bloomberg's daughter?" He had read that the daughter of Michael Bloomberg, former mayor of New York, was a serious rider and spent a lot of time in Wellington.

"No, no, not him, *the Boss*," Amber said.

Now Braddock got it. "Oh, Bruce Springsteen's daughter. Yeah, I think she was on the U.S. equestrian team for the Olympics."

"Yes, exactly. Jessica's her name."

That seemed to be all the legs that conversation had.

"Do you work?" he plowed on.

"Well, I'm a part-time real estate agent. You know, for my friends and stuff."

Braddock translated that to mean *dilettante*.

He nodded enthusiastically anyway. "Houses, condos or what?"

"Whatever they want," she said.

And that subject seemed to run out of gas.

He felt an obligation to keep the conversation rolling.

"So, what do you do for fun?" he asked.

Oh, Christ, did he really ask that?

A sultry smile crept across her deeply tanned face. "That's why I'm here."

Quick. Something. Anything. "Ah, do you know Frank Diehl?"

"Of course I know Frank. Everyone does. He runs the show."

"How about Larry Carr?"

She shook her head. "Poor Larry. I really liked him. He was a fun guy. Is he…was he a friend of yours?"

"Yes, he was. Both. A fun guy and a friend of mine."

"I miss him," Amber said, looking to her right. "Oh, speak of the devil, there's Frank."

Braddock swung around to see a man dressed in a midnight blue suit—a little shiny but extremely well cut—and a pink tie. None of the other men there wore ties except Diehl. He was tall, well-built, and had salt-and-pepper hair that was combed straight back and curled around his ears. He had big, expressive green eyes and a bearing that you'd see in a politician who would walk in and take over a room.

Diehl tapped Amber on the shoulder as he walked past her and said, "Hello, love."

"Hey, Frank," she said, but he was already out of earshot.

"So that's Frank," Braddock said. He couldn't help but being impressed.

"Yup, that's Frank," Amber said. "So where were we?"

"Talking about Larry Carr, Frank's former partner."

She turned to him, surprised. "Larry Carr was Frank's partner?"

"Yes. I figured you knew."

"I had no idea."

"Well, let me ask you this…this is a pretty small club. How'd the two of them seem to get along?"

She shrugged. "Fine, I guess. I mean, I never really noticed."

A waiter came up to them. "Do you know what you folks would like to order?"

"Sorry," Braddock said. "We haven't had a chance to look at the menu. Give us a few minutes, please."

The waiter nodded and walked away as Braddock took a glance at the menu and finished off his wine. Then he stood up.

"Well, I'm going to introduce myself to Frank, since I'm new and all," Braddock said. "Would you mind ordering me a medium rare steak if the waiter comes back."

"Sure, but don't be too long," Amber said.

As he walked away, he caught himself thinking, would a one-night stand be so bad? What was the big deal? It was just a little hanky-panky. Totally meaningless.

Then he silently reprimanded himself; he was sounding like all the other dirt balls out there.

He walked over to the table where Frank Diehl was sitting. There were only six eight-person tables, all filled, plus two couples sitting at the bar.

"'Scuse me, Frank," he said, and Diehl turned and looked up at him. "I'm a new member and just wanted to introduce myself. Matt Braddock is my name. We spoke briefly the other day."

"Oh, hi, Matt. You become a member, huh?" Diehl said, like *How'd that slip through the cracks?*

"Yeah, just joined. Larry Carr was a good friend of mine."

Diehl nodded. "I remember you saying." His eyes bored into Braddock's. "Hey, how 'bout I buy you a drink over at the bar?"

"Sure, that would be nice," Braddock said. He was still uncertain about what to do with the libidinous Amber. A little slam-bam-thank-you-ma'am? Why not? It wasn't like he and Leah were an item. If they were, they were the only ones who knew about it. There it was again…him thinking like a dirt ball!

He followed Diehl over to the bar and they both sat. The bartender came over to them. "Mr. Diehl," the bartender said. "The usual?"

Diehl nodded.

"And you, sir?" the bartender said to Braddock.

"I'll have a Meyers and tonic. Not too much ice," Braddock said.

Diehl turned to Braddock. "So, Matt, why do I get the idea you're stalking me?"

A direct man. He liked that. "Well, I guess you could say that," Braddock said. "Why do I get the idea you're trying to avoid me?"

Diehl chuckled. "Well, I guess you could say that," he echoed. "Question is, why is a big shot mergers-and-acquisitions guy from Wall Street playing detective?"

"Former mergers-and-acquisitions guy," Braddock said. "And the answer is simple. 'Cause a friend of mine was killed and I want to know why, and I want the guy who did it put away."

"That's noble," Diehl said. "And you think I might know something about it?"

"I have no idea. I just wanted to talk to you since you were his business partner."

Diehl held up his hands. "We're talking."

"Yeah, but only because I joined your club."

"All right, all right. What's the question?"

"I'll start with a softball. Why'd you and Larry become partners?"

"That's easy. Not that it's any of your business. But we met at a time I was quietly looking for an investor. I was illiquid, having just bought a big building complex. He mentioned having just sold his business, and one thing led to another, and we became partners. He had some good ideas how to improve my website and it worked."

"Like what?"

"Well, none of it was rocket science. He just studied the competition and noticed that they were barraging potential customers with promotions. Like 'Sixty percent off if you sign up in the next twelve hours,' and stuff like that. So, we did some of those things, and it turned out to be a home run. Can't argue with a million new subscribers."

Braddock nodded.

Their drinks came and Diehl took a long pull on something clear. Something in the vodka or tequila family, Braddock guessed. He noticed that Diehl had a scar on his right hand that looked like maybe someone had driven a spike into it.

"Did you ever have any disagreement over the management of the business?" Braddock asked.

"Damn right we did. That's what makes for good partners."

Braddock nodded. "But nothing that ever made you want to…undo the partnership, let's say."

Diehl took another quick sip of his drink. "I'm gonna give you a straight answer to that question. Then you get one more question and then we're done, 'cause I'm doing you a favor now and I don't owe you a damn thing. Got me?"

He seemed to spit out the last statement and question.

"Yep, I get you. Let's hear the straight answer."

"All right. So about ten years ago, we had a member here who…let's just say, came here incognito. He later became well-known. You could even say he's a *household name* now."

"Okay?"

"Turned out he used a bogus name when he joined. When I found out who he was I checked him out because he wasn't well-known at that time. He went to an Ivy League school, fought in Iraq or Afghanistan, I forgot which, and everyone here liked him." Diehl laughed and shook his head. "I'll never forget, he'd wear this blond wig that looked real when he came here. But one time it came off in the middle of…well, you can guess. The girl he was with was this hot, little TV reporter—she's not a member anymore. Anyway, she told me about the incident a week or so later. About him being a—what did she call him—oh yeah, a very *hands-on* member."

Diehl took another sip of his drink. Braddock had no clue where he was going with this.

"So anyway, after a couple of years and Congressman X becomes Senator X, getting more and more well-known, with talk of him being a presidential candidate, he quits coming here. Figured he'd get recognized, I guess. Probably found himself a nice mistress somewhere. So back after Larry had been here a while, I told him about it, and his reaction was like, *Holy shit! You gotta be kidding me!* I was kinda surprised and he starts talking a mile a minute, rubbing his hands together, and said something like, *That's the silver bullet we need.* I said, whoa, whoa, what are you talking about—"

Braddock heard footsteps and turned to see Amber, who gave him a pouty look. "Hey, Matt, your steak is getting cold and I'm getting lonely."

Diehl laughed and Braddock touched her on the arm. "I'll be right there. Just finishing up something."

"You better be," she said and turned and walked away. And what a walk it was.

"She's a hot one," said Diehl.

"Okay, so I figured out who you're talking about. What happened next?"

"Yeah well, it's obvious who I'm talking about. So I go, *Silver bullet, what the hell are you talking about?* and it turns out Larry's a major contributor to the Democratic party in Connecticut and Florida and he wants to use this to take down…you know who."

"Jim Nicastro, beloved U.S. senator from the great state of Florida."

Diehl nodded.

"Wow…that's incredible."

"No shit. So I say, in so many words, no fuckin' way, Larry. No way my club, which is all about discretion and confidentially, is gonna get compromised and used as a pawn here. Plus, I don't give a shit about politics. Hell, I don't even vote—they're all a bunch of corrupt bastards anyway."

"Okay, but what was the upshot? Obviously, it never came out or I'd have read about it and Nicastro'd be dead in the water as a candidate."

"I talked Larry out of it. I told him if he did anything with it, he'd be in violation of our partnership charter and forfeit his interest or some bullshit like that. I mean that crazy sonofabitch really wanted to nail the guy."

"So that was the end of it?"

Diehl nodded.

"So now I get my last question, right?"

Diehl chuckled. "Yeah, then I suggest you go take care of business with Amber."

Braddock took a quick sip of his drink. "Speaking of the partnership, Catherine Carr told me she got this certified letter saying her previous partnership interest had been decreased from fifty to thirty-three and a third."

Diehl nodded. "Oh, that. Here's the deal, Matt: I got this very aggressive lawyer who thinks that the way to score points with me is to be a total hard-ass. He dreamed that up. It's really got no teeth to it. My lawyer's claim is that because Larry's dead and is no longer contributing in a hands-on sense, that sixteen and a third percent goes away."

"Sixteen and two thirds, to be exact."

"Whatever. Tell Catherine to ignore it. I don't even know why I went along with it. Her lawyer would blow it out of the water anyway."

"That's what I told her."

Diehl shrugged. "Like I said, ignore the damn thing. All right, we're done here." He stood and glanced over at Amber. "Time for you to go...get after it."

Diehl put out his hand and Braddock shook it.

"Well, welcome to Narcissism," Diehl said. "Oh, hey, next time you come here why don't you bring Leah?"

"How do you know about her?"

"I know everything, my friend."

THIRTY

As far as taking care of business went, he didn't. Despite all the reasons to do as Diehl suggested—which were plentiful—he chickened out. He just couldn't bring himself to go through with it.

When he returned to the table where his lukewarm steak and the red-hot Amber were waiting, he patted her shoulder and said how he had a pounding migraine headache and had to leave. He couldn't come up with anything better. She looked disappointed, but what could she say. So she said the obvious "feel better" and handed him a card. He decided to keep it. *Hey, you never know.*

*****

Frank Diehl had a meeting the next morning at his twenty-fifth-floor office at Phillips Point in West Palm. It was a building he didn't own, though he had thrown a few low-ball offers at the managing owner and hadn't even gotten a counter. He had heard through the grapevine that they were about to lose a major tenant that had two floors in the building and figured after that happened, they'd be more receptive to his offer.

Len Davidovich was his right-hand man. He didn't have an impressive sounding title, though. In fact, he had no title at all because Diehl didn't believe in titles. The two men were in the conference room. Len was wearing blue jeans and drinking a Coke and Diehl was in shorts drinking Starbucks. There was no dress code at Diehl Ventures so halter tops, flip-flops, and cut-off jeans were not a rarity.

"Okay, first of all," Diehl said. "See what you can find out about a guy named Matt Braddock. He lives down in Delray and some place up north. Used to be a big player on Wall Street."

Davidovich had a notepad out. "Got it."

"So catch me up on our pool hustlers?"

Davidovich smiled and nodded. "They're doing awesome, as usual. Hunter's knocking it out of the park. He's working with that one, Rainey."

"Oh, yeah, she's a hot one."

"Smokin' hot."

"Why don't you give 'em a bonus. Say, a grand a piece. Don't want 'em thinking about going off on their own."

"Done."

"So we got eight teams working the pools, right?"

"Yup. Exactly. Five at buildings in Palm Beach. Two in Boca and one in Delray. So the grand total last week was eighty-five thousand. Like I said, Hunter and Rainey alone did over fifteen K."

"So what's the net?"

"Right around seventy K."

Diehl was good at math. "So, over three million, seven hundred thou a year?"

"Exactly, but it drops way down in the summer months when the pigeons fly north. I'm projecting we do about $2.5 million this calendar year."

"That ain't too shabby."

"No kidding."

"Then Narcissism, another two million or so."

Davidovich nodded. "And all the buildings."

Diehl smiled broadly. "I can't count that high."

"Hey, speaking of raises, boss…"

"I was?"

"Well, actually, a bonus."

"You want a bonus? For what?"

"I don't know. For doing a good overall job."

"Look, Len, you'll get a bonus when I think you deserve a bonus. Not when *you* think you deserve one. You got me?"

Davidovich threw up his hands. "Okay, okay."

"But just 'cause you caught me in a generous mood. I'll raise your salary by two grand a month."

Davidovich frowned. "Is that it? For me busting my ass like I do?"

Diehl leaned across the table. "Seriously. You're a long way from irreplaceable. I like you, you do a good job, but don't push it."

Davidovich put up his hands. "Okay, thanks. I didn't mean to push it."

"Hey, while I'm being generous," Diehl said, "I want you to tell that jackass lawyer of ours to withdraw that thing with Catherine Carr. Know what I'm talking about?"

"Yeah, sure, that thing about cutting her share."

"Exactly. That's a pretty damn cruel thing. She did just become a widow after all."

THIRTY-ONE

After Braddock had finished all his newspapers, including a thorough read of the *Financial Times*, he dialed Jason Fisher's number. As was his habit, he had gotten up at six fifteen, made his coffee, and gone out onto his oceanfront balcony at six thirty. It was a pleasant way to wake up, plus he always felt he got a jump on the day by being fully informed on the news of the world by 8:00 a.m. Today was a little different, though, as he was actually waiting for a reasonable hour to call Jason Fisher. He deemed eight o'clock on a Sunday morning to be a reasonable hour, though most people probably wouldn't agree with him on that. Especially Jason Fisher.

"Jesus Christ, man, it's eight in the morning on Sunday," was how Fisher answered his phone.

"Sorry, Jason, but we need to talk. A lot's been going on that I gotta catch you up on. Won't take more than a half hour of your time," though he knew it would probably take a lot more than that.

"Okay, okay, there's a place near me, I'll meet your there at nine thirty," Fisher said and gave him the name. "Oh, and by the way, Matt, you're buying."

"I'm good with that, I'll see you then."

Now he had to kill another hour before he made his second call of the morning. To Leah, who he was already missing like crazy, although it had only been a little over a day since he had seen her last. He realized that this was definitely getting serious—at least for him—because he hadn't felt this way in a long time. He wanted to look into her beautiful eyes, hear her unrestrained laugh, smell her sun-bleached hair... Christ, he was sounding like an eighteen-year-old with a first-date crush.

Okay...so what was wrong with that? he thought.

To kill time, he did Wordle, then took a shot at *The New York Times* crossword puzzle, but he was too distracted for that, getting only six words. He kept looking at his watch. Time had never seemed to go by so slowly.

At 8:59 he started to dial her number but waited until his iPhone said 9:00 to hit the call button.

Anticlimactic. He got her voicemail.

"Hey, Leah, it's Matt. I was wondering if you'd join me for brunch at the club. Get back to me and let me know, please."

He clicked off.

Twenty minutes later, when he was walking to his car, his iPhone rang. It was Leah. He was excited, but he had to tone it down.

"Good morning," he said. "How are you?"

"Good morning. I'm fine," she said. "Yes, I would love to join you."

"Eggs Benedict and a Bloody Mary? How could you say no to that?"

"One of my favorite combinations. What time were you thinking?"

"Say one o'clock? I can swing by and pick you up, or would you rather just meet me there?"

"I'll just meet you," she said. "I'll be the girl in the hot pink blouse."

He almost said, *you mean the hot girl in the hot pink blouse,* but didn't dare come across as that lovestruck teenager.

He arrived at the coffee shop Fisher had designated at 9:25 and ordered coffee, even though he'd already had his requisite two mugs. Fisher arrived ten minutes later with Tambor Malmstrom, which was a surprise.

"What a treat," Braddock said. "I got a two-fer."

Fisher chuckled. "What you got is another guy to buy breakfast for."

"Hey, go crazy. Steak and eggs, whatever."

Sure enough, Fisher and Malmstrom both ordered steak and eggs, then Fisher glanced over at Braddock.

"So what's up? What's so pressing that you drag me away from mowing my lawn?" Fisher said.

"Well, first of all, I want to tell you about Larry Carr's partner. I met him last night and he's a real piece of work."

"Yeah," Fisher said. "We know all about Frank Diehl. Dream-mates, Narcissism. Half the real estate in West Palm."

Braddock leaned close to him. "How'd you find that out?"

"I told you. I got a contact at Palm Beach PD," Fisher said. "We're having lunch with him tomorrow."

"Did he mention anything about Jim Nicastro?"

"No, what *about* Jim Nicastro?"

"So, in fact, you *don't* know all about Frank Diehl," Braddock said, rubbing it in.

Then he told them about what Diehl had told him about the blond wig on the head of the leading presidential candidate in the Republican party.

"So your point is?" Fisher said, after Braddock finished up. "Let me guess? That Jim Nicastro killed him, or had one of his henchmen kill him, so Carr wouldn't get the word out about his swinger days."

Braddock shook his head. "No, I don't believe that at all. It's way too far-fetched plus I doubt Frank Diehl would ever tell anybody about it. Nicastro being an active, one-time member of Narcissism, I mean."

"But Diehl told you?" Tambor Malmstrom pointed out.

"True, but I think it was partly to get me off his back. And 'cause he figured I wouldn't tell anybody."

"But here you are telling us," Malmstrom said.

"True again, but this is where it stops. Agreed?"

Fisher and Malmstrom both nodded as their steak and eggs were delivered by their waitress.

"Oh, man, that looks good," Braddock said. "Looks like real steak instead of that minute-steak you usually get."

"Hey, we only dine at the finest places," Fisher said.

"You mean when someone else is picking up the tab?"

"Exactly," Fisher said. "Why aren't you eating?"

"'Cause I'm doing a big brunch later on. Eggs Benedict, maybe a couple of Bloody Marys, the whole shooting match."

"Lucky you," Malmstrom said. "Sounds good."

"So what do you guys have? Anything?"

Fisher snickered, glanced over at Malmstrom, then back at Braddock. "We'll let you be the judge. You want to go first, Tam?"

"Sure. So we had someone come forward—an Island Club member—and say they saw a man walk from the direction of building

4 toward that stand of trees on the fifth hole the day Carr was killed. Thing is it was a cloudy day, as you probably remember, but he was wearing wraparound shades and a big, floppy golf hat."

"Like he was trying to disguise himself?"

"That's the idea," Malmstrom said. "We also found some footprints on a little beach on the Intracoastal right behind the trees. We took a mold and turns out the shoe size is a fifteen. Not a lot of guys going around with size fifteens unless they play football or hoops."

Fisher put down his fork. "Which brings up another possibility—that a boat could have dropped the hitter there, then he hides in the trees and pops Carr," he said. "Oh, and by the way, we've got a pretty good idea who floppy hat is."

"Who?"

"Can't tell you until we get a positive ID," Fisher said.

"Are you just trying to tease me or something?"

"Nope," Fisher said. "Just playin' it by the book."

"Then there's Whispering Pines that you brought up before," said Malmstrom, referring to the trailer park just to the north of the Island Club that stretched from the ocean to the Intracoastal.

"What about it?"

"Well, there's still the possibility someone from there could have done it. It's a short hike from those trailers to the trees."

"Yeah, but why would someone from Whispering Pines want to do it?" Braddock asked.

"Until we got on the case, we had no idea about the hostility between the Island Club and Whispering Pines."

"Hostility? What hostility? What are you talking about?"

"How long have you been a member at the club, Matt?" Fisher asked.

"Five years."

"Well maybe it was before your time," Fisher said. "But we interviewed a couple of old-timers at Whispering Pines and this one guy told us about how the quote-unquote *dead guy* first wanted to buy the park along with some other Island Club members, then when that blew up wanted to have it condemned by the government."

The detective took a bite of his steak.

"Wait, what? Is the quote-unquote *dead guy* supposed to be Larry Carr? I have no clue what you're talking about here," Braddock said.

"Okay," Fisher said, putting up his hands. "According to this guy, who struck me as pretty credible, the dead guy—Carr—headed a group of men who wanted to buy Whispering Pines, knock it all down and redevelop it into ultra-high-end condos and a luxury hotel. They supposedly used a Canadian developer as a front."

"You mean a buyer to disguise their identities?"

"Bingo."

"Okay, I heard all about the Canadian developer, but never anything about him being a front. Each trailer owner was offered a million bucks, but the deal never happened."

"Exactly. So anyway, that blew up, I'm not exactly sure why, and then this group—"

"Again, headed by the so-called *dead guy*, i.e., Carr—" Malmstrom added, picking up his toast and taking a bite.

"Tried to get the government to condemn it as being a so-called 'blight on the landscape' or some shit," Fisher said, "then turn it into a public park."

"But that's crazy on a million levels, not the least of which is the fact that there are two public parks within a couple miles of Whispering Pines."

Fisher shrugged. "What can I tell you? That's what this guy told us. He said that Carr was a big muck-a-muck with the Democratic party, too, and was trying to put pressure on the government to condemn it."

"Well, the big muck-a-muck part is apparently true," Braddock said.

"So why don't you believe the rest of it?" Malmstrom asked. "Oh, I just remembered something else: another thing this guy said was, he—meaning the quote-unquote *dead guy* again—referred to the trailers as 'ugly little tin cans that stick out like sore thumbs and bring down home values all around them.'"

Braddock shook his head and thought for a few moments. "If he actually said that then he didn't know what he was talking about. The people who live there love it. And they should. I've met a bunch of them. One guy there who I got to know, asked me to go fishing on his boat out of the marina there. Caught my first swordfish. Plus, they have this beautiful clubhouse—I got invited to a barbecue there once. They got a million activities: bridge club, glee club, they put on a play every year and have this big art show. I bought a painting there. Even have their own TV station."

Fisher laughed. "You sound like the damn chamber of commerce."

"Yeah, why don't you just move there?" Malmstrom said.

"I'm serious. I love the place."

"We got that," Fisher said, looking at his watch. "Okay, the half-hour you promised this was going to take is now fifty-five minutes."

"Wait a minute," Braddock said. "One thing doesn't make sense: that whole thing you just described—Larry Carr trying to buy Whispering Pines by using a bogus developer. Then trying to have the government condemn it, which is like a hundred-to-one longshot, at best—took place at least five years ago, right?"

"Right," Fisher said. "And I know exactly where you're going, so why would anyone from Whispering Pines want to kill him when that whole thing is ancient history and way back in the rearview mirror?"

"Yeah, exactly."

"The answer is that a couple months back, these government cars start showing up at Whispering Pines. Guys taking pictures of everything. And supposedly even a drone buzzing around overhead."

Braddock shook his head. "I don't know, man," he said. "Now you're going a little sci-fi on me."

"Maybe," Malmstrom said. "But word was that Carr had a high-ranking government guy in his pocket and was taking another run at it."

"Hey, how would you feel if you thought someone was going to take your place away from you?" Fisher said. "Real or imagined?"

Braddock nodded. "Yeah, I hear you. But you don't have one specific suspect at Whispering Pines?"

"No," Fisher said, "we don't."

"Tell him about the slug," Malmstrom said to Fisher.

"Oh, yeah," Fisher said, wiping his mouth with a napkin. "Saved the best for last. So one of the missing pieces has always been the slug that killed Carr. We did a trajectory test from the stand of trees, which is eight feet higher than where Carr was standing when he got shot, then subtracted four and a half feet from that, which was where he got shot in the chest. That gave us a field where the slug had to have ended up. We went out there at the crack of dawn on Friday with four techs, did a grid search, and after half an hour found the slug."

"No shit," Braddock said. "That's a major find."

"Damn right," Fisher said. "Potentially tells us what the murder weapon was. Lab hasn't gotten back to us with the results yet. Now you know everything we know."

Braddock shook his head slowly and deliberately "Well, I've got to hand it to you guys," he said. "You've sure as hell been doing your homework. I'm not quite sure where we are in all this, though."

"We're getting there, man," Malmstrom said.

"Yeah, we're gonna break it soon," Fisher added.

"I really am impressed at all you've done," Braddock said.

"You shouldn't be," Fisher said. "We're just doing our jobs."

"You know what rule number one in the cop handbook is, Matt?" Malmstrom asked.

"What's that?"

"'Get off your lazy, fat ass and go knock on doors.'"

THIRTY-TWO

Braddock was still overwhelmed with all that Fisher and Malmstrom had told him as he drove back to his condominium. He had to admit it: he had totally underestimated them. And though they didn't have a suspect in jail, they had made a hell of a lot of progress. Braddock believed Fisher when he said, *We're gonna break it soon.* But, as was his nature, whether he was playing a sport or hungry to complete a billion-dollar business deal, he couldn't help but feel competitive with Fisher and Malmstrom. Yes, they were all on the same team, but he still wanted to be instrumental in catching Larry Carr's killer.

*****

Shortly after he got back to his condominium, he got a call back from his daughter Nell.

"Hey, kid, 'bout time."

"You just called last night," she said. "You expect me to call you back five minutes after you left the message?"

"Yup."

"Don't be a jerk," she said. "So how's everything with you?"

"Good. I've been missing you. I can't wait to see you in—what is it?—just a little over a month."

"Me. too. What do you feel like doing out here?"

"I don't know, maybe hit one of the vineyards again. That was fun. Go into San Francisco for dinner one night. See the sights a little. That city never gets old to me."

"Okay, so what's your preference for dinner, Scoma's or Mersea? I'll make a reservation."

"I don't care. Your call—they both have great views."

132

"All right, I'll book Mersea."

"So, how's that paper coming along?"

Nell laughed. "Hey, I called you, didn't I? I'm working my ass off out here."

"Hey, hey."

"Oh, come on, Pop... I can't say 'ass'? Okay, I'm working my fanny off."

He laughed. "Good to hear."

*****

As advertised, Leah Bliss was wearing a hot pink blouse. Below which was a short, cream-colored skirt. Below which were her fabulous, tanned legs.

She was standing next to a table where a couple was sitting. He knew the couple by sight, having been introduced to them a while back.

"Hey, Sam," he said to the husband, then turned to the wife. "How are you, Joanne?"

"Hey, Matt," said Sam.

"Hello, Matt," said Joanne. "Beautiful day."

"Sure is," Matt said. "Well, great to see you guys."

He and Leah walked over to a table, which was near the swimming pool.

Braddock pulled out Leah's chair. She sat down and shaded her eyes. "So, bring on the Hollandaise sauce."

"Absolutely," Braddock said. "You've got food and drink on your mind, I see."

"Always."

On cue, a waitress came to their table and they both ordered Bloody Marys—Leah's with Tito's vodka, Braddock with the house vodka.

"So how was your date last night?"

Talk about out of the blue. "Uh, what do you mean?" he said and blushed.

"Oh, struck a nerve, I see."

"Just for the record, I was on my way home at 9:45," he said. "I almost called you."

"You should have," she said. "I was missing you."

Damn, he thought, *I should have called her.*

"All right, I'm going to make a full confession now," he said.

"You don't have to, you know."

"I want to," he said. "I went back to Narcissism."

Her response was pure incredulity, complete with a one-inch mouth drop. "Get out of here!"

"I assure you, it was strictly business."

"Yeah, I'm sure... I think they call it monkey business."

He shook his head and explained, leaving out the part about Jim Nicastro. It took the better part of a Bloody Mary and a half.

"Wow, you're taking this sleuthing business very seriously," she said when he was done.

"I know. Maybe too seriously."

"I kind of admire you for it, though," she said. "But do you think it's dangerous?"

It was such an obvious question, but one he'd never really given any serious thought to.

"Now that you mention it, it might be," he said. "I mean, I am trying to catch a killer. But I'm working with two Delray homicide cops who're doing all the heavy lifting."

"The shoot-out at the end and everything?"

He laughed. "Yeah, exactly."

"Yes, but still, if the guy who did it finds out you're after him...I mean like, say it's that guy who owns Narcissism, he might be kind of a rough customer. Packing heat and all."

"Yeah, you're right," he said, but it still wasn't enough to get him to stop or even slow down.

"I'm just saying—"

"Hey, Matt," came a voice behind Braddock.

Braddock turned to see Jack Vandevere and his wife, Sally, with Chris Coolidge.

"Hey, fellas," he said, and introduced everyone, though it turned out that Leah knew Sally Vandevere.

As the women started talking, Braddock stood and turned to Vandevere and Coolidge. "Hey, I've been meaning to ask you guys," Braddock said. "Besides us, who else would have known we had the game scheduled that morning Larry was killed?"

Vandevere's eyes went from Braddock to Coolidge. "I don't know...it's not exactly big news. Our golf games, I mean. Why?"

"Well, see, it's just that whoever shot Larry would seem to have known we were playing then, you know?"

Coolidge nodded. "I see what you mean. So you're still playing amateur detective?"

Vandevere laughed.

"Hey, man, I just want this guy caught," Braddock said. "We might be getting closer."

"Who's we?" Coolidge asked.

"Me and the cops."

"Good to hear," Vandevere said and added, "Well, good luck with it."

"We gotta sit down," Coolidge said. "I'll give you a call about our next game."

Braddock nodded, as the Vandeveres and Coolidge said good-bye and walked over to their table.

"Golf buddies," Braddock explained as he turned back to Leah.

"I gathered," Leah said. "I've never played with her, but I hear Sally Vandevere's good."

Braddock lowered his voice. "Nah, you'd crush her."

Leah laughed. "You didn't see me play yesterday. I drowned three balls."

"Welcome to the club," he said. "Hey, I was thinking, it's a perfect day for a boat ride. What do you say?"

"Fishing, you mean?"

"Nah, just cruise up and down the Intracoastal. We could bring along a couple more of these"—he raised his almost-empty glass—"and make it a booze cruise."

She raised her glass. "Let's do it. Do I need to change or anything?"

"Nope. We'll just go straight from here to the boat. It's five minutes from here. All I need to do is call my captain... Come to think of it, why do we even need him?"

As they were about to leave, Braddock spotted a grizzled man coming in their direction. It was Atticus Oliver.

"Look out," Braddock murmured in Leah's ear. "Incoming."

Atticus, wide grin on his face, stopped just short of their table. "Hey, kiddies, how's the romance blossoming?"

He said it so loud you could have heard him on the other side of the pool.

"Easy, Atticus," Braddock said. "You're not asking the whole world."

"Oops, sorry," he said, glancing at Leah. "You are just as cute as a button."

Braddock was afraid the old man might pinch her cheek…or worse.

"Well, thank you, that is nice of you to say," Leah said, with a megawatt smile.

"So I just thought you kiddies might want to hear about my latest conversation with Lucy Mitchell"—that was Braddock's cue to stand—"on the croquet court."

"We'd love to, Atticus," Braddock said, on his feet now, "but we're late for a boat ride."

*****

They had the bartender at the Island Club mix up four more Bloody Marys.

"I always loved a good roadie," Leah said carrying two red plastic cups. "But I think I'm only good for one more."

"Yeah, well, just in case," Braddock said. "We'll put them in the boat's refrigerator."

They drove the short distance to the marina on George Bush Boulevard on the Intracoastal and got aboard the *Blue Alibi*.

"What a beautiful boat," Leah said as they approached it.

Braddock patted the bow. "Thanks. Bet it's feeling a little bit neglected," he said. "I haven't used it much lately."

Five minutes later they shoved off from the dock heading north.

"Do you know why the bridge seems to always be in the up position?" Leah said, pointing to the bridge on George Bush Boulevard.

Braddock nodded. "It's been like that forever—a month at least. It's broken. What I heard is they need to get some part from like Czechoslovakia or somewhere."

"Seriously?"

"So I heard."

They went further north along a golf course in Gulf Stream, past houses and condominium buildings.

"So we're coming up to the Little Club par three, then the Island Club par three, both designed by—I'm sure you know—Pete Dye."

Leah raised her hand. "Wait a minute. Not so fast, Pete Dye and his wife, Alice. People seem to forget about her, but she was pretty involved in designing a lot of courses."

"You're right. Very involved actually. She also was a hell of a golfer and won a bunch of tournaments in the seventies and eighties."

"Oh, I didn't know that," Leah said.

"Yup," Braddock said, his voice turning solemn, "and coming up is the scene of the crime."

Braddock pointed at the fifth hole of the Island Club.

"Does it still kind of give you the creeps?" Leah asked, shading her eyes.

"It gives me something. I'm not quite sure what."

They kept sailing in silence.

"And to the left you have the scene of our first date," Braddock said, pointing at the Prime Catch.

"That was fun," Leah said.

About another mile farther north Braddock said, pointing at the Two Georges, "And that's where Atticus Oliver told us about Lucy Mitchell's, ah, affliction."

Leah laughed. "You mean, acute…"

"Yeah, that."

They then turned around and went south to Linton Boulevard at the south end of Delray Beach. Then they reversed direction and went back to the marina at George Bush Boulevard.

As Braddock was steering the *Blue Alibi* up to the dock, he got a call on his phone. He didn't answer it as docking the boat required his full concentration.

He turned to Leah. "I have a job for you."

"I'm ready. What do you want me to do?"

"Take the line on the port side of the bow and when we get close jump onto the dock and hold the line taut."

"Aye, aye, Captain. I just translated that all into English and I'm ready," she said, and she walked toward the bow of the boat.

Braddock had been known to "nudge" the dock a little more than he had meant to do in the past, but this time he brought it in perfectly. Leah, without being prompted, jumped onto the dock and hitched a line to a cleat on the dock.

"Atta girl," Braddock shouted from the wheel. "You know more than you let on."

She shot him a thumbs-up. "Just full of surprises."

"Good job."

Leah went and cleated two other lines as Braddock shut down the engine and jumped onto the dock.

"I'm impressed," he said for the second time that day. The first was to Fisher and Malmstrom.

"I'm not a complete landlubber," Leah said, grabbing his hand. He could get used to this, he thought, as he took his phone out of his pocket with his other hand.

He looked at the missed call. It was a Palm Beach number. At first, he thought maybe Frank Diehl. Then he remembered it was actually Neil Carr's number.

He can wait.

"That was so much fun," Leah said. "I love sightseeing from a boat. It's so much nicer than driving. You see so much more."

"I agree," Braddock said, looking at his watch. It was a little after five p.m. "So what do you want to do now?"

"Oh, goodie, so *date day* isn't over yet?"

"Not unless you want it to be," he said as they walked to his car.

"I don't. So it's too early to eat again and I had my quota of alcohol for the day, so…got any ideas?"

"Yes, in fact, I do," Braddock said. "I would love to see your paintings."

She clapped her hands. "Done! I would love to show you my paintings."

"Well, what are we waiting for," he said, holding the car door for her. "Let's go. I just need to make a quick call first."

"Last night's date?"

He laughed. "I've already forgotten her name," he said. "Besides it was business, remember?"

She smiled. "So you say."

He walked around, got into the driver's seat, dialed Neil Carr's number, and turned to Leah. "It's the brother of Larry Carr."

She nodded.

Neil answered.

"Hey, Neil," he said. "It's Matt Braddock getting back to you."

"Oh, hey, Matt. I just wanted to see how you're coming along. What's new on Larry's murder?"

"Well, a lot actually, but nothing that's…what I'd call a smoking gun yet. Can I fill you in later, maybe call you tomorrow? I'm kind of in the middle of something."

Leah smiled and nodded.

"Yeah, sure, but I just wanted to tell you something else. Promise, I'll do it quickly."

"Yeah okay, I just don't have a lot of time right now."

"Okay, so I was at my building's pool just reading a paperback and this guy comes up to me. Nice-looking young guy, tells me he likes my bathing suit and asked me where I got it. So I tell him and we're just talking and about five minutes later this woman…I mean a really attractive woman, twenty-five or so, comes up to us—"

"Hey, Neil, I'm sorry, but I've got to cut you off. How 'bout I give you a call first thing tomorrow morning?"

"Yeah, okay, that's fine," Neil said. "It's a pretty bizarre story and I didn't really have anyone else to tell it to."

"I gotcha. Talk to you tomorrow morning, Neil," Braddock said, and he clicked off and started the car engine.

"What was that about?" Leah asked.

"I'm not really sure. But maybe another person in need of my well-honed detective services."

"I just heard something about a very attractive twenty-five-year-old woman."

Braddock smiled. "Yeah, and if you're a fifty-five-year-old alcoholic like Neil Carr, that probably could only mean nothing but trouble."

THIRTY-THREE

L eah's paintings were abstract, but not so abstract that you couldn't make out human figures, along with landscape elements as well—he could make out trees and the ocean and mountains in the background of one.

She had six completed paintings resting against two walls and another one on a large easel that seemed to be about halfway along.

"I love all of them," Braddock said, walking up to one, "but this is my favorite." It was of a small group of people up to their knees in water, with a craggy cliff in the background, but the figures were all impressionistic, bordering on the abstract.

"That one's from my California phase," Leah said. "A little place called Capitola."

"Where's that?"

"A seaside town not far from Santa Cruz," Leah said. "I'm not quite sure why I ended up there. Except it's got a lot of great restaurants."

"How long were you out there?"

"Well, I lived in Montecito for three years," Leah said. "After my divorce. I wanted to get away from the east coast for a while."

"I hear you. I did the same, but not so far afield."

"Where'd you go?"

"Maine. Ended up buying a house there."

"Oh, yeah, you mentioned that. Where is it again?"

"A place called Christmas Cove. I just go up there and kind of veg out."

"I've always loved that expression," Leah said, turning to him and putting her arms around him.

He took the hint and kissed her. At first gently, but the passion began to build as it had on the beach two nights before.

Finally, Leah pulled back and looked him in the eye.

"I've got an idea," she said.

"Let's hear it."

"Why don't we veg out in front of the tube tonight? Watch something on Netflix or Hulu. I'll cook one of my famous pasta dishes."

"Sounds perfect," he said.

*****

Leah had gotten adventurous and cooked them shrimp scampi. Braddock liked it so much he had seconds while watching the fourth season of *Goliath*.

"Okay, I have a trivia question for you," Leah said, putting down her pasta bowl on the table in front of them. "How many times has Billy Bob"—she was referring to the show's star, Billy Bob Thornton—"been married?"

"Um, I don't know...twelve?"

She laughed and poked his arm. "No, only six. And I have even more info on the subject."

"Do tell."

"Each one, with the exception of number six, lasted two years."

Braddock laughed. "How do you come up with stuff like that?"

She shrugged. "I don't know much about normal things, but stuff like this, I know cold."

"I don't know if I'd ever cut loose Angelina Jolie."

"Yeah, but word is she's kinda weird."

"I'd say that makes two of 'em."

"Yeah, but I love *him*."

"Well, maybe he'll come find you and make you wife number seven."

She put up her hands. "I don't love him that much."

The kissing resumed. And resumed.

Finally, Leah pulled back. "So, I'm thinking—"

"—I was too," Braddock said. "Time for me to go?"

"But I didn't—"

He put his fingers to her lips. "There's plenty of time," he said getting up.

Leah was on the couch, her mouth open in what looked like at least mild disbelief. Then she got up, walked up to him. "One last kiss," she said and kissed him long and hard.

"It better not be the last one."

"Don't worry."

THIRTY-FOUR

On the short drive across the street to his condominium, Braddock had just enough time to berate himself. Well, not exactly berate. More like wonder why he had acted the way he had.

In his entire history, he had never once turned down a woman's offer as he just had. What had come over him? What the hell was he thinking? Was he trying to prove to her that he was not in it for the sex? Was he trying to postpone it with the belief that it would be even better in the future? Was he...? Damned if he knew.

He chuckled to himself, at least he hadn't used the migraine thing again.

*****

As promised, Braddock called Neil Carr the next morning.

Carr's tale was indeed bizarre.

"So I'll just cut to the chase, 'cause I know you're a busy man," Neil said. "So as I told you, this really attractive woman came up to me and this guy at my pool, and shortly after that, the guy took off. Said he was going to the men's room or something. Only thing is he didn't come back...well, until later."

"When was this again?"

"Saturday. Just the day before yesterday," Neil said. "So, the woman apparently found me irresistible, and one thing lead to another and before I know it we're up in my condo doin' the horizontal rhumba—" and just in case Braddock didn't get it— "Screwing our brains out."

"You're kidding," Braddock said, looking out as the sun rose higher in the sky, the stack of newspapers at his feet.

"No, and this was no alcohol-fueled fantasy, by the way," Neil said. "This was reality. So at one point I hear this noise, like a footstep on my wood floor, and look up and there's the guy from the pool with a camera in his hand. And he goes, 'Say cheese.' So I jump out of bed, put on my bathrobe and confront the sonofabitch, who's standing there with the camera."

"What did you say?"

"What do you think I said? I said, get the hell out of here, I'll have you arrested for trespassing. Something like that."

"And he goes, all smug and everything, 'Okay, Neil, you do that, and I'll show these photos to the missus.' He actually called her that, 'the missus.'"

"But you told me your wife died a few months before. Cancer, right?"

"Right. So I said to the guy, 'You go right ahead and do that, you stupid asshole'—or words to that effect—'you'll find her in a cemetery in Greenwich, Connecticut.'"

"What did he say?"

"He pointed at my ring. 'But—' I cut him off and said, 'Is it written somewhere that a man can't wear a wedding ring after his wife dies?' Then I told him to get the hell out of there and take his hooker girlfriend Rainey with him…though, I must admit, I was kinda sad to see her go."

"Wow, only in Palm Beach, I guess," Braddock said. "But my question is, Neil, why are you telling me this?"

Neil didn't say anything for a few moments. "That's a fair question," he said finally, and laughed. "I just had to tell someone about the whole crazy thing, plus I guess I thought the Sherlock Holmes in you might somehow be interested."

THIRTY-FIVE

A half hour after Braddock spoke to Neil Carr, his phone rang again. It was Jason Fisher.

"Two days in a row," Braddock said. "Lucky me."

"I just had lunch with that Palm Beach detective I told you about and you gotta hear this."

"Oh, right. Charlie somebody, right?"

"Yeah, Charlie Crawford," Fisher said. "So there're several websites that law enforcement can go to for background information on people—like one called FDLE in Florida which stands for Florida Department of Law Enforcement. And a couple of others."

"Good to know."

"Anyway, Crawford was trying to find out more about your friend, Frank Diehl, after I told him about Diehl's business connection to Larry Carr. He spends a bunch of time on all these sites, then gives me a call back. You ready?"

"Yeah, what did he find out?"

"So it turns out that Diehl grew up in California and started out life as a wannabe actor named Caleb Jensen. Then, after that went nowhere, he ended up having a brief career as a porn star. Went by the catchy name of Pistol Pete."

Braddock laughed "Oh, my God, you're kidding, how lame is that?"

"Yeah, I know. So after a couple years of that he somehow ends up on the other side of the camera, as a director of porn flicks. And, little known fact, one of his *films* was actually nominated for the porn equivalent of Best Picture Award."

"Wow. You can actually find out stuff like that on cop sites?" Braddock asked.

"Yeah, guess so. I don't use 'em much."

"Gotta question for you, Jason."

"Fire away."

"Why didn't *you* look into Diehl on those sites?"

Fisher was silent for a few moments. "What are you trying to say, Matt?" he said finally. "That my Palm Beach detective friend is doing his job better than me?"

"Oh, Jason, don't get your nose all out of joint," Braddock said, wryly. "If you're offended, don't be. It was just a simple question."

"Christ, man, here I'm trying to be helpful, and you take me out at the knees."

"Come on, get over yourself," Braddock said. "While that's all very interesting, question is where does it go? What's it prove? What's it got to do with the case?"

"I know. That was my reaction. Just thought you'd want to know."

"How 'bout, did this guy Crawford find any police record for Diehl. A sheet, I guess you guys call it?"

"Nope, guy's clean."

"Well, like I said, as much as that little trip down memory lane about Pistol Pete Diehl is quasi-interesting, it ain't got shit to do with solving Carr's murder."

"Okay, okay, then I won't call you anymore if you're just gonna bite my head off every time I do."

*****

Not knowing what he could do to advance his murder case, Braddock turned to advancing his case with Leah Bliss.

She picked up on the second ring.

"Hey, if I didn't gush enough last night, I love your paintings," he said.

"You did and I'm flattered," she said. "How are you anyway?"

"Missing you," he said. "I've got a place picked out on my wall for that one I really love. The Capitola one."

"How much is in your bank account?" she said.

"Ah…"

"I'm kidding. You get the friends and family discount. By the way, you have very good taste; that's my favorite too."

"Good to hear," he said. "So we've done the boat ride, the walk on the beach, the paintings, the night at Narcissism, what's next?"

"I've got an idea," Leah said. "There's this speaker I'd really like to hear at the Four Arts in Palm Beach. Would you be interested?"

"The Four Arts? *Cul-chah*? Sure, I'm in."

"Don't you want to know who it is?"

"I trust you."

"It's Carl Hiaasen."

"I love him. He's funny as hell. When is it?"

"Tomorrow night."

Braddock groaned dramatically. "How am I supposed to wait a whole day and a half until I see you?"

"Well, you could join me at the flower show this afternoon."

Braddock chuckled. "Hey, I love flowers as much as the next guy, but I got a golf game."

"They always have such beautiful rainbow roses."

"I am sorely tempted," Braddock said. "But I don't want to have three guys pissed-off at me. What about a little beach barbeque tonight?"

"I'd love that. Where?"

"On my balcony."

"What time?"

"Say, seven."

"Perfect. What can I bring?"

"Just your beautiful self."

*****

"That is the thickest steak I've ever seen," Leah said watching the beef sizzle on Braddock's grill. "Where'd you get it?"

"A place called Atlantic Meats. I'm a regular."

"A meat and potatoes guy, huh?" she said, taking a sip of white wine.

"Meat and potatoes *and* ice cream."

Leah laughed. "You might want to throw a salad into the mix every once in a while."

"I do," he said, raising his glass to her. "Smothered with nice, fattening, blue cheese dressing."

She shook her head. "Why is it you don't have an ounce of fat on you?"

He pulled at his stomach. "Oh, that's not true, I got a little pooch here."

"That's nothing," she said, sitting.

"So how was the flower show?"

"It was great, but things like that—a roomful of women— always turn into a gossip fest."

He sat down next to her, keeping an eye on the steak. "So what's the latest?"

"Gossip, you mean?"

He nodded.

"Well, of course, there's always something about Larry Carr's murder and nonstop speculation about who did it."

"Who are the leading suspects?"

"Well, see that's the thing, nobody really has a clue. But I heard the name Phil Keevil… Do you know who he is?"

He sure did. Phil Keevil was a local curmudgeon who could be counted on to be negative on just about every conceivable subject. He'd gripe about the food at the Island Club. He'd dis the golf pro for the cost of a golf cart. He'd rail at the club valet for being "grumpy." Like he should talk.

"What did they say about Phil?" he asked, already unable to picture the man as a sharpshooter.

"Just that he hates everyone and everything, so it must have been him, their reasoning goes," Leah said, raising her hands. "Plus, something about him having a business issue with Larry."

Braddock was beginning to think a lot of people had business issues with Carr. Carr's brother, Neil, Frank Diehl, some of the members of Whispering Pines. Probably others that he hadn't even heard about yet. He reminded himself that he wanted to talk to his friend at Whispering Pines to see if he could shed any light on Carr's effort to have it condemned by the government and how that might have been a motive to silence him. That scenario still seemed like a stretch, though.

"Did it come up what that business issue might be?" he asked.

"No, but he and Larry both lived in Darien, Connecticut, and there seemed to be some history of bad blood."

Then, as he pictured Keevil in his mind, he suddenly had a revelation. Keevil, a large man, had about the biggest feet he'd ever seen. Could he be the phantom size-fifteen shooter?

"What?" Leah asked. "Looked like you just had a brainstorm."

He shrugged. "Nothing. Just remembered something about Keevil. Probably meaningless."

But he wasn't so sure it was.

As he pictured the giant footprint on the beach off the fifth hole of the Island Club, Leah's phone rang.

She glanced down at the number and seemed to recoil. Her long eyelashes started flicking and she got to her feet. "Sorry, but I've got to take this."

She walked through the sliders to the living room and went to a far corner.

Braddock got up and went over to the grill and flipped the steak. He glanced over at her inside and all he could hear was a low murmur. Five minutes later, she walked back outside.

"Is everything okay?" he asked tentatively, but he could see it wasn't.

"Matt, I'm going to have to leave. I'm sorry, but I just need to go," she said offering no explanation.

"Can I walk—"

"Thanks, I'm okay."

But clearly, she was far from okay.

THIRTY-SIX

The next morning, Braddock took out a carton of orange juice from his refrigerator. It was on the same shelf as his half-eaten steak from the night before. He had cooked it to perfection and was sorry Leah hadn't joined him. After he'd eaten his steak and potatoes—and asparagus—the night before, and polished off a big bowl of ice cream, he had gone out on the balcony with a glass of red wine and thought.

He thought about what could have upset Leah so much that she left without even a goodbye kiss. That had become a nice part of their routine. But, of course, he had no way of knowing what it could have been. He thought about Phil Keevil and his huge feet and how he didn't come close to fitting the profile of a killer, but needed to know what the "bad blood" was, which Leah had mentioned hearing about. If it were even true. Gossip fests had never been known to provide the gospel truth.

Finally, unable to answer any questions or come to any new conclusions, he had gone to bed a somewhat frustrated man.

Now, he poured the orange juice and put it on a tray where his steaming mug of coffee sat. Then he went to the front door, opened it, and bent down and picked up his stack of newspapers. He walked to the kitchen counter, lifted up his tray with one hand, the newspapers in the other, and walked out to the balcony. It was his morning ritual. He sat down and sank into the plush, padded chair that he always sat in and gazed out at the ocean. The view of the lawn in the foreground, then the beach and the ocean stretching out over the horizon always gave him a refreshing jolt to kick off the new day. To his left he saw a couple strolling on the beach, not a rare sight, except at 6:30 a.m., well before most beach strollers got going. He lifted his coffee cup and took a sip and just as he put it down, he heard a sharp noise and the glass slider shattered behind him.

Instinctively, he dived to the balcony floor, landing on his outdoor carpet. He knew it had been a gunshot. Next he heard what he thought was a woman screaming and his first thought was that maybe the woman in the adjacent condominium had been hit. But that didn't make sense, since he had only heard the one shot. He crawled inside, careful not to cut his hands and knees on the glass. He got to his kitchen and stood up behind the island where he had left his cell phone. He started to dial 911, but then hit the red button and speed-dialed Jason Fisher, who lived only five minutes away.

"Jesus, you again?" groaned Fisher, "What now?"

"Someone just took a shot at me. I'm in my condo."

No hesitation. "I'll be there right away," and Fisher clicked off.

Within a few minutes, he heard the sound of distant sirens that seemed to be coming from all directions, but Jason Fisher got there first. Braddock heard a pounding on his front door and heard Fisher shout, "It's me, Fisher!" He opened it to find an out-of-breath Fisher.

Braddock had had a chance to change out of his white bathrobe into running shorts, a T-shirt, and slip-on sneakers.

"You all right?" Fisher asked, looking Braddock over.

"Yeah, I'm fine. My slider isn't," Braddock said, pointing.

"Tell me exactly what happened?" Fisher said. "By the way, did you call 911?"

"No, just called you. Someone else must have," Braddock said. "So I was out on my balcony having my first cup of coffee and reading my papers and...do we want to go out there?"

"No, not until the perimeter's been searched and cleared," Fisher said. "So seems like the shot came from the east? From the beach, maybe?"

"Yeah, definitely," Braddock said and pointed. "My only exposure is to the east. As you can see, the north and south sides are solid walls."

"All right, you stay here," Fisher said. "I'm gonna go check out the beach. Cops or first responders will probably be here any minute and I called Malmstrom from my car."

Braddock shook his head and exhaled. "My neighbors aren't gonna be real happy."

Fisher, on his way to the front door, turned. "Hey, man, you're lucky to be alive."

*****

Ten minutes later the condo was crawling with cops, first responders, a crime scene tech and Tambor Malmstrom. Braddock recognized some of the faces from the scene on the fifth hole after Larry Carr had been killed.

"It's got to be someone I know," were Braddock's first words to Malmstrom.

"Why do you say that?" Malmstrom said. He was wearing blue jeans and a Nirvana T-shirt.

"Your kid lend you that?" Braddock asked, pointing at the T-shirt.

"Grabbed whatever was handy," Malmstrom said. "Why do you think it's someone you know?"

"'Cause who else would know I was going to be sitting on my porch at six thirty in the morning?"

Malmstrom stroked his chin and thought a moment. "Your friends know that? I mean, is that like common knowledge or something?"

Braddock nodded. "Good point. Not like I've told a lot of people about my daily MO."

Over Malmstrom's shoulder, Braddock saw Jason Fisher walk in the front door.

"A couple surprised the shooter at the beach," Fisher said to Braddock. "Maybe why he missed. He took off down the beach to the south and they called 911."

"Did they get a good look at him?" Malmstrom asked.

"Just said he was lying in the dune with a rifle the guy described as 'short.' Blue pants, shades, and a floppy hat."

"'Short?'" Malmstrom said. "Any more detail than that?"

"That was it. He just said it looked like a short-barreled rifle with a wood stock."

"Like maybe a sawed-off Mauser 98 or something?" Malmstrom said, apparently a gun expert.

"I don't know," Fisher said, turning to a man in uniform. "I need you to do a BOLO for a suspect in blue pants, a black T-shirt, sunglasses, floppy hat with a short rifle. Also, get two guys to stop pedestrian traffic on the beach and tape off the whole area."

Fisher turned back to Braddock. "You got any idea at all who this guy might be?"

"Nobody other than the ones we were talking about on Sunday," Braddock said with a shrug.

He decided not to throw Phil Keevil, the size-fifteen man, into the mix until he had a chance to poke around a little about the alleged "bad blood" between him and Carr. There was no point in the Delray detectives treating him as a possible suspect until then.

"What would be nice would be to find a size-fifteen footprint on the beach," Malmstrom said.

"Yeah, obvious problem is we can't get any good footprints on the beach," Fisher said. "But maybe south of here where he got off the beach."

"Yeah, we had that rain last night." Malmstrom said with a nod. "Softened up the ground a little."

"Let's go check out the balcony," Fisher said to Braddock and Malmstrom.

The three walked out to the balcony, tiptoeing around shards of broken glass.

Braddock pointed to his chair, anticipating Fisher's question. "That's where I was sitting."

Fisher nodded. "So seems like you were lucky that couple came along and distracted the shooter. Though maybe he was just a shitty shot."

"He wasn't with Larry Carr," said Braddock.

"True. So let's talk motive."

"Wouldn't you say that it's as simple as him knowing that I'm going around asking a bunch of questions, trying to help catch him?" Braddock asked.

He didn't want to use the word "investigating" since Fisher might take issue with the word.

"Yeah," Fisher said. "I guess that's probably the long and the short of it." He chuckled and eyed Braddock hard. "So how do you like detective work so far?"

Braddock didn't smile. "About as much as being a bathroom attendant. I'm thinking about going back to fishing and golf…as soon as we wrap this up."

"As soon as *we* wrap this up? Are you crazy?" Fisher said. "You want to keep going? You must have a death wish or something."

"Hey, look, the way I figure it is I'm already in the killer's crosshairs. Now that he failed, he's gotta know that I'm gonna make myself a much harder target. If he tries again, I'll be ready for him."

"What? Are you gonna get into a shootout with the guy?"

Malmstrom laughed. "Last time I checked you don't know shit about guns,"

"Yeah, which clearly you do," Braddock said to Malmstrom. "What was that rifle you mentioned?"

Fisher put up a hand to Malmstrom as a man and a woman walked in wearing blue windbreakers with *Crime Scene* logos.

"I'm gonna go talk to them," Fisher said.

Malmstrom nodded, then turned to Braddock. "Jason hates it when I launch into gun talk, which is probably why he found something else to do. So, what I mentioned was a sawed-off Mauser 98. It's a short-barreled rifle made by a German company and, as you probably know, the Germans are very big in gun-making and munitions. Mauser, Heckler & Koch, Ziegenhahn & Sohn"—he patted his shoulder holster—"SIG Sauer—"

"Glock?"

"No, Glocks are actually made in Austria. Krupp's another one. Anyway, as the name implies, it has a short stock and a short barrel, measuring as little as twenty-six inches long. I've even seen some at gun shows that have no stock at all, just a pistol-grip. Only problem is the shorter the barrel the less accurate they are."

Braddock nodded. "You really know your stuff."

"So maybe this guy used a Mauser 98 because he thought it was easier to hide since rifles typically are more like forty-one, forty-two inches long."

"Makes sense."

Fisher walked back to them. "I told them to keep an eye out for footprints. One of 'em spotted the slug, too, which they're digging out of the wall."

"Oh, good," Malmstrom said. "Now we'll be able to tell the caliber of the rifle used."

"You missed a good conversation about German guns," Braddock said to Fisher.

Fisher rolled his eyes. "I'm familiar with the spiel."

"So, what now?" Braddock asked.

"Seems like I've heard this question before," Fisher said. "Now it's more of the same. Just keep doing what we've been doing. We'll crack it."

"Seems like I've heard that before, too," Braddock echoed.

THIRTY-SEVEN

As, of course, would be expected, the shot fired at Braddock was the talk at the Island Club. Braddock's phone started ringing while the law enforcement contingent was still there and didn't stop until late that night. Braddock didn't answer any of the calls. The only one he planned to take was Leah Bliss's, but by three in the afternoon, she had not phoned him.

A new wrinkle was the news media. At ten o'clock, Braddock heard the unmistakable whirring of a helicopter's propeller, and it sounded very close. He walked to the edge of his living room, near his balcony, and saw that the helicopter was hovering just above the top of his building with a woman photographer, one foot on the chopper's skid, snapping off photos with a camera that had a long telephoto lens.

Tambor Malmstrom, before he left, came in from outside. "So, by my count we got trucks from the local affiliates of CBS, NBC, ABC, FOX and—believe it or not—the Weather Channel, plus a shitload of reporters from every paper between Boca and Palm Beach."

"Oh, great," Braddock said, once again thinking about how irate Island Club members would be about all the unwanted publicity and—getting a little paranoid now—how they might want to kick him out, just like a group had tried to do with loose-lipped Atticus Oliver.

*****

At least his neighbors were respectful. None of them had come by his condo to ask how he was doing, a guise for peeking in his condo and craning their necks to see the bullet hole. But at five in the afternoon, his buzzer rang. He ignored it. A minute later it rang again. He guessed it might be a friend who lived on the second floor and walked toward the door.

He opened it and was pleasantly surprised. It was Leah Bliss.

She didn't say a word, just fell into his arms. Then she kissed him and looked up into his eyes. "You poor boy, how are you?"

"Alive. And mostly well. And, since you got here, much better."

She kissed him again. "I just can't believe something like that can happen here. I mean, here we are in this idyllic little community, spared from all the bad stuff in 'the real world.'"

He nodded. "Or so we thought."

"So what are you going to do now?"

"You mean, as far as Larry Carr's murder goes, or life in general?"

"Both."

"Be less visible for one, although you can't be much less visible than sitting on your balcony drinking coffee and reading the papers at six thirty in the morning. Can we talk about you for a change?"

"You mean, why I took off in such a hurry last night?"

"For starters."

"I'm not quite ready for that conversation yet," she said. "You wouldn't *believe* all the reporters and cameras out in front."

"I've heard. Not to mention in helicopters, and I just saw a photographer cross the yellow tape in back."

"Aren't the police guarding you?"

"Supposedly there are two undercovers. But maybe they're both in front now."

Leah shook her head. "When I came in, I overheard a short conversation. This older woman asked a reporter what happened, and the reporter said, 'Someone tried to kill a famous Wall Street tycoon.'"

Braddock slapped his forehead with the heel of his hand. "Oh Christ, that's all I need."

"Famous, huh?"

"Yeah, to about three people."

"Modest Matt."

"I don't need this, Leah."

"I understand."

"Okay, but enough about Matt. *Please*, can we talk about Leah now?"

"I guess we have to sooner or later," she said. "All right...so that was my former live-in boyfriend who called last night."

Braddock nodded.

"He wants to sue me for 'violation of the laws of co-habitation.'"

"What? Are you kidding? What does that even mean?"

"I'm not entirely sure yet, but I'm guessing it has to do with him losing his big job in New York and looking to me as some kind of substitute for that income."

Braddock cocked his head. "Can I ask you a really tacky question?"

She sighed. "Go ahead."

"Are you rich?"

"Um...rich enough. And not real keen on giving it away for no good reason."

"I gotcha. I wouldn't be either. Have you looked into these so-called laws of co-habitation?"

"Most of last night and all of today. Let's just say, it's murky."

"Don't you have to have some kind of written agreement, like a pre-nup, for him to have any case at all?"

"The short answer is 'yes.' But you know how it is, you can sue anyone for anything. Regardless of how baseless and ridiculous it might be."

"That I know," said Braddock. "I totally get why that threw you for a loop last night."

She smiled. "By the way, how was the steak?"

"Delicious. There's still a lot left. All I need to do is heat it up for you. Will you stay for dinner?"

No hesitation. "Yes. And this steak talk is getting me hungry."

"You want me to heat it up now?"

"Not quite yet. Maybe an hour or so."

"What do you want to do in the meantime?"

"Just talk... Dazzle me by recounting your years as a *Wall Street tycoon?*"

He laughed.

"Nothing dazzling about it. I went to work. Went home. Went back the next morning. Rinse, repeat... Ugh, I can't believe I just said that. Talk about the latest lame cliché."

*****

Leah said it was the best steak she had ever had. Reheated or not. Braddock thought she might have been exaggerating a bit, but it was good. She ate almost all of what was left. Braddock had a few bites that were left over and also made himself a hamburger.

"So what do you want to do now?" Leah said, putting down her fork and smiling up at Braddock.

"I been thinking about that," he said. "So I have these two rituals I do every year, probably for at least the last fifteen."

"Oh, yeah, and what would they be?"

"One, I reread *The Catcher in the Rye*; and two, I watch *The Talented Mr. Ripley.*"

"Hmm. Interesting," Leah said.

"And since I don't think you'd have much interest in sitting around and watching me read *The Catcher in the Rye*, how would you feel about watching *The Talented Mr. Ripley* with me?"

Leah leaned back in her chair. "Is that with Matt Damon and Jude Law?"

He nodded.

"I think I've seen it and remember liking it."

"Matt Damon, Jude Law, Gwyneth Paltrow and the best...Philip Seymour Hoffman."

"Oh, yeah, I miss that man. He was amazing," she said. "So let's do it."

Braddock's cell phone rang. He looked down at it. *Jason Fisher.*

He held up his hand to Leah and whispered, "One sec."

She nodded.

"Catch him yet?" Braddock asked.

"No, but we're on it," Fisher said. "How you doin'?"

"Is that why you called? To check up on me?"

"Yeah, why?"

"That's very touching, Jason."

"Cut the bullshit. I need to keep you alive so I can hear your brilliant deductions."

Braddock laughed. "I don't remember having one yet."

"Yeah, well then, you're due. Just try to stay alive, huh?"

*****

Halfway through *The Talented Mr. Ripley* the kissing began again. With gusto and exuberance. It was ten minutes after Jude Law got clubbed to death with an oar by Matt Damon, which one wouldn't normally think of as a prelude to romance.

It ramped up this time, as it had in the past, but now featuring hands going in places they hadn't gone before. Like Leah's hand inside Braddock's shirt. Followed by Braddock's hand unclipping Leah's bra. Followed by a great deal of heavy breathing and feverish squirming.

Then came the only words spoken for a while, as Leah tugged at his hand. "Come on, let's go."

He wasn't *so* out of practice that he had to ask, *Where?*

THIRTY-EIGHT

"Did it make you nervous at all last night being in bed with a guy someone tried to kill?" Braddock asked Leah as he slathered strawberry jam on a piece of toast. It was the final ingredient in the breakfast spread he was preparing for her. The first two were a Swiss cheese omelette and crispy bacon, which sat on a large plate. They were inside, Leah sitting at the island. Braddock normally would have been outside on the balcony, but not today. Not for a long time, maybe.

"No," she said, "for one thing I didn't think about it. But if I had, logic would have been that the guy who shot at you would be lying low."

"Good logic," Braddock said, placing the toast on her plate and handing it to her.

Leah smiled and rubbed her hands together. "Oh, that looks so good. All you ever do is cook for me."

He smiled. "Is that *all?*"

"Well..." she said, smiling then digging into her omelette.

"So I didn't hear any snoring at all," Braddock said. "What you do is this kind of cute little humming noise."

"Really? I always thought it was snoring," Leah said. "Well, what you do is hog the bed. Arms and legs all over the place. I had to keep moving around to find a spot. It's lucky you have a king-size bed."

"Sorry about that. I'll try to stay on my own side."

She smiled at him. "Don't worry, it was well worth it," she said. "This omelette, by the way"—she gave him the thumbs-up—"incredible."

He smiled back at her. "Glad you like it. So what are you going to do today?"

160

"Oh, God," she said, putting her hands up to her head, "I guess I've got to get my lawyer up in New York to deal with this thing from Bill."

"That's his name?"

She nodded.

"Hopefully your lawyer will say it's a nuisance case."

"Well, it is. I never said I'd give him anything if it ended. He never said he'd give me anything."

"Doesn't sound like you've got anything to worry about."

"I hope not," Leah said. "What about you? What are you going to do?"

"A couple of things. First of all, if you'll join me, I want to look into trips. Nothing major, I just think it would be nice to get out of Dodge at least for a few days. Like to the Bahamas or the Keys, maybe."

"Count me in. Just give me a little time to deal with this legal thing," she said enthusiastically. "Would we take your boat?"

"Yes, if we went to the Bahamas, but not the Keys."

"Just drive there?"

He nodded.

"I am so up for that," she said, with a broad smile. "Either one."

Braddock's cell phone rang. Surprisingly, at 8:30 a.m., it was the first of the day, versus yesterday when he guessed he'd probably had fifty. Maybe it was old news by now, maybe he'd been forgotten. He hoped so but doubted it. It said C. Carr on the display. He decided to answer it.

"Good morning, Cath," he said.

"Well, that's the question, *is* it a good morning?"

"A hell of a lot better than yesterday morning."

"Oh, my God. I just can't believe something like that—"

"I know. I'm fine, though."

"Well, can I bring you something?" He flashed to a quick image of Leah hiding under his bed. "Do you need anything at all?"

"No, I'm fine," he said, then remembered Phil Keevil. "But I have a question."

"Ask away."

"So, Phil Keevil. I know he's from Darien, too. Did he and Larry have any issues?"

"Oh, Christ, Phil Keevil seems to have issues with just about everyone."

"I know, but anything of any substance with Larry?"

"Let me think…"

Braddock glanced out the window and saw a man in dark pants and a long-sleeved shirt walking around in back. He recognized him as an undercover who Jason Fisher had introduced him to the day before. Braddock could only imagine he must be hot as hell out there. It was already up to eighty-five degrees.

"There was something about Larry hiring a man away from Keevil's company. I know that Keevil was really mad about it."

"Mad enough to want to kill him?"

"I don't know about that."

"What were the particulars? Do you remember?"

"Um, not really. I just remember him confronting Larry once at the club. Seemed like Phil had a lot to drink, and Larry tried to walk away from him, but Phil grabbed him by the shoulder."

"Oh, so it got physical, too."

"Yeah, but it didn't really go anywhere. Larry turned to him and gave him a nasty look…well, as you know, Larry could be pretty intimidating."

"So Keevil backed off?"

"Yes, exactly. And that's about all I know about it. You're not thinking that Phil—"

"I'm not thinking anything. Just that his name came up and I figured I'd ask you."

"Off the record…*no*, on the record, I'm not a big fan of the man."

"You're not alone," Braddock said. "Well, thanks for calling, Cath."

"You're welcome and if you do need anything, just give me a call."

"Will do." He clicked off.

"Phil Keevil, huh?" Leah asked. "That name I heard with the flower gals."

"Yeah, but he's probably guilty of nothing more than being habitually cranky."

Braddock went back to scrolling on his computer.

After a few minutes, Leah finished her breakfast, wiped her mouth with a napkin, and stood up.

"Well, I don't mean to eat and run, but I've got to deal with this ridiculous lawsuit thing."

"Whoa, whoa, whoa," said Braddock, standing up and putting his arms around her. "You're not getting out of here so easily."

She smiled at him and gave him a kiss on the lips. "I know what you're thinking."

"What?"

"One for the road?"

*****

It was ten thirty when Leah finally left. Braddock got back on his computer, researching both places to stay and things to do in the Bahamas and the Keys. It was kind of a toss-up, though he had a friend who had a house in a place called Lyford Cay in Nassau.

Then he shut his computer down and made a call he had been intending to make for the last two days. It was to a man named Roger Santaw, his friend from Whispering Pines, with whom he had once gone deep-sea fishing. Santaw answered right away.

"Holy shit, Matt," Santaw said, "I heard what happened. You okay?"

"Yeah. A little excitement to kick off the morning yesterday."

"But you're all right?"

"Yeah, I'm fine. My glass slider's not doing too well, though."

"They got any idea who it might've been?"

"No, not yet. A couple theories, I guess," Braddock said. "So, Rog, I want to ask you about something."

"Shoot."

"Did you hear anything or know anything about my friend who was killed, Larry Carr?"

"Only *after* he got killed. There was a lot of talk here about how he and a bunch of other guys tried to buy the Pines under whatchamacallit——an assumed name. Then when that fell through, they supposedly tried to get the state of Florida to condemn it as a 'blighted ghetto' or some shit."

"So I'm sure there were a lot of people who were up in arms about it."

"Oh, yeah, two guys in particular," Santaw said. "Then the whole thing kind of went away for like a year or two but came back a couple months ago."

"Came back? How do you mean?"

"Some congressman from here was pushing to get the Pines condemned again. Word was, he got a very large contribution from an anonymous source."

"No kidding. So people figured Carr was behind it?"

"Yeah, definitely, that was what *everyone* thought."

"So those two men you mentioned, what did they say…or do, exactly?"

"Well, one of them—younger guy, Iraq war vet—went door to door and got signatures on a petition to sue Carr for…what was it? Defamation and slander, I think it was. Something like that. The other guy, kind of a hothead and rabble-rouser, was saying to anyone who'd listen that we should 'whack the sonofabitch.'"

"Really?"

"Yeah, you believe it? And I know I don't need to say this, but you never heard any of this from me."

"Don't worry. This is all just between us. Anything else?"

"Nah, that was pretty much it. But supposedly the one guy I mentioned had pledges of over fifty thousand dollars to hire a lawyer and sue Carr."

"For defamation?"

"Yeah, there was more to it than that, but that's the gist. Vet's name is Greg Jeter. Hothead's name is Holden Mishkin."

"Hey, thanks, man, I really appreciate the info," Braddock said, scribbling notes on a pad. "Let's get out there again and catch some fish."

"Anytime you want. I got nothin' but time."

*****

Braddock's next call was to Jason Fisher.

"All quiet on the home front?" Fisher answered.

"Yeah, I haven't left here since it happened."

"You seen my guys guarding you?"

"Yeah, I'm looking down at one right now. I guess the other guy's in front."

"I'd say the last thing the hitter's gonna do at this point is make another attempt."

"I agree," Braddock said. "So I want to catch you up on a few things. Add some names to the mix."

He told Fisher about the men Roger Santaw mentioned: Greg Jeter and Holden Mishkin, Then about Phil Keevil.

"Okay, I already interviewed that guy Mishkin, your 'whack-the-sonofabitch' guy."

"And?"

"He's totally harmless, just got a big mouth. You've run across the type. All bark and no bite."

"You're pretty sure about that?"

"Absolutely sure. He's a guy in a wheelchair who's a chain smoker and has nothing better to do with his time than spout off crazy stuff and get people riled up. But I'll give the other guy, the vet, a call. At least we can assume he knows how to shoot."

"And you'll talk to Keevil?"

"Yeah, he's a name I remember hearing once before."

"I don't think you're gonna warm up to him much."

"Unlike the other people I've met at your club."

"Are you being sarcastic?"

"No, dead serious. Seems like they're a hell of a lot of nice people there, based on the ones I've met."

"Well, thank you, Detective, glad you approve."

"But then…there's you," Fisher said, deadpan.

Dead air.

"That was a joke, Matt."

THIRTY-NINE

L eah and Braddock ended up sailing to the Bahamas the next morning. He had made the trip before, and it was a relatively easy ride over. He debated whether to take his captain or not and ended up deciding it would be a lot more romantic if it were just Leah and him. His captain, Chuck Day, would be a third wheel. The one thing he had to make sure was that the weather would cooperate. He knew he'd need Day for rough seas, but good weather was forecast for the week.

Braddock was at the helm of the *Blue Alibi* an hour after they departed from the marina at George Bush Boulevard. It was five miles up to Boynton Beach inlet, where they passed under a fixed bridge and then out to sea. Braddock figured that going thirty-five knots an hour meant they'd get to Nassau in about five and a half hours.

Leah was sunbathing on the bow with a paperback in hand.

About ten nautical miles out, Braddock looked down at her and was in for a pleasant surprise: she had removed her bikini top. She caught his eye as he looked down at her, shaded her eyes and said, "I hope this is permissible?"

"Permissible? Hell, girl, it's encouraged."

She laughed and went back to her book.

*****

It took them a little less than five hours to get to the marina at Lyford Cay. It was just past two in the afternoon. By now, Leah had her top back on, and her tan seemed even darker to Braddock, who had spent a lot of time at the *Blue Alibi*'s wheel gazing down at her from the bridge.

As she had done before, she expertly jumped onto the dock and hitched the bow line to the forward most cleat, then did the same for the ones at the middle of the boat and the stern.

"Nice job, matey," Braddock said, giving her a kiss as he jumped onto the dock.

"Thanks, Cap," Leah said, giving him a salute.

"At ease," he said. "How about some lunch?"

"Are we going to check into our room first?"

Braddock had called his friend, who was a member of the Lyford Cay Club, and asked him if he would contact the club and make a three-night reservation for them at one of the club cottages. As Braddock remembered, having been there once before when he was married, the club had about twenty cozy cottages all with spectacular views of the ocean.

"It's up to you," Braddock said. "I was thinking it might be nice to go get a quick shower at the pool, then take a swim, and I wouldn't mind a rum cocktail or two."

"Sounds good to me. Grog…isn't that what we sailors call it?"

He bumped her fist. "Exactly."

*****

They were on their second rum drink and lunch seemed to have been forgotten, at least for the moment.

"My new favorite drink," Leah said, raising her glass.

They were sitting side by side on chaise lounges overlooking a pool where a mother and three children were swimming in the shallow end.

"I thought you might like 'em," Braddock said, raising his glass. The potent drinks were called Southsides, and Braddock explained he had been introduced to them at a club on Long Island several years back.

"Does your friend live near here?" Leah asked.

"Not that far; a nice, secluded part of the island," Braddock said. "My friend Dick likes his privacy."

"So we're going there for dinner tomorrow night?" Leah asked, finishing off her drink.

"Yup, you'll like his wife too. Very bright and very opinionated. She kind of reminds me of you."

"Oh yeah, how so?" Leah asked.

"Well, she's funny for one thing. Sweet, for another. Beautiful, for a third."

"Aw, Matt, you think I'm sweet. That's so…sweet."

"Well, thanks. Never been called that before."

Leah glanced over at the three girls in the pool. "Those little girls remind you of your daughter?"

"Funny, I was just thinking that. I remember going to her swim meets. She was a little minnow." Braddock sighed. "I miss those days."

A man and a woman walked by them. The man gave Leah a sneak peek and nodded to Braddock.

"Lovely day," said the woman with an English accent and kept walking.

"Sure is," said Leah.

Braddock smiled at Leah. "I was thinking…"

"About?" Leah asked, smiling back at him.

"Maybe we want to check into our cottage?"

"Is that code?" she asked.

He nodded slowly, smiled, and stood up.

*****

"I got a little too much sun on my shoulders," Leah said, lying naked in the king-size four-poster bed. A one-thousand-count sheet covered her lower half and Matt Braddock covered her upper half.

"Want me to get some lotion from the bathroom?" Braddock asked.

She shook her head. "You stay right here. I'm not letting you out of this bed," she said. "Know what this kind of reminds me of?"

"What?"

"A honeymoon."

"I know what you mean. A honeymoon with no marriage—the best of both worlds."

"Aw? That's kind of mean," she said, giving him a light slap on his shoulder.

"No, I meant—"

She laughed. "I know…no strings."

"Exactly," he said, glancing at his watch. "Christ, it's five fifteen, where'd the time go?"

She laughed. "Where do you think?"

He patted her thigh. "I don't know about you, but I'm officially starved."

"We can have an early dinner."

"I doubt they open the dining room before six."

"That's perfect," Leah said. "We go get our stuff at the boat, shower, dress, and it's six o'clock."

"Really? All that'd take me fifteen minutes."

"'Cause you're a guy."

*****

They had a delicious dinner at one of Lyford Cay's dining rooms. Leah had lamb and Braddock had swordfish and they polished off a bottle and a half of wine. There were other couples dining there and the same mother with the three daughters they had seen earlier at the pool.

One of the girls, who Braddock guessed was about seven, waved at him and that made him feel good.

"She likes you," Leah said.

"All you have to do is smile," Braddock said.

"Where do you suppose the husband is?"

"I was just thinking about that," Braddock said, wistfully. "Working on a deal maybe. Kinda thing I wasted too much time on."

"Why do you say that?" Leah said, putting her hand on his.

"I don't know. In retrospect, I would have liked to have gone to more of my kids' games and school plays, stuff like that. I would have done just fine if I did a few less deals."

"But that was your job."

He nodded. "That was my job," he said, glumly. "Then my son was killed, and I had a million regrets. I mean, he was a really good athlete. I saw a grand total of about three of his games. But at least I could tell how excited he was to see me at them. Anyway, it is what it was. Life is filled with regrets, to state the obvious."

She kissed her fingers, put them to his lips and nodded. "Yes, I've got a few."

"Not having kids, you mean?"

She nodded.

"You still have time."

"Oh, I don't know about that, but I'll tell you a little secret."

"Tell me."

"I froze my eggs."

He squeezed her hand. "That was a hell of a good idea."

"Cost me a lot, but I think it was worth it."

"So what do you want? Boy or a girl?"

"Healthy."

He gave her a gentle fist bump. "That's the right answer."

FORTY

They woke up in a tangle. Braddock slid his arm out from under her. It was eight thirty, the latest he had slept in a long time. He had a flash of regret about leaving town without letting Jason Fisher know, but he wouldn't have changed a thing. Looking at his phone, he saw he'd missed three calls from Fisher.

He decided to call him. See what he'd missed. He got out of bed, put on a white terrycloth bathrobe, put his phone in its pocket, and went out to the porch of the cottage overlooking the ocean. It was not a lot different from his view at home, although his Delray vista had been marred in his mind by the sniper shot.

He dialed Fisher.

"I've been trying to reach you," the detective said as urgently as Braddock had ever heard him say anything.

"I decided to take a little break. I'm in Nassau."

"Really? Just when this thing's heating up," Fisher said, his tone meant to convey guilt.

"Hey, relax. As you'll recall, someone tried to kill me. That may be no big deal to you, but it is to me. I thought getting out of town for a while was a good idea."

"Sorry, man, it's just... So let me catch you up. First of all, that guy at Whispering Pines, the Iraq vet, he's in the clear."

"Why?"

"Simple. He's Black and our subject's white. Second of all, is this guy Keevil."

"Yeah?"

"Turns out he's like this champion at skeet shooting at his club up in Connecticut. Matter of fact, guys up there call him...you ready for this? *Sure Shot.*"

"No kidding?"

"Yup, and this I just found out. I spoke to a woman named Faye Mayhew, who told me Keevil got rejected a while ago when he tried to get into that club in West Palm."

"Narcissism, you mean? Larry Carr's club?"

"Exactly."

"Holy shit. So he blamed Carr for that?"

"I guess. And then there's those size-fifteen shoes."

Braddock whistled. "Man, that's a lot of evidence."

"Don't ya think? I've left three calls on the guy's machine. No call back."

"Well, look, Jason, I'm gonna be back tomorrow, probably early afternoon."

"By then Keevil might be in jail," Fisher said. "Tried and convicted."

Braddock laughed. "We can hope, but we both know that the wheels of justice move at a snail's pace."

FORTY-ONE

He went back to bed, and they didn't get out of it until a little after eleven. After a very late breakfast or very early lunch, depending on whether a crab salad and cheeseburger qualify as breakfast or lunch, they decided to play golf.

Leah outdrove him on the first hole by five yards.

"I seem to recall you're very competitive," Braddock said as he lined up his second shot on the par four.

"Oh, yeah. As I told you, when you've got three older brothers and you're struggling to get noticed, you have to be," she said and smiled. "Wanna play for money...or your boat maybe?"

He laughed as he addressed his ball. "Listen to you. Hey, I'm trying to hit my shot here."

He swung and almost missed it completely. To golfers, it's known as a shank, usually a cause for a long string of expletives.

"Just glad I didn't bet," he grumbled.

"We still can," Leah said, taking a practice swing in front of her ball.

"A buck a hole," he said. "Not counting this one."

She laughed. "Hey, big spender."

"You want it or not?"

"You're on," she said, and, of course, hit her shot onto the green, fifteen feet from the pin. She turned to him. "Lucky you didn't bet this one. Saved yourself a buck."

*****

"What do you feel like doing now?" Braddock asked as he counted out thirteen dollars on the eighteenth hole and handed it to her.

"Keep playing," she said. "I could get rich."

He laughed as he slapped the last dollar into her hand. "You want to go into town, Paradise Island, or Baha Mar?"

"What are they? Don't forget, I've never been here before."

"Well, Nassau town is about what you'd expect. Kind of a tourist trap, lots of T-shirt shops."

"I've got all the T-shirts I'll ever need."

"And Paradise Island has been around forever. A bunch of casinos in the hotels. Baha Mar is new, opened up a few years ago. I've never been there, but more gambling and hotels."

"I'm happy to stay right here." Then she shot him a big smile. "As far as gambling goes…well…I'll stick to golf."

Braddock shook his head. "Don't rub it in."

"Okay, but before I do anything," Leah said, "I need to check in with my six-hundred-dollar-an-hour lawyer and get his read on that bullshit Bill thing."

Braddock laughed. "Is that what you're calling him now?"

"Ever since the lawsuit," Leah said. "He always used to be *nice* Bill or *charming* Bill."

"But not *sweet* Bill."

"No, no, that's reserved for you."

Braddock smiled as they reached their cottage. "Just checking… Go make your call."

*****

Almost exactly an hour later, she came inside to where Braddock was reading a book he'd found on a bookshelf in the cottage.

Braddock looked up at her. "I can't tell from your look whether you're happy or pissed."

"A little of both," Leah said. "My lawyer said that Bill's suit was essentially meritless, but that his lawyer was pushing hard to go forward with it anyway."

"Know what that sounds like to me?" Braddock said. "Bill and his lawyer are looking to hold you up. Get a settlement."

"Bingo. That's exactly what my lawyer said. That we should offer them some money to quote-unquote, *go away*."

"Did he say how much?"

Leah walked over to him and stroked the back of his neck. "Put it this way, I'd have to win a hell of a lot of golf games to give 'em what my lawyer suggested."

"How much?"

"Half a million."

"Oh, Jesus, really?"

"Yeah, well, easy for him. It's not his money."

"So what did you say?"

"I said, 'Offer 'em a hundred thousand and tell 'em to go fuck themselves if they want more.'"

Braddock wrapped his arm around her leg. "You said that?"

"Yeah, I mean, the whole thing's ridiculous."

"I hear you. So what did he say? Your lawyer?"

"He just said 'okay.' Then I looked at my watch and said, 'By the way, it's been exactly one hour and one minute, and if you try to round that off to two hours, you're gonna have one very pissed off client.' Then I hung up on him."

"Atta girl, you tell 'em. So when do you expect to hear back?"

"Oh, that's the other thing: I told him to tell the other lawyer that the offer was only good for an hour. If his client doesn't take it, see you in court."

Braddock reached up with his fist and bumped hers. "Boy, I never want to get on the wrong side of you."

"I never want you to," she said, caressing his cheek.

"So what do you want to do? Go check out Paradise Island or Baha Mar? We could actually go there by boat. Or Nassau, or just sit by the pool, or, God forbid, play more golf? You know, make you even richer?"

She laughed and put her hand on his neck again. "I got a better idea."

FORTY-TWO

"There's another thing I love about you," Braddock said, looking up at her, above him.

"What's that?"

"You're insatiable."

She just smiled.

Braddock looked at his watch. It was 3:30 p.m.

"We haven't moved from this place all day. Want to go take a swim?"

The pool was a short walk away.

"Let's do it," she said, as her cell phone rang.

She picked it up from the bedside table and looked at it.

"My lawyer," she said, then clicked speakerphone.

"Hello, Craig."

"Well, we got ourselves a deal. All they want is for you to pay his legal fees."

"Fuck *that*!" Leah said without hesitation. "No way in hell. Bye, Craig."

She clicked off.

"Man, you're tough. Turned into quite the little f-bomber too…and I must say, I kind of like it."

She slowly shook her head. "But that's such bullshit. Next time he calls, I'm gonna drop it to fifty grand. I mean, what a negotiator that doofus is—he wanted me to pay four hundred grand more than where we ended up."

"Swim?" he asked.

She nodded. "Swim."

"I don't think we're going to have time for much of anything after that," he said. "We're due at Dick and Jane's at six thirty."

She cocked her head. "Those are really their names? Dick and Jane?"

"Well, I think he wants to be called Richard now. Now that he's gotten so damn rich."

"Oh, is that how it works?"

"Yes, so I would be…Matthew. And you would be—"

"—Leah."

"Exactly."

"Glad we straightened that out."

*****

Braddock had read an article somewhere about his friend and dinner host, Richard Fairchild, having had a colossal feud with a neighbor named Jarmo Koskinen, who he remembered was a Canadian billionaire. And shortly after they arrived and were having their first cocktail, Fairchild launched into the whole mess about Koskinen. It went on for about ten minutes before Fairchild took a breath and let his guests speak.

"So now I remember reading about him. In *Vanity Fair* or something," Leah said. "Seems like Jeffrey Epstein had nothing on him. Young girls, drugging them and doing all sorts of horrible things to them, right?"

Fairchild nodded. "Oh, yes, he's a horrible man. Even his two sons ended up suing him. Get this, for rape!"

"Wait," Leah said. "What do you mean?"

"The charge was, or is—I don't know whether the trial has taken place or not—that Koskinen had hookers force his sons to have sex with them when they were like twelve or thirteen."

"You're kidding," Braddock said. "How sick is that?"

Jane Fairchild nodded vigorously. "You should see his house. It's the tackiest thing imaginable. Supposedly it's designed to be like a Mayan temple." She shrugged, raised her arms and gave them quizzical looks. "Go figure, right?"

"He's got a nightclub, a massive aquarium with sharks in it—"

"Don't forget the sex dungeon," Jane said.

"Oh, yeah, this room described as a sex dungeon," Fairchild added.

"Whatever that might be," Jane added.

"He and I got into it over a million things," Fairchild said. "Noise; the fact that he was illegally dredging sand offshore to increase the size of his property; traffic roaring past our house at all hours. Hell, we bought this place to get away from it all. I sued the guy; he counter-sued," Fairchild said. "What a disaster!"

"That's incredible," Braddock said. "So, he's just down the road from here?"

"Yeah, at the end of the peninsula," Fairchild said. "He'd have these parties. Bring in teenage girls by the truckload, music blaring so loud you could hear it at the other end of the island. I mean, it was a horror show."

"Was?"

"Yeah, the guy's in jail now. Thank God."

"He claimed that Richard was an international drug dealer—"

"International gun dealer, too," Fairchild chimed in. "Never owned a gun in my life."

"That's not all," Jane said to her husband. "Tell 'em the rest."

"Oh yeah, that I was a secret member of the KKK. That I had masterminded the biggest insider trading operation in Wall Street history…oh, God, you name it."

Braddock shook his head in disbelief. "Last time I checked you ran a low-key hedge fund?"

"Yeah, well, what can I tell you?" Fairchild said, turning to Leah. "So enough about our nightmare. Tell us about you and why you're wasting your time with this guy."

They all laughed, though it wasn't that funny.

"Well, not much to tell," she said. "We've been seeing each other for just a couple of weeks."

Seeing a lot of each other, Braddock thought. *Like every square inch!*

"We met on a golf course," he added, "where she regularly takes small fortunes off me."

"Matt's gotta work on his putting," Leah said.

"So are you in Delray just for the season?" Jane asked Leah.

"Yes, Southport, Connecticut, the rest of the time."

"Oh, I love Southport," Jane said.

"Yes, it's a nice little village."

Fairchild turned to Braddock. "So, Matt, besides losing to a *girl* at golf, what else have you been up to?"

Braddock had decided beforehand that he wasn't going to go anywhere near the whole Carr investigation with the Fairchilds. His reasoning was that if he brought it up it would dominate the conversation for the rest of the evening and he'd have to answer a million questions, when all he really wanted to do was give the subject a rest.

"Well, just kind of taking it easy," he said in answer to Fairchild's question. "I'm on a couple of boards and I've got my boat and my golf, which keep me as busy as I want to be. How about you, how many more years do you figure you have left?"

Fairchild beamed—the conversation was back on him. "I'm still a young buck. Just turned fifty. Maybe retire at sixty. As long as I can figure out what to do with myself."

Jane laughed. "As long as he doesn't hang around the house all day."

Dinner was pleasant enough, though Richard continued to hog the monologue and told them more than they needed to know about the spectacular returns of Great Western Capital and all his philanthropic endeavors. Braddock wondered if he was like that back when *he* was in shoes similar to Fairchild's. He hoped not. He was certain that he never talked about the philanthropies that he supported unless someone asked him about them.

Just before they left, Jane put her hand on Braddock's arm and said, "We're going over to Harbour Island tomorrow. Want to come with us?"

Leah's big blue eyes seemed to brighten. "Oh, yes," she said to Braddock. "Let's go! I've always wanted to go there."

"Can we tell you first thing in the morning? I may have to get back to Delray," Braddock explained.

Leah looked disappointed but didn't say anything and they said their goodbyes soon after that.

They got back to the cottage at just past ten.

Amazingly, they both were too tired for any more lovemaking, though, at some point in the middle of the night, they launched into another full-scale passion session.

FORTY-THREE

Braddock was awakened by the ringing of his cell phone. He reached over Leah and picked it up off of the bedside table.

"Hello?" he whispered, slipping out of bed so as not to wake Leah.

"Hey, Matt, it's Fisher."

Braddock could tell by his tone this was not the *we-nailed-the-sonofabitch* call he'd been hoping for. He went outside and sat on the steps of the cottage.

"I spoke to Keevil last night and he's off the hook."

"Why?"

"Simple. He had two ironclad alibis—for Carr and you. When Carr got shot, he was playing tennis with three other guys. I checked it out with the pro at the tennis courts who saw him there. When the shot was taken at you, he was out of town. Up in Vero Beach. I checked that out too."

"Shit."

"I know. So I don't know what we've got at this point, but we'll come up with something."

"I sure as hell hope so."

"When are you coming back?"

Braddock thought about last night's Harbour Island invitation. "Well, I was thinking about...nah, I'll be back later today."

"Okay," Fisher said. "Hope you have calm seas."

Shit, shit, shit, Braddock said to himself. Then, one more time. *Shit.*

Maybe it was time to throw in the towel, hang up his gumshoes. Where had it gotten him? A lot of people thinking he had lost it, trying to find his friend's killer. Kind of noble, some seemed to think, but a little wacky too, most people definitely thought. And now he had Leah… What more did he need?

Speaking of Leah, he heard her footsteps. She opened the door and sat down beside him on the steps, wearing only a long-sleeved shirt of his from the night before.

"Good morning," she said.

"Good morning," he said and gave her a kiss.

"What was that all about?"

"The call?"

She nodded.

"My detective friend telling me that we're back to square one."

"Oh, sorry."

"What do you think about this whole thing?"

"You mean, you trying to catch Larry Carr's killer?"

He nodded.

"Well, on one hand I think it's kind of admirable."

"And on the other?"

"Kinda dangerous. I mean, look what happened," she said. "I was going to say something about it to you."

"Okay, go ahead."

"Okay, here goes. So…I like you and don't want anything to happen to you. I mean, just the idea of someone taking a shot at you, trying to kill you, scares the hell out of me. How is that worth the risk?"

Braddock looked out at the ocean and squinted. "That is a very good question. Maybe it hasn't sunk in yet?"

Leah grabbed his arm. "Are you kidding? That a bullet went whizzing past your head? How can that not have sunk in?"

It seemed to echo something Fisher had said. "Now that you put it that way."

"Well, that *is* what happened."

He nodded. "If you don't mind, let's change the subject."

"Okay, I'm game, but I hope you heard me."

"I did."

"Good," she said, "Okay, so the new subject is…famous Jimmy Buffett quotes."

Braddock laughed. "I like his music but don't know about his famous quotes."

"Well, maybe only one. 'There's nothing worth saying or hearing after two in the morning.' Something like that anyway."

"Probably pretty true," he said, waiting to hear more.

"Except in this case. In the middle of last night, to be exact…"

"What happened in the middle of the night is a fond memory, but what was said?"

"You really don't remember?"

"Um…"

"I said, 'I love you.'"

"Oh my God. You did? Well, I love you back."

"Are you just saying that?"

"Hell, no, I mean it."

"It's pretty quick," Leah said.

"What does it matter?"

She leaned toward him and kissed him. "So, it's official. I love you; you love me. Now it's time for you to retire from the sleuth business before you get hurt. And speaking of Harbour Island?"

"We were?"

"No, but let's."

"Okay."

"Have you ever been there?"

"Yes, about five years ago. I've got to admit, it a very cool place. Great restaurants and amazing beaches."

"So what are we waiting for? Call up Jane Fairchild and say we're on."

Braddock let out a long sigh. "How about this? If I *promise* to take you there soon… I just…I just really need to get back to Delray."

"What for? So that guy can take another shot at you? Did you not hear anything I just said two minutes ago?"

Braddock patted her on the shoulder. "Is this our first fight?"

She laughed. "If so, it's not much of one. Seriously, why do you want to go back there when we're fifty miles away from Harbour Island?"

"I just…I—"

"You keep saying that."

He laughed, then turned serious. "I need to get back there. It's just something I have to deal with and finish off. We're so close."

She didn't look convinced.

FORTY-FOUR

As Braddock navigated under the eighteen-foot bridge at Boynton Beach at five in the afternoon, he got a call.

He looked at the display. It said, "Frank Diehl."

She saw it, too, and rolled her eyes, as if to say, "Don't forget our conversation about you retiring from the sleuth business."

"Hello, Frank."

"Hey, Matt, haven't seen you at Narcissism in the last few days. Amber's been asking about you."

Braddock was suddenly glad he hadn't put Diehl on speaker. "I'm just getting back from a trip to Nassau. What's up?"

"One of the girls at the club told me something Larry Carr told her. Thought you might be interested."

"Okay, what was that?"

"Said Larry told her he had a business problem with some guy that wouldn't go away. Told me she said to him, 'But I thought you were retired.' 'I am,' Larry said. 'But this is something that goes back before I sold my company.'"

"Anything more?"

"That was pretty much it."

"But why would Carr be confiding in this woman in the first place? He never struck me as the type of guy to go around spilling his guts about business."

"Couldn't tell ya," Diehl said. "Maybe they just ran out of stuff to talk about."

"Okay, well thanks. I appreciate the call. If she tells you anything else that you think might be useful, let me know."

"I will. In the meantime, what do I tell Amber?"

"It's over."

Diehl laughed. "Before it even started."

FORTY-FIVE

Braddock woke up alone in his bed. He didn't like it much. He had gotten used to Leah being there. The first thing he did was go to his balcony with a large pair of binoculars. Maybe Leah was right: maybe he had been a little too casual about the fact that a bullet went "whizzing" by his head three days ago. He scanned one side of the beach to the other side. Nothing. No early surfers out there and the yoga group didn't meet on the beach for another fifteen minutes.

He went and made a Swiss cheese omelette, toast, and coffee. Then, balancing a tray in one hand and his newspapers in the other, he went and sat down in his favorite chair on the balcony. But in between bites he kept looking out to the beach, only occasionally glancing at the papers. The whole need to be on the lookout for a possible shooter was a major irritation. Is this how it would always be if the shooter wasn't caught soon...or ever?

At a little past nine, he called Catherine Carr.

"There's a rumor going around about you, Matt," Catherine said before he could get "hello" out.

He caught a trace of tease in her tone. He suspected he knew what the rumor was and groaned.

"A certain blue-eyed blonde?"

"What's the question, Cath?"

"Well, is it true?"

"I know several blue-eyed blondes."

Catherine laughed. "Don't play coy."

Braddock laughed with her. "You know, here I called to ask *you* as question, and you jumped the gun on me. So here's my question to you: Do you know anything about Larry having some ongoing business issue with someone from his old working days? Frank Diehl called me and said he heard something like that."

"Well, of course, there was his brother Neil, but I think they had more or less patched it up. Even though they didn't talk much."

"No, not Neil, someone else."

"Um, sorry, can't help you on that," Catherine said, then back to the subject of Leah. "Story is that certain blue-eyed blonde was spotted on your boat coming back from somewhere in the Bahamas."

Now how the hell was it possible that someone had pieced all that *together?*

"Sorry, Cath, don't know what you're talking about. Gotta go now."

He decided to go for a swim at the Island Club pool, half hoping that Leah might be there. Instead, Jack Vandevere was.

"Hey, Matt, understand you went on a little boat trip?" Vandevere greeted him.

Not him too! Christ... He knew Leah was not the leak.

"Yeah," was all Braddock said. "Hey, you feel like playing a few holes?"

"Now?"

"Maybe in an hour or so. I could use a little exercise."

"Sure," Vandevere said, looking at his watch. "Say at ten forty-five?"

"Perfect. I'll see you then."

Braddock dived in and did half a lap underwater. He got out, toweled himself off and headed up to his condominium to get dressed for golf.

*****

On the second hole, Braddock launched his drive—a nine-iron—into the water. Many of the greens at the Island Club were quite easy to reach from the tees. One of the exceptions was the fifth hole, the one that ran along the Intracoastal and where Larry Carr had been shot.

"That's unlike you," Jack Vandevere said of the second hole. "This is usually your birdie hole."

It was true. For whatever reason Braddock usually birdied the second hole, but his mind was elsewhere at the moment. He was back on the case, despite Leah's appeal, and wanting to speak to the woman who told Frank Diehl that Larry Carr had had a long-standing business problem with a certain man. He figured if he really grilled the woman, she might be able to come up with a name, a description, something.

He launched his next drive into the water again.

"Jesus, man," said Vandevere. "Hope you got a lot of balls."

The good news was that there was only one more hole where he'd have to drive over water.

The next hole, the third, also ran along the Intracoastal. One had to seriously hook a drive to land in the water on it. Which was exactly what he did.

"I've never seen you hook before," Vandevere commiserated with Braddock. "Usually it's a slice."

On the fourth, he concentrated really hard and got a par.

"That's more like it, huh?" Vandevere said as Braddock plucked his ball from the hole.

Braddock nodded and the two walked over to the fifth tee.

"I call this hole Coolidge's nemesis," Vandevere said, as he teed up his ball.

"What do you mean?" Braddock asked.

"Talk about a hook," Vandevere said and pointed. "You don't play with him as much as I do, but he always ends up in the trees here."

Braddock nodded, as his mind raced back to the morning Larry Carr was killed.

"But the day Larry was shot," Braddock said, "we all hit the fairway, right?"

Vandevere took a practice swing. "No, Coolidge hit a really high one. Into the woods as usual. I remember hearing it hit a tree. Made a loud *thwack*."

Braddock nodded. When it was his turn to drive, he deliberately aimed for the trees on the left. He succeeded. He and Vandevere left the tee, Braddock headed for the trees, Vandevere to the middle of the fairway.

Braddock didn't care if he found his ball or not as he walked into the trees. He just stopped and looked through the trees over at Vandevere.

Interesting: he could see Vandevere, but no way Vandevere could see him.

Even *he* could have shot Larry Carr from this close.

FORTY-SIX

Braddock played horrible, distracted golf for the next thirteen holes. To the point that he didn't even take practice swings. He just needed to finish, get off the course, and call Jason Fisher.

Despite his distraction, Braddock made a long putt on the eighteenth hole. Vandevere took off his cap and walked over to him.

"Nice putt," he said, shaking Braddock's hand. "But what the hell happened on all the others? You weren't up to your usual standards."

"Yeah, I don't know. That's golf, I guess. Somedays you got it, most days you don't," Braddock said pulling out his wallet and stuffing a bunch of bills into Vandevere's waiting hand. He had been doing this way too much lately. If he didn't run out of balls, he'd run out of money.

"Well, pleasure doing business with you," said Vandevere.

"Hey, I have a question for you," Braddock said, pulling a five-iron out of his golf bag. "You know how long this is? Ballpark?"

"I know better than ballpark. Standard irons are between thirty-four and thirty-five and a half inches long."

Braddock nodded and put the club back in his bag.

"Want to do it again tomorrow?" Vandevere asked.

"Thanks, Jack, but I think I'm going to have my hands full."

"You *think*?"

"I *know*."

*****

He couldn't wait to speak to Jason Fisher and called him the second he walked into his condominium.

Fisher answered. "You back?"

"Yeah, got in last night," Braddock said. "I think I might know who did it."

"Didn't you say that before?" Fisher asked, skeptically.

"No, this time I'm eighty-percent sure."

"How you gonna get it to a hundred percent?"

"I need to talk to a few more people."

"Who do you think it is?"

"Chris Coolidge. He was playing in our foursome that day Carr was killed."

"Wait? How—"

"On the fifth hole, he drove his ball into the woods. Took the shot from there."

"How'd he get the gun?"

"I been thinking about that. He either hid it there beforehand or had it in his bag. Tambor suspected the rifle used to shoot at me might have been sawed-off. I think he said twenty-six inches. That could easily fit into a bag. Clubs are normally between thirty-four and thirty-five and a half inches long."

Fisher let out a long stream of air. "No shit? But what was the guy's motive?"

"That's what I'm trying to figure out. There was never any love lost between Coolidge and Carr, that's for damn sure. I just always thought it was two macho guys being competitive. You know, shooting jabs back and forth all the time."

"*Shooting* being the operative word."

Braddock chuckled. "Yeah, right."

"All right, so I'm not going to do anything about Coolidge for the moment. But tell me when you dig up enough to nail him. And Matt—"

"Yeah?"

"Sooner is better than later."

"I got that."

Braddock clicked off and dialed Catherine Carr.

"Hey, lover boy."

"Don't start... Can I come over and see you?"

"Sure. What's up?"

"The usual. A few more questions."

"I'm here."

"I'll be right over."

He walked over to her building, up to the second floor, and knocked on her door.

She opened it right away.

"Hi," she said. "This about Larry, I presume?"

"Yes."

"You're a dog with a bone, I swear."

"I know. But for the right reasons, I hope."

She waved him in. "Come on in."

He walked over to the club chair he always sat in. He cautioned himself on the way over to proceed cautiously or Chris Coolidge might catch wind that Braddock was asking questions about him being a killer.

"I need you to promise me you won't say a word about what we're about to discuss," he said.

She smiled. "I promise. Scout's honor."

"No, I'm really serious. You can't say a word."

She put up her hands. "Okay, okay, I got it. Not one word. Swear on a stack of Bibles."

"Okay, so what was the relationship between Larry and Chris Coolidge?"

"Relationship?" she repeated with a laugh. "Unless you know something I don't know, Larry only had relationships with women."

"Okay, sorry, let me rephrase that: was there any bad blood between them that you know of?"

She cocked her head. "Didn't you just ask me this about Phil Keevil?"

"Yes I did, but turned out there was nothing there."

"So…now you're moving on to Chris?"

"I know, it sounds a little unlikely…"

"A little?"

Braddock put his hands up. "It's just—"

"Look, Matt, I'd like to help you, but all I know about Chris Coolidge is that Larry hated losing money to him at golf and he definitely wasn't one of his favorite people. In fact, I always wondered why he played with him at all."

"Anything else?"

Catherine cocked her head, then laughed. "I remember this one thing: Larry told me how Chris was always boasting about being the great, great—or maybe great, great, great—grandson of the president of the United States. Like that was his only claim to fame."

Braddock laughed too. "Oh yeah, I remember. Good ol' Calvin Coolidge."

"Yeah, exactly. As Larry said… 'in the top ten of the worst U.S. presidents.'"

Braddock nodded. "Yeah, he was kind of a lightweight." He stood up. "Okay, well thanks," he said. "I promise not to come around tomorrow asking about a new guy."

"Hey, don't worry about it," she said. "But maybe you should be spending your time with your new lady friend."

*****

Braddock went back to his condominium and made two more calls. The first one was to Frank Diehl. He reached him and asked for the name and phone number of the woman who had told Diehl about Larry Carr's longstanding "problem" with a man. He was a little surprised that Diehl obliged him without a question or an argument.

He called the woman—her name was Lisa Frechetti—and got her voicemail. He asked her to please call him back.

Then he called Faye Mayhew, the woman Carr almost divorced Catherine to marry.

"Hello?"

"Hi, Faye, it's Matt Braddock, Larry Carr's friend."

"Hello, Matt."

"So I was wondering if I could come see you again. I just have a few more questions."

"Sure, I'm around all afternoon."

"Can we say…two o'clock?"

"Sure. See you then."

In the meantime, Lisa Frechetti called back.

After brief pleasantries, Braddock launched right in.

"So, Frank said Larry Carr told you about a man who he had 'a problem' with. Did he say what the man's name was or what the issues were, by any chance?"

"Um, let me think. It was all kinda general. Not really anything too specific. Something to do with when Larry sold his company. I think he had a big banking company up in New Jersey." Close enough, Braddock thought. "Something about the man claiming Larry owed him money for something."

Braddock had the feeling that was as much as he was going to get out of her. But he figured he'd give it one last try.

"Did Larry say what this man did—to claim Larry owed him money?"

"No, sorry, that's all I remember."

"Okay, well, thank you."

"Now, I have a question for you."

"Sure, fire away."

"One of the girls at the club said you were pretty cute. When are you going to come to Narcissism next? I'd love to meet you."

"Ah, I'm not too sure. I'm kind of busy at the moment." Though his real answer was, *Not in this lifetime.* "Thanks again, Lisa."

*****

He was sitting in Faye Mayhew's living room looking out at the Intracoastal five stories below.

"Don't you have a boat, Matt?" Faye asked.

"Yes, how'd you know?"

"Because I saw you go past last night," Faye said. "Was that Leah Bliss with you?"

"Yes, yes it was," Braddock said.

Busted. Again. So now everyone in the whole world knew.

"She's really nice."

"Yes, she is. So, as I mentioned, I have a few more questions about Larry."

"I'll help if I can," she said, brushing back a wisp of red hair from her eyes.

"I think there's a man down here who Larry had…let's just say, a problem with. An issue. Something that probably went back a few years, I think. Maybe having to do with the sale of his reinsurance business."

Faye nodded. "I know exactly who you mean. Chris Coolidge."

Braddock felt a flutter in his stomach.

"And do you know what exactly it was about?"

"I sure do. Chris was, or is, a business broker. Sold businesses, or at least tried to. Larry told me he was never very successful at it. Anyway—and mind you this is all according to Larry, and Chris may have a completely different story—but Chris claimed he was instrumental in finding the buyer of Larry's business."

"But Larry didn't agree?"

"Not at all. Told me that he had known the CEO of the company that bought his company half his life. And that he had gone directly to him, but Chris claimed later that he had a meeting with the CFO of the company that bought Larry's and gave him a lot of financials which enticed him and the CEO to want to buy it. Which Larry said, by the way, was all BS."

"Do you have any idea how much Larry's company sold for?"

"I know exactly—120 million. Plus, the buyer bought his office building in Stamford for another 8.5 million."

Braddock did some quick calculations, knowing that business brokers usually asked for a commission of five percent of a company's sales price and usually got something closer to three percent. Five percent would have been around six million dollars.

"Do you know if Chris had any written agreement with Larry that said he was representing him?"

"No, he didn't. But Larry told me that he would have honored an oral agreement and paid him if he really was the so-called 'procuring cause' for the deal. I remember that was the phrase Larry used, 'procuring cause.'"

"So Chris got nothing?"

"And deserved nothing."

"Sounds like it," Braddock said.

"Larry also told me about one time at a dinner party, or maybe it was dinner at the Island Club—yes, that's what it was—where Chris ambushed him in the men's room and laid into him about how because Larry screwed him, he couldn't invest in this tech start-up. Where a hundred-dollar investment went on to being worth ten thousand dollars a year later, or some nonsense. Larry said it was like he was blaming him for practically everything that went wrong in his entire miserable life."

"Like what else?"

"Hmm, what was it? Something about how he had to live in Florida all year round, when all of his rich friends took off to places like Watch Hill, Nantucket, Northeast Harbor, Maine, or wherever in the summertime."

"Wow. He actually said that?"

Faye nodded.

"But wait, he must have been up there, at least part of the year, doing business? Like trying to sell Larry's business, or claiming to anyway? And maybe brokering other business deals?"

"I asked him that, too. Larry, I mean. And he said he heard Coolidge stayed in the guest house of his mother-in-law's house in Norwalk," Faye said, shaking her head slowly. "Which is a far cry from Nantucket or Watch Hill."

"So this all came out in the men's room confrontation?"

"Yes. He kind of cornered Larry and let him have it with all this nonsensical stuff. A whole diatribe about how Larry had singlehandedly ruined his life."

Braddock shook his head. "That's pretty incredible," he said. "When did this happen?"

"Not too long ago. A month at the most."

"Oh really, that recently?"

"Yes, three weeks to a month, I'd say."

Braddock got to his feet, put out his hand. "Thank you so much. I really appreciate it."

"You're very welcome," Faye said, shaking his hand. "I hope it was helpful in some way."

"Oh, definitely. You gave me a lot to think about."

"Well, good. Glad to hear it," Faye said.

"Now…just one last thing: I need to swear you to secrecy."

"Don't worry," she said. "I just listen to gossip…I never repeat it."

"Good to hear."

Faye smiled broadly. "Oh hey, give my best to your friend, Leah."

FORTY-SEVEN

Braddock went back to his condominium and called Jason Fisher. "Jackpot," he said proudly. "Chris Coolidge is our guy. A hundred percent."

He proceeded to tell Fisher about his conversation with Lisa Frechetti, and then the more substantive one with Faye Mayhew.

"All right," Fisher said. "That's definitely enough for me to haul him in for a hard interrogation."

Braddock was disappointed. "But not charge him?"

"No, we're not there yet. I mean, I could go for *suspicion of murder*, but that's got no real teeth to it. We need definitive proof."

"Okay, so what exactly are you saying?"

"We interrogate him about the whole thing, since he was there when Larry Carr was shot—"

"'Cause he did it."

"Wait, not so fast," Fisher said. "Then we ask him where he was when someone took the shot at you."

"And he'll say either asleep or having breakfast," Braddock said. "Something like that."

"Is he married?"

"No. Far as I know he's been separated from his wife for a year or so. I don't think he's divorced, though."

"So, no wife to alibi him. But also no one to dispute what he says."

Braddock exhaled long and loud. "So far, this isn't going anywhere."

"I'm sorry, but it's not like we have a smoking gun."

"Yeah, I know. Seems like we got nothing."

"Not true. We've got motive and a suspect who was at the Carr murder scene."

"Okay, so you're going to talk to him...then what?"

"I don't know. It depends on what comes out of the interrogation. By the way, what kind of a car does Coolidge drive?"

"Why does that matter?"

"What kind, Matt?"

"A black BMW. I'm guessing three or four years old."

"Thanks. I'll get back to you."

*****

Jason Fisher had put in four calls to Chris Coolidge in the last five hours and had heard nothing back. Though that was not surprising, he decided to go straight to Coolidge's condominium at the Island Club and question him. He called Braddock, got Coolidge's address, and drove there.

A minute after he pressed the buzzer, a man opened the door. He looked to be a shade over six feet tall, with mousy brown hair and teeth that seemed to barely fit into his small mouth.

"Mr. Coolidge?"

"Yes. Are you the detective who called?"

"Yes, Detective Fisher. Can I ask you a few questions?"

"Sure. I was just about to call you back. I've had my hands full."

Fisher took a step forward. "Can I come inside?"

"Yeah, sure. Come on in," he said, turning and going inside. "Place is kind of a mess. My cleaning lady comes tomorrow."

Coolidge pointed at two club chairs and a brown leather couch and Fisher sat down in one of the club chairs. Coolidge sat in the leather couch.

"So what is this all about?" Coolidge asked. "All those calls—must be important."

"I'm one of the lead detectives on the murder case of Larry Carr."

"I figured this had something to do with that."

"You mind if I take notes?" Fisher asked, holding up his iPad.

"Be my guest."

"Okay, so I know that you were playing golf with Mr. Carr when the murder took place. Where exactly were you when the shot was fired?"

"Looking for my ball," Coolidge said. "I hit it into the trees along the Intracoastal."

"So did you hear the shot?"

"I sure did. It was like a cracking sound."

"And what did you do when you heard it?"

"Well, I looked over at the other three on the fairway and saw Carr on the ground. Then I ran over there."

"Were you scared that the shooter might keep shooting?"

"I gotta admit that did occur to me."

"So why'd you run over there?"

"Well, my natural instinct was to try to help. Not that there was really anything I could do. Another guy, Matt Braddock, was already doing what he could to help Larry, but we all realized pretty quickly he was dead."

Fisher punched away on his iPad for a few moments. "Okay, four days ago, as I'm sure you've heard, a shot was fired at Mr. Braddock. Where were you at that time? It was about 6:30 a.m."

"I don't get up until seven thirty or eight, so I would have been sound asleep."

Fisher nodded and abruptly changed the subject. "I understand that you and Mr. Carr had some serious…disagreements in the past. Having to do with the sale of his company up in Connecticut."

"I don't know who you've been talking to, or where you got that, but obviously we got along, or we wouldn't be playing golf that day."

Makes sense, Fisher thought, but then the old *Godfather* adage came to mind: "Keep your friends close and your enemies closer."

"So that isn't true, that you two had serious differences?"

"Look, man," Coolidge said, rubbing his chin. "That was over a year ago. I got over it."

"Yes, but sometimes things…let's just say, linger. Know what I mean?"

"No, I don't. Are you really suggesting I had something to do with Carr's murder? What? Shot him with my seven-iron maybe?"

"Just asking questions, Mr. Coolidge. Someone mentioned something about you confronting Mr. Carr in the men's room at the Island Club. Said something about him stiffing you on the sale of his company. How that meant you couldn't buy some hot tech stock. Seems like that was only a few weeks ago, a month maybe. So when you say, 'I got over it,' did you really?"

"I don't know what you're talking about."

"So you never had a conversation with Mr. Carr in the men's room as described."

"Hey, look, guys have a few drinks and say shit. That ever happened to you, Detective?"

"Something about you having to live in Florida year 'round when all your rich friends go to fancy places up north in the summer."

Coolidge shook his head and his eyes got slitty. "What other bullshit hearsay you gonna throw at me, Detective?"

"Like I said before, just asking questions."

Coolidge took a long look out his window, then his eyes came back to Fisher. "So bottom-line it for me: You think I killed Larry Carr, is that it? And don't keep saying you're just asking questions."

"Well, that *is* all I'm doing."

Coolidge thrust himself up quickly out of the couch. "Okay, well, I've patiently answered your questions, but I'm now officially done."

Fisher stood up. "Okay, fair enough. I appreciate your time, and…have a nice day."

"I will," Coolidge said. "Now that we're done with this absurd conversation."

FORTY-EIGHT

Braddock's phone rang early in the afternoon.

He looked down at it. It was Faye Mayhew.

"Hi, Faye."

"Hey, Matt," she said. "I remembered a couple other things Larry told me about Chris Coolidge."

"Tell me."

"How he was so desperate to make that commission on the sale of Larry's business and building. How he had split up with his wife and was planning to marry this other woman. Even promised her he was about to get very rich."

"You mean, on the commission from Larry's business and building?"

"Exactly. Then, when it never happened, I heard the woman lost interest."

"A tale as old as time?"

Faye laughed. "But then Coolidge went limping back to his wife, and even she didn't want him anymore."

"Wow. I almost feel sorry for him," Braddock said. "This wasn't around the time of the famous men's room confrontation at the Island Club, was it?"

"No. This was back when Coolidge was pleading—begging was more like it—for Larry to pay that damn commission. Said he'd take half of it, but Larry said, 'For what? You didn't do anything.' This was right after the deal happened. As I remember, he just barged into Larry's office uninvited."

"Well thanks, this is good info. Anything else?"

Faye laughed again. "Isn't that enough?"

"It sure is."

"So sounds like maybe Chris Coolidge is your—what do you call it—leading suspect?"

Braddock nodded. "Put it this way, he's definitely in our top one."

*****

Braddock was impatient to hear about Jason Fisher's interview with Chris Coolidge, so he called him.

"So?" he said simply, when Fisher answered.

"Is that a question?"

"Damn right. Tell me how it went with Coolidge."

"It got a little hostile at the end. Of course, he denied everything. Said he was sound asleep when you got shot at."

"So, like I asked before, where are we?"

"I know you're not gonna like to hear this, but we need more. So what I did—"

"Let me ask you this: Are we *ever* gonna get this guy?" Braddock implored, his tone laced with scorn.

"If you let me finish, for Chrissakes," Fisher said. "So what I did was I went to a judge, laid out the whole thing on Coolidge, and got a search warrant for his condominium."

"Now you're talking."

"Changing your tune, huh?" Fisher said. "So if you want to tag along—in a very unofficial, off-the-record capacity—you can."

"When?"

"Now."

"I'll meet you there."

Braddock went straight to Chris Coolidge's condominium and waited outside his door. He didn't have to wait long for Fisher and Tambor Malmstrom to show up, warrant in hand.

"You guys gonna have your guns out?" Braddock asked.

"We're a little more subtle than that," Fisher said, and Braddock noticed that Fisher's right hand was in his jacket pocket, and he could make out the outline of the short barrel of a pistol. Malmstrom's right hand was inside his jacket and Braddock could see the strap of his shoulder holster.

Braddock smiled. "Should I hit the buzzer?"

"Be my guest," said Fisher.

A few moments later they heard footsteps and the door opened.

It was a short woman in sweatpants and a white T-shirt.

Fisher took a step toward her. "Hi, is Mr. Coolidge here?"

"Oh, no sir," she said in a Hispanic accent. "He left."

"Left for where?" Fisher asked.

"I don't know, sir," she said. "He just packed a suitcase and said he was going away."

"But not where?"

"Sorry."

"You're his cleaning lady, right?"

She nodded.

Fisher glanced at Malmstrom and nodded. He showed the woman the warrant. "Okay, we are police detectives and I have a search warrant signed by a judge giving us the right to search Mr. Coolidge's condominium."

The cleaning lady looked like she only understood half of what he said and didn't move.

"We are going to search the condo," Fisher said, brushing past her. Malmstrom and Braddock followed.

Malmstrom turned to her. "What's your name?"

"Juanita."

"Okay, Juanita. I'm sorry for the surprise. You can keep doing what you were doing. We won't take too long."

She nodded uneasily.

Braddock turned to Fisher, who was headed toward what appeared to be the master bedroom. "What exactly are we looking for?"

"A Mauser 98 would be nice, but we'll settle for anything that shoots eight-millimeter ammo," Fisher said, going over to a bureau, and opening the top drawer. "Don't forget, it could be as short as two feet long."

Unlike in cop shows on TV, where cops toss around clothes and belongings haphazardly, Fisher was neat and orderly in how he went through the drawers of the dresser. Braddock went to Coolidge's vast walk-in closet searching for a rifle or anything else that would tie Coolidge to the shootings.

A half hour later, they had come up with nothing that connected Coolidge to the crimes. Fisher spent ten minutes going through the contents of a desk in a third bedroom, which Coolidge clearly used as an office. He was sitting in the desk chair.

He turned to Braddock when he heard him come up behind him and showed him a handful of papers.

"What is it?" Braddock asked.

"Foreclosure papers on this place from a couple months back. Guy was in tough shape financially," Fisher said, shaking his head. "Not sure how he can even afford that cleaning lady."

"Amazing," Braddock said. "I would have never known."

He was finding that to be the case with several men he thought he knew.

"But no rifle," Fisher said, shrugging. "Guess we might as well hit it. And find out where Coolidge went."

Braddock nodded, and they turned and walked out of the bedroom.

Malmstrom was in the kitchen.

"Come on, Tambor," Fisher said. "We're done here."

Malmstrom nodded.

Fisher walked over to the cleaning lady and took out his iPad. "Can you give me your phone number, please? In case we have some questions for you."

She nodded and complied.

"Does Mr. Coolidge let you in when you come, or do you have your own keys?" Fisher asked.

She took two keys out of the pocket of her sweatpants and held them up.

"Okay, thank you," Fisher said, and headed for the door, with Malmstrom and Braddock right behind him.

They walked out into the corridor, where Braddock saw a series of doors on the other side of the corridor, all fairly close together.

"Hey, wait a minute," he said. "Those are storage units for the different condos."

Fisher nodded. "Tambor, go get the keys from the cleaning lady. Good thinking," he said to Braddock.

Malmstrom came back out of Coolidge's condominium holding up the keys. The first one didn't fit, but the second one did.

Malmstrom opened the door to the storage unit. In plain sight was a set of dusty old golf clubs and a two-foot stack of replacement tiles for the kitchen floor. The storage space was only big enough to hold one person, so Fisher walked in, put a hand in his pants pocket, and pulled out blue nitrile gloves, then put them on.

There were some metal shelves on the far wall. On the top shelf was a stack of old hardcover books, some kitchen pots and four sets of light bulbs in their packaging. On the next shelf down were three cans of tennis balls, a twelve-pack of Callaway golf balls and a square box of something in between them.

Fisher picked up the box and examined it as Braddock and Malmstrom moved closer to see what it was.

"Well, what do you know," Fisher said, handing the box to Malmstrom, who had also donned gloves.

"Well, whaddaya know is right," Malmstrom said to Fisher with a broad smile. "This is ammo for a Mauser 98, and something tells me this is gonna match up to that slug we found on the golf course."

Fisher turned to Braddock. "Okay…in answer to your question, Matt, 'Are we ever gonna get this guy?' Damn right we're gonna get this guy."

"Yeah, but we have no idea where he is. He could be anywhere."

"He could be," Fisher said, taking out his iPhone, calling up an app, and studying it, "but it just so happens…right now he's about, um, seventy miles south of Jacksonville, going north on I-95."

Braddock smiled like he hadn't since he'd last laid eyes on Leah. "Holy shit. How'd—"

"Remember when I asked you what kind of car Coolidge drove?"

Braddock nodded.

"So I slipped a little GPS tracker into his grille," Fisher said. Then, noticing Braddock's excited look, "And no, you can't go with us to arrest him."

"Come on, man—"

"No way in hell. Guy's got a Mauser 98 on him," Fisher said. "Ain't gonna happen."

FORTY-NINE

Fisher and Malmstrom had a quick debate about how to play it with the fugitive Chris Coolidge.

"My best guess is he's heading up north somewhere. Maybe Connecticut, where he used to live," Fisher said.

"We could catch a flight to, say, Richmond or D.C., and just wait for him on 95," Malmstrom said.

"Hey, I'd like to catch him in person as much as you would, but the best thing is to get him right away," Fisher said.

"So you mean contact the staties up in the Jacksonville area to pick him up?"

Fisher nodded, reaching for his cell phone. "Exactly. Then we can lead-foot it up there and bring him back."

*****

There were three state troopers following the black BMW, far enough back so Chris Coolidge couldn't spot their cars. One of them had confirmed, using high-powered binoculars, that the license plate matched Coolidge's. Up ahead ten miles—some twenty miles south of the Florida border—two more state troopers waited at a rest stop. A state police chopper was on standby in case they needed it.

"All right, we got him in a squeeze," lead state trooper Callahan said. "Let's take him down. Don't forget, guy's armed and dangerous."

"Roger that," radioed the two other troopers following Callahan's vehicle.

"You guys at the rest stop, we're probably not gonna need you, but we'll keep you in the loop."

The two troopers in separate cars at the rest stop rogered Callahan back.

"Okay, let's do it," said Callahan. "I'll get on his ass, order him to pull over, then when he does, I'll get around him, you two take the rear."

And with that, Callahan accelerated and within a minute was on the bumper of the black BMW.

Callahan clicked on his loudspeaker mic. "You in the BMW, pull over to the shoulder. Right now."

Coolidge did as he was instructed, and Callahan pulled in front of him and parked thirty yards ahead.

Callahan opened his door and, with a portable megaphone in hand, crouched behind it. "Get out of your vehicle and put your hands on top of your car."

The two other troopers, one with a shotgun and the other a service revolver, crouched behind open car doors twenty yards behind Coolidge's car, their weapons aimed.

Coolidge got out of the car and put his hands on top of it.

All three troopers moved toward him. Callahan, pistol in hand, got there first.

"Is your name Chris Coolidge?"

Coolidge nodded.

"You're under arrest for the murder of"—he checked a scrap of paper—"of Lawrence Carr in Delray Beach, Florida. Put your hands behind your back."

Coolidge did as he was told without a word of protest. There were wide sweat stains on his shirt under his armpits and beads of sweat on his forehead.

Callahan cuffed him and led him to his car. He held Coolidge's head down after instructing him to get in the back seat.

Callahan went around and got into the driver's seat. He turned back to Coolidge.

"We're going to put your car on a flatbed, and it'll be taken back down to Delray."

"How much is that gonna cost me?" Coolidge asked.

"I wouldn't worry about that," Callahan said. "You got way bigger problems."

FIFTY

Jason Fisher told Braddock about his conversation with Chris Coolidge in his jail cell and also one he had with Coolidge's estranged wife, who now lived up in Palm Beach Gardens, Florida.

"His wife described him as a really bitter guy who felt that he had been screwed his whole life. He had grown up in a wealthy family and just pissed away everything he ever made or inherited. She said Larry Carr was just the latest person he blamed for everything that had gone wrong in his life."

"I guess they split up because he was messing around with another woman," Braddock said. "Way I heard it, he told this other woman he was about to make millions on a deal—the one with Carr—but when that blew up, she was out of there."

"Yeah, that's pretty close to what the wife said. So, he came back to her, and she said in so many words, 'I want no part of you.'"

Braddock shook his head. "It's amazing how someone can seem so damn normal when that's the last thing they are."

"I hear you," Fisher said. "So, then I had a long talk with Coolidge in the interview room."

"And I bet he claimed he was innocent, like they all do? Had nothing to do with any of it? Didn't have a clue what you were talking about? That he was just taking a nice, leisurely drive up north?"

Fisher shook his head. "I headed him off at the pass. Said that we had a match between the slugs we found on the fifth hole and the one we took out of your wall and the Mauser 98 in the trunk of his car."

"He had it with him, huh?"

"Yeah, but probably to dispose of, not use again."

"Sure as hell not against three state troopers."

Fisher nodded.

"And that was it? He confessed?"

"No, he hasn't confessed yet. He may never, but it doesn't matter. The evidence hangs him," Fisher said. "Funny thing is, me and Malmstrom were interviewing him and it's like the guy's *still* obsessed by Larry Carr. Kept saying how he used to prance around in thousand-dollar alligator golf shoes on the course, order five-hundred-dollar bottles of wine at the Island Club, while screwing half the women in Palm Beach County."

"That's a whole lot of screwing," Braddock said.

Fisher laughed. "Everything Carr did, seemed to drive Coolidge batshit. He said something like, 'The guy could have at least thrown me a bone, for putting the deal together on his business.'"

"Which clearly he didn't."

"Yeah, I know," Fisher said. "But he said, 'Bottom line, the guy went through life screwing people—women literally, and men just for the fun of it.'"

FIFTY-ONE

Braddock called Leah Bliss after he hung up with Fisher. First, he told her all about the capture of Chris Coolidge and what Coolidge's motive had been for killing Larry Carr.

She listened raptly to the lengthy story.

"So, are you ready?" he asked at the end.

"Ready for what?"

"To go to Harbour Island," he said. "Case closed and I'm officially done playing amateur detective. As you suggested, I am officially retiring from the sleuth game."

"It's about time," she said. "Congratulations. I don't know what I'm more excited about, you not being in danger anymore or going to Harbour Island."

"How 'bout both?"

"Perfect!" she said. "When do we shove off, Cap?"

"Tomorrow morning."

"How far is it?"

"Just a little farther than Nassau."

"Oh, I am so excited."

*****

They got to Harbour Island, just off of Eleuthera, in record time and Braddock couldn't help but notice, when Leah tanned herself on the deck of the *Blue Alibi,* that her breasts had now darkened to a deep mahogany hue.

They had a reservation at a hotel called Pink Sands on Chapel Street, where Braddock had stayed the one time he had gone to Harbour Island. As he recalled, Pink Sands was similar to Lyford Cay in that it had a number of private cottages. Some of them were a short walk to the ocean, others were a little farther away and had their own pools. They were staying at one of the cottages called Frangipani, which had a pool and was just a short distance away from the reception building where they checked in. The tall black woman at the reception desk with teeth as white as Aspen snow had just explained the easiest way to get to the beach and a place called the Blue Bar, which was on the beach.

Braddock turned to Leah. "I guess we look like people who hang out in bars?" he said, a smile on his face.

The woman at the desk laughed. "Most of our guests want to know where to get a…libation. There's food too."

"We like food, too," Leah said.

"Are you tennis players, by chance?" the woman asked. "Because the courts are very near you."

"Bad ones," Braddock said, then glancing at Leah. "Well, I should just speak for myself. She's probably very good."

"We didn't bring racquets," Leah said.

"Well, if you want, we have ones here."

"Cool. Thanks," Leah said. "We may take you up on that."

*****

Carrying their light bags, they walked the short distance to Frangipani, a yellow Bahamian-style stucco cottage surrounded by palm trees. They walked inside and Leah's eyes widened. "Oh my God, it almost blinding, it's so white" she said approvingly. The one-bedroom cottage had a high tray ceiling, and the king-size bed had a pure white canopy over it. The only non-white color in the room came from the vibrant green fan fronds in a vase next to the bed, and a thick rattan headboard. The cottage had a white coquina stone floor and the whole interior appeared clean and fresh.

"Wow! I love it," Leah said.

"More than Lyford Cay?" Braddock asked, taking her bag and putting his and hers down on a white sofa.

"Um, I'd call it a toss-up," Leah said. "I'm not a big fan of that expression *to die for* but this truly is…*to die for.*"

She went into the bathroom and swooned a little more. "So nice," she said simply.

It was two in the afternoon now.

Braddock eyed Leah, smiled, and flicked his head at the bed. "Looks pretty inviting."

"You are just incorrigible," she said. "We did enough of that in Lyford Cay to last a lifetime."

"Aw, come on."

"What? Just a quickie, you mean," she said, shaking her head. "Later, lover boy. Let's go exploring."

"Okay," Braddock said, reluctantly. "The beach?"

She nodded and walked to the door with him right behind her.

The beach was—as advertised—pink, or at least had a pink tinge to it. It didn't take long before they ended up at the Blue Bar.

"Speaking of things we did enough of in Lyford Cay to last a lifetime," Leah said sitting down on a rattan barstool.

"What? Rum drinks?"

She nodded. "Grog. But I'm ready for another."

"Just one?"

"We'll see."

They ordered two different exotic rum drinks, which were delivered complete with maraschino cherries and little paper umbrellas on top.

Leah had been Googling on her iPhone.

"What are you looking for?" Braddock asked.

She took a sip of her drink. "Um, yummy… Well, I'm finding a ton of places that rent golf carts. Only problem is, no golf course so far." She looked up at him. "I was hoping to take some more money off you."

"Ah, I've got bad news for you. No golf courses on Harbour Island."

"No?" she said, disappointed.

"I think the nearest one…might just be Lyford," he said. "The reason you're finding so many places that rent golf carts is because that's the preferred means of transportation on the island."

She nodded. "So what are we going to do?"

Braddock turned to the bartender, a portly black man with one large gold tooth, and gave him a little wave.

"Yes, sir?" the bartender said.

"Do you happen to know any bonefish guides, by any chance?" he asked.

"It just so happens I do," the bartender said. "My brother Llewellyn. One of the best on the island. Do you want to go out?"

Braddock turned to Leah. "You ever do any bonefishing?"

She shook her head. "Never have, but I'm game."

Braddock turned back to the bartender. "Could you give him a call? See if he's free?"

"Sure. When do you want to go?"

Braddock turned to Leah, who smiled and answered for them both: "No time like the present."

Braddock turned back to the bartender. "Now?"

The bartender, whose name turned out to be Raymond, called his brother. Llewellyn was free and gave them directions to a dock where he'd meet them.

"Okay, we're all set," Braddock said, "I'm just going to hit the head, then let's go."

He walked to the nearby men's room and took out his cell phone and hit a number he had on speed dial.

Delray Detective Jason Fisher answered. "Hey, Matt, what's up?"

"I've got a little job for you."

*****

They finished up their drinks and, forty-five minutes later, met Llewellyn at the appointed dock. From twenty feet away, Braddock saw Llewellyn had a gold tooth just like his brother's.

Leah noticed too.

"Maybe it was a two-for-one sale," she whispered.

They introduced themselves—Llewellyn said to call him "Wellie"—and ten minutes later they were out on the water. Wellie first gave Leah a quick tutorial on the art of bonfishing. She seemed to get the hang of it pretty quickly, which both Braddock and Wellie were impressed by since there was a real art to it, which usually took a while to acquire.

Wellie explained that it was best for them to fish one at a time so he could concentrate on helping them individually.

Braddock went first. The idea was that Wellie would spot a bonefish, then Braddock would quickly cast near the fish. Two minutes into it, Wellie pointed. "There!"

Braddock didn't see the fish but cast anyway.

"Just missed him," Wellie said.

"I never even saw him," Braddock said, glancing at Leah. "Did you?"

She shook her head.

"They really blend in," Wellie said, then pointed. "Over there!"

Again, Braddock didn't see the fish but cast his line anyway.

"Good cast," Wellie said, but then shook his head. "He's gone."

This went on for another twenty minutes. Finally, Braddock glanced over at Leah and shrugged. "I struck out. You're up."

"You don't want to try a little longer?"

"Nah, your turn," Braddock said, turning to Wellie. "Okay, Wellie, find her a fish."

A minute or two later he did. And despite her expert cast, the fish either wasn't interested or swam away. This went on for another fifteen minutes until, finally Leah said:

"Okay Wellie. I give up. They just aren't biting today."

When they got back to the dock, Wellie offered to discount the price they had agreed on, but Braddock wouldn't hear of it.

"It wasn't your fault we couldn't catch them. They were there." They thanked him and walked down the dock. Leah turned to him when they were just out of earshot of Wellie.

"I don't think they exist," she said.

*****

"Want to play a little tennis?" Braddock said when they got back to Pink Sands.

"Sure," she said. "I got a feeling that hitting a tennis ball is a lot easier than snagging a bonefish."

Their tennis outfits were hardly Wimbledon all-whites. They both had sneakers, though. Leah wore a teal T-shirt and short beige shorts, not hard on the eye. Braddock wore a splashy Hawaiian shirt over light blue shorts. They just rallied and never got around to playing actual games. If they had, Braddock knew, she would have whipped him.

It was six o'clock when they got back to Frangipani. They took a shower together and were getting ready for an early dinner, when Braddock's phone rang.

He looked down at the display. "Jason Fisher, the detective," he said. "Wonder what he's calling about?"

Leah groaned and rolled her eyes as Braddock clicked the green button and put the call on speaker. "Hey Jason, what's up?"

"Got bad news for you, Matt. Chris Coolidge escaped from jail."

"You gotta be kidding me. When?"

"Just a little while ago. Took off in one of our squad cars. I'm gonna need you back here. Where are you?"

"A million miles away. No way!"

"Come on, man. You can't bail on me now."

Leah shook her head furiously, her eyes ablaze.

"Come on, man," Fisher said. "I really need ya."

Braddock let out a long stream of air. "Oh Christ"—then glancing at Leah—"hang on a second, Jason."

He put a hand over his cell phone and lowered his voice. "What can I do? It's my case. Sorry, we gotta pack up."

Leah Bliss looked like she was going to haul off and smack him. Or at the very least, start hurling f-bombs. "Are you *crazy*?" was all she could get out.

Slowly, his frown turned into a wide smile.

"What?" she said.

"You know what today is?" he asked, the smile now a vast, impish grin.

"Um, first of April," she said, then burst out laughing. "Why you big jerk, you!"

Braddock raised the cell phone and spoke. "Good job, Jason."

"April Fools," Fisher said, and left them alone.

EPILOGUE

Two months later, Catherine Carr called Braddock on his cell phone.

"So, Matt, I'd really like to meet your new lady friend who I've heard so much about."

Braddock had just docked his boat after an afternoon fishing trip. "I'd love to have you meet her too," he said, tying a line around a cleat.

"Well, how about a double date then?"

"Sure. Who's the lucky man?" Braddock asked.

"Um, I'll give you a clue. It's someone…you know," Catherine said. "Come on, you're good at solving mysteries."

"That's no clue," Braddock said. "I know a lot of men."

"Well then, you'll just have to wait and see," she said. "I made a reservation for four at the club this Saturday at seven. Does that work for you two?"

"Yup, works for me, let me just check with Leah and get back to you."

*****

Braddock picked up Leah just before seven on Saturday. Normally, she'd walk the short distance to the club from her condominium, but it was raining.

"So what do you know about Catherine's *friend?*" Leah asked as they made the short drive to the main club.

"No clue. She just said it's somebody I know."

Leah laughed. "So that narrows it down to—what?—a couple thousand men."

"Yeah, that's about right."

Braddock pulled up to the valet at the porte cochere of the club and they both got out of the car and went inside. They walked up to the hostess. "Hi, Karen," Braddock said. "We're meeting Ms. Carr and her...guest."

"Ms. Carr isn't here yet, Mr. Braddock. May I seat you at your table?"

"Yes, please." And they followed her to a far corner of the dining room.

"Dying of curiosity, aren't you?" Leah said, as they sat down.

"Yeah, kinda," Braddock said, then the waiter came up to them and they ordered drinks.

"I'm glad she's going out again," Braddock said. "Hopefully with a man who'll treat her better than Larry did."

"Wouldn't that be just about anyone?" Leah said.

Braddock cocked his head. "The man had his good qualities," he said.

"You're being charitable," Leah said, as he saw Catherine Carr across the room with a man behind her.

"Holy shit!" Braddock said, lowering his voice, as Leah turned to see the couple coming toward them.

"Who is it?" Leah said.

Braddock whispered. "The proprietor of your favorite nightclub."

*****

Braddock gave Catherine a kiss and did the introductions: Leah to Catherine, then Leah to Frank Diehl.

Diehl was wearing the same perfectly-cut midnight blue suit and tie that he was wearing when Braddock met him at Narcissism. It was overkill for the low-key Island Club.

The waiter took Catherine's and Diehl's drink orders, then they all looked at the menu and ordered.

"So I understand you two had a nice trip to the Bahamas a while back," Diehl said to Leah.

"Yes, it was heaven," Leah said.

"Frangipani, huh?" Diehl said.

"What?"

"Where you stayed."

Braddock frowned, clearly irked. "How do you know that?"

"A little birdie," Diehl said with a grin.

"How long have you been at the Island Club, Leah?" Catherine asked.

"Oh, only about three or four months, but I love it," Leah said. "Great bunch of people and plenty to do."

"Matt mentioned you were a painter," Catherine said.

"I believe my exact words were, 'girl's a real Picasso,'" Braddock said.

"Or was it Matisse?" Catherine said.

"Matt's been known to exaggerate a little," Leah said, patting his arm.

Diehl took a sip of his vodka and leaned back in his chair. "So what's your next case, Matt?"

Braddock chuckled. "I'm done with all that. Once was more than enough. Back to being a bad golfer."

"Just because you lose to a girl, Matt," Leah said, "doesn't make you a bad golfer."

"Rub it in," said Braddock.

Catherine laughed and stood up. "You'll excuse me for a moment,"

"I'm going to join you," said Leah.

They walked away in the direction of the ladies' room.

"Very attractive woman," Diehl said of Leah.

Braddock nodded. "Both of 'em."

"So, Matt...you pretty confident you got the right guy?" Diehl asked. "Coolidge or whatever."

"Now that you ask, I always thought you looked like a pretty good suspect, Frank," Braddock said. "But then, we got a match on the murder weapon."

"And those tests are always foolproof?" Diehl said.

"I don't know. I'm not exactly a seasoned crime scene investigator," Braddock said. "Why? You got another theory?"

Diehl shrugged. "Not really," he said, dialing up an earnest look. "Well, just the obvious."

"Which is?"

"You know, oldest motive in the book: killing a man to get a woman."

"Funny. That did occur to me when you two walked in here," Braddock said. "And, if I was a suspicious man, I'd say you did a good job of getting that woman, Lisa Frechetti, to point the finger at Coolidge."

Diehl shrugged again. "I just thought you'd want to hear what she had to say. Just trying to be helpful."

Braddock gave Diehl a cold eye. "And, now that I think about it, I wouldn't be at all surprised if you got Larry Carr's old girlfriend, Faye Mayhew, to spin things a little."

"Who?"

Braddock shook his head. "Come on, Frank, that wasn't convincing at all."

The two women walked out of the ladies' room and the men gave them both adoring smiles.

THE END

PALM BEACH BETRAYERS

Exclusive sample from Charlie Crawford Palm Beach Mysteries Book 13

CHAPTER ONE

Mort Ott glanced over at Charlie Crawford and shook his head in disgust. They were in the Palm Beach County Courthouse on Dixie Highway in West Palm Beach, attending the murder trial of Maynard Kressy, a local pediatrician Crawford and Ott had arrested six months before and charged with the murder of a twelve-year-old boy whose body was never found.

Two eyewitnesses had testified that they had seen Kressy with the boy shortly after his disappearance from his home on Peruvian Avenue in Palm Beach. Kressy had been suspected of being in possession of child pornography and when Crawford and Ott got a search warrant for his house, also on Peruvian, they'd found seven file cabinets full of kiddie porn. Most damning was the discovery of the boy's name scrawled on the back of a prescription pad atop Kressy's desk.

The problem was that Maynard Kressy, who was the millionaire son of a prominent car dealer in the Philadelphia suburbs, had a cadre of defense attorneys that made OJ's dream team look like a bunch of pikers. One of them had made the unfounded assertion that the boy had run away the year before he had disappeared. The prosecutor immediately challenged it and said there was no hard evidence to substantiate that, but it was too late, the damage had been done, the jury had heard it.

At that point, Ott had leaned toward Crawford in the spectator section of the courthouse and said under his breath, "We're fucked."

Coupled with the fact that no body had been found, this had become an even tougher case to prove, though "no body" cases had been prosecuted successfully, most notably in the famous case of Robert Durst, the New York real estate heir. Kressy, dubbed the "Palm Beach *Pedo*-trician" by one of the local papers, claimed that all the pornographic material found in his house actually belonged to a mysterious "male roommate" named Christopher, who also had never been located. Crawford and Ott were convinced that Kressy had invented Christopher and that, in fact, he never existed, and the prosecutor did his best to support that by bringing several witnesses to the stand— neighbors of Kressy— who swore they had never seen anyone fitting the description near Kressy's home.

Kressy's lawyers relentlessly questioned the two witnesses who said they saw Kressy with the boy. One of them was a Hispanic man who had about a fifty-word English vocabulary and worked as a landscaper at a house across the street. He turned out to be an illegal alien from Guatemala, who got flustered and rattled on the stand and seemed to say that the young boy could actually have been a young girl.

The other witness, it turned out, had been convicted twice for drunk driving, and when pressed hard, admitted that she'd "had a few drinks" when she spotted Kressy with the boy.

It got worse.

Kressy also claimed, through one of his attorneys, that after they arrested him and brought him in for questioning, Crawford and Ott had repeatedly called him a "pervert" and a "pedophile" and beat him "mercilessly" in a "torture room." When the prosecutor produced several photographs of Kressy after the alleged beatings took place, with no bruises, no contusions, no marks of any kind on his face or upper body, the defense attorney quickly added that the detectives had, "kicked him repeatedly in the groin area." He went on to say, "besides, these guys knew exactly what they were doing, they've been around. Including that one who came from the mean streets of New York City. They knew how to beat Dr. Kressy. Those two beat him with a rubber hose which doesn't leave any bruises or marks."

Crawford still couldn't believe the guy had referred to his former stomping grounds as "the mean streets of New York City." He wanted to leap out of his seat and strangle the guy, but Ott put a firm hand on his upper leg. "Chill," he said firmly under his breath.

And so this trial ended in the manner that unsuccessful rape cases often ended: the victim ended up being portrayed as the villain.

Ott turned to Crawford a little later and said under his breath, "Now we're *really* fucked."

And fucked they were, when the jury proclaimed Maynard Kressy not guilty after deliberating a mere forty-five minutes.

After bear-hugging his five attorneys and raising his fist to the ceiling, Kressy looked back in triumph at Crawford and Ott and defiantly flipped them the finger. This time Crawford had to restrain Ott.

It got even worse.

After leaving the courthouse, Kressy read a statement and conducted a Q & A with the throng of assembled reporters and media people. Before at least twenty-five microphones clustered around a hastily-improvised lectern, Kressy puffed out his chest and addressed the crowd:

"I'd like to thank my brilliant lawyers for their unflagging efforts on my behalf, for believing in me from the beginning of this put-up job of a trial. I'd also like to thank the jurors who saw through the smears and underhanded tactics of the prosecutor, and the judge for his fair and judicious handling of this sham trial. And, lastly, I'd like to say justice prevailed, not the brutal, sadistic methods of the two corrupt and disreputable detectives, Crawford and Ott. They should be the ones put on trial, not me."

It was lucky Crawford and Ott weren't around to hear that. They were already beelining it to their favorite West Palm Beach cop bar, Mookie's Tap-a-Key.

TWO

"You believe that shit?" Ott said, shaking his head in disgust again, as he got behind the wheel of the Ford Crown Vic for the short ride to Mookie's.

He had been doing that a lot lately. Shaking his head.

And going to Mookie's.

Both men had seen bad verdicts before, but this was certainly in Crawford's top five, all-time worst ones. The more he thought about it, the more he realized, it was the worst *ever*.

They walked into Mookie's. The usual lunch crowd of mutts and miscreants were in attendance. Crawford and Ott went to the bar, nodded at the bartender/owner John Scarlata, and ordered stiff ones, with draft beer chasers.

"I heard," Scarlata told them simply, pointing to the TV, which was tuned to a local news station.

"What did they say?" Crawford asked Scarlata.

"The perv gave a news conference. Thanked all the assholes who let him walk, then said you and Mort ought to be on trial, not him."

Ott slammed his draft beer down on the bar. "You gotta be fuckin' kidding."

Crawford put his hand on Ott's arm. "Don't let it get you crazy."

"Reporters were eating it up," Scarlata added. "What that jack-off was saying."

"Motherfuckers," Ott growled and downed his draft. "I mean, what's the point if they all get off?"

Scarlata, an ex-cop, leaned across the bar. "'Member that wing nut Robert Blake? Played that detective with that stupid bird on his shoulder?"

Crawford nodded. "Yeah, what about him?"

"He got off," Scarlata said.

"Killed his wife, right?" Crawford said.

"Yeah, and get this, he was her tenth husband."

Ott laughed. "How do you know worthless shit like that, Scar?"

"I don't know," Scarlata said. "Mighta been on Jeopardy or something?"

"How 'bout that lunatic Phil Spector?" Crawford said. "He got off first time. Shot that woman in the mouth and said she killed herself."

"Yeah, but they nailed his ass the second go 'round," Scarlata replied.

"Fuckin' sicko," was all Ott had to say on the subject.

"And then there was OJ," Crawford said, tearing the wrapper off a Slim Jim.

Ott nodded. "And then there was OJ."

*****

It was two hours later, and it was safe to say that Crawford and Ott were in the bag. A few cops buying them drinks and several sympathy rounds from John Scarlata had hastened the process.

"I just can't get that kid out of my head, Charlie," Ott said, referring to the missing and presumed-dead boy, Bobby Mittgang. "That photo of him on the skateboard…cute little guy."

Crawford nodded as Ott took a pull of his beer.

"I mean it," Ott said. "I'm giving serious thought to quitting. Like I said, what's the point? I bet that woman movie producer gets off too. I mean, talk about someone who can afford Johnnie Cochran, Robert Kardashian, *and* F. Lee Bailey."

"Yeah, if they weren't all dead," Crawford said.

They were referring to a woman named Janny Hasleiter, whom they had arrested for the murder of Antonia von Habsburg, proprietor of an ultra-high-end dating service, clandestinely used by many rich, *married* Palm Beach men.

"I don't know," Crawford said. "With her, I think it's gonna stick. Don't forget, the guy she hired to do it's testifying against her."

"You mean, unless he gets paid off or something happens to him in prison."

Crawford had no answer to that.

"I mean, Charlie, let's face it, it's stacked against us. You're rich, you skate."

"So what are you gonna do after you hang it up?" Crawford asked, eyeing the unappetizing-looking boiled eggs in a giant, murky-looking glass jar behind the bar.

"I don't know," Ott said. "Maybe join the circus...or Wall Street."

Crawford laughed. "I could see if my brother, Cam, would hire you."

Ott laughed. "What's he do again?" he asked, polishing off drink number...ten or eleven.

"He runs a company on Wall Street that specializes in arbitrage...whatever the hell that might be," Crawford said. "He tried to explain it to me once but after a while my head exploded."

Ott pulled out his iPhone and went to Wikipedia. "Okay, here you go: says, *In economics and finance, arbitrage is the practice of taking advantage of a difference in prices in two or more markets,* semicolon, *striking a combination of matching deals to capitalize on the difference,* comma, *the profit being the difference between the market prices at which the unit is traded...* period. It goes on to say, *When used by academics, an arbitrage is a transaction that involves no negative cash flow at any probabilistic or temporal state and a positive cash flow in at least one state.* Period."

He turned to Crawford and smiled. "Got it?"

"I was with you up to, 'probabilistic or temporal state,' then my head exploded again."

"There's more... Want to hear it?"

"No," Crawford said. "Let's talk football."

"Go Browns." Ott originally hailed from Cleveland.

"Tell you the truth, I think you might be better cut out for the circus," Crawford said. "You could be that guy shot out of a cannon, or maybe a sword swallower."

"Nah, I picture myself more as a fearless lion tamer."

They ordered another round and refills on Slim Jims and bags of barbecue potato chips.

"I don't know," Crawford said, doing his damnedest to try to sound sober. "Can't say I got any bright ideas how we get our reputations back."

Ott slowly shook his head. "You mean 'cause we stand accused of kicking a perv in the nuts and flogging him with rubber hoses."

Crawford nodded.

"I got one," Ott said.

"Let's hear."

No hesitation. "Kill the lying motherfucker," Ott said. "Shut him the fuck up."

"Seriously?"

"I'm *dead* serious."

THREE

Five days later, Maynard Kressy's body was found at his house on Peruvian Avenue. He had been shot once in the back of his head and was slumped over his computer, which was open to a social media messenger app, where men chatted and shared videos and still images of young boys being sexually abused.

Charlie Crawford and Mort Ott, being Palm Beach's only homicide detectives, arrived at the scene twenty minutes after Kressy's terrified cleaning lady called 911. Two uniformed cops were already there when Crawford and Ott walked into Kressy's house, then into the ground-floor bedroom he used as an office.

"Couldn't have happened to a nicer guy, huh?" one of the uniforms named Witmer said to Crawford.

Crawford glared at him. "Knock it off," he said. "This is a murder victim."

Witmer backed away, suitably chastened.

Ott took notes describing the condition of the dead body on his iPad as Crawford clicked away on his cell phone, getting photos from all angles.

"Big question is," Ott said, "how'd the shooter sneak up on him without being heard?"

Crawford glanced down at the thick carpet. "It could be done if Kressy was focused on the computer and the volume was up."

It was then that Crawford and Ott looked down at the image on the computer screen.

Ott groaned. Crawford looked away.

"Didn't take him long to get back to that," Ott said, loud enough so only Crawford could hear.

Crawford just nodded. "I'm gonna look around and see if it was forced entry or not."

"I kinda remember from the trial that he didn't lock up when he was here."

Crawford nodded, then turned to Witmer behind him. "Any signs of forced entry?"

"We haven't had a chance to look," Witmer said. "Got here just a few minutes before you."

Crawford turned to the other uniform, Mendez. "You see anything suspicious when you first got here?"

"No," said Mendez. "Cleaning lady let us in and took us straight to the vic."

Crawford nodded. "Where's she?"

"Think she might be upstairs," Witmer said. "She was really freaked."

"All right," Crawford said. "Why don't you guys go string up tape around the house."

Witmer and Mendez nodded and walked toward the front door.

Crawford turned to Ott. "I'm gonna talk to the cleaning lady."

Ott nodded and continued to type notes into his iPad as Crawford walked out of the room.

He walked up the staircase and got to the top. "Hello?" he called out.

A short Hispanic woman in sweatpants and a bottle of cleaning liquid in hand came to the door of one of the bedrooms.

"I'm Detective Crawford. Can I speak to you for a few moments?"

She nodded nervously.

"What's your name?" Crawford asked, taking out his iPhone.

"Blanca."

"Okay, Blanca. Please tell me what happened when you came to work this morning?"

She swallowed and nodded. "Well, I walked in and called for Dr. Maynard…to tell him I was here."

"Did you have a key?"

"I did, but he always left the door open for me."

Crawford nodded. "So then what?"

"I kept calling out, 'Dr. Maynard, Dr. Maynard,' so he'd know I was here. He didn't answer, so I started cleaning the kitchen as I always do first. Then about fifteen or twenty minutes later I went into his office and—" She put her hands up to her mouth and burst out crying.

His instinct was to put a comforting hand on her shoulder but he didn't. Instead he smiled his best consoling smile. "Take your time, Blanca, take your time."

"I-I-I was so shocked and scared… someone might still be here."

"You mean the person who did it?"

"Yes," Blanca said, "I just ran out of the house to my car, got in and locked all the doors. Then I called 911 on my phone."

"And what? Did you stay there until the two officers arrived?" She nodded.

"That was smart," Crawford said. "And then you led the officers to where Mr. Kressy had been shot."

She nodded again.

"And you never saw or heard anything when you first got to the house?"

"No, I did not."

Crawford thought for a few moments. "How much does Mr. Kressy pay you for cleaning?"

"Ninety dollars."

Crawford reached for his wallet and took out three twenties and two tens and handed it to her. "Sorry. I only have eighty. You might as well go home now."

"But I haven't finished."

"That's okay."

She nodded.

"Thank you for the information," Crawford said. "I appreciate it."

She nodded and Crawford walked back down the stairs.

When he got to the bottom, the front door opened and two crime scene techs walked in. One was Micki Ganz, the other Dominica McCarthy. Under the radar, Dominica and Crawford had a "special relationship," which just about everyone in the Palm Beach Police Department knew about, despite the pair's efforts to keep it quiet.

"Hey," Crawford said, slightly uncomfortably to Dominica, because they hadn't seen each other in more than three weeks.

"Hey," she said back at him.

"Hey, Mick," he said to Ganz.

"Hey, Charlie."

"Follow me," Crawford said, and the three took the short walk to Kressy's office.

Then Crawford turned to the techs. "One shot to the back of the head," he said. "Besides the slug, I don't know what else you're gonna find. Looks like someone just snuck in and popped him."

"Maybe that guy 'Christopher,'" Ott said to the techs. "Came to get his porn."

"Who?" Dominica asked.

"Guy who Kressy claimed at trial owned all the porn we found here," Crawford explained.

"Thing is," Ott said, "we never thought there was such a person."

"All right, we're on it," Dominica said, turning to Ganz. "You want to locate the slug? I'll concentrate on the vic."

Ganz nodded.

Crawford's cell phone rang. He looked down at the display. It just said, *Norm.*

Norm Rutledge was Chief of the Palm Beach Police Department and the partners' direct boss.

"Hey, Norm."

"Hey, Crawford," Rutledge said. "I heard about Kressy. Are you at the scene now?"

"Yeah, I am."

"What happened?"

"He was shot once in the head."

Nothing for a moment, then: "I'm not sure it's a real good idea that you and Ott take the case."

"I get why you're saying that," Crawford said, "but who else could you put on it?"

"I don't know. I gotta think about it," Rutledge said. "Stop by when you're done there and we'll talk about it. Ott too."

"Okay. We're not going to be here much longer."

Crawford went back to the bedroom office where Kressy had been shot. Dominica looked up at him.

"ME coming?" he asked her, meaning the medical examiner.

Dominica nodded. "He'll be along. You know how he likes to take his time."

Crawford smiled. "I sure do. So when you guys have a guess on time of death, will you let me know?"

Dominica nodded again. "My initial reaction is last night sometime. Based on the blood coagulation. But we'll be able to pin it down to a ballpark window a little later."

Crawford nodded. "Okay, Mort," Crawford said, and Ott looked up. "Not much more we can do. Let's leave it in the hands of the experts. Rutledge wants to have a chat with us."

Ott winced and groaned. "Oh, swell."

FOUR

Chief of Police Norm Rutledge, never one to be called a snappy dresser, favored brown suits and loud ties. Today it was the chocolate brown suit with orange pinstripes and a purple tie. *GQ* he was not. Not that Crawford and Ott were, though Crawford at six-three and 180, and handsome without much fuss, had been mistaken a few times for that polo player in the Ralph Lauren ads.

Ott, on the other hand, a roly-poly 230, five-eight and ninety percent bald, had been mistaken for the Palm Beach Police Department janitor on numerous occasions. Might have had something to do with his snazzy Earth shoes from the Nixon era.

Crawford and Ott took their usual seats facing Rutledge in his office.

"I've got real concerns about this one," Rutledge started out.

"I understand," Crawford said.

"You mean, 'cause of the trial?" Ott asked.

"'Course I mean 'cause of the trial," Rutledge said. "What the hell else would I mean?"

Ott put up his hands. "Easy, Norm. You didn't believe any of that shit, did you?"

"Doesn't matter what I believe," Rutledge said. "There're a shitload of people out there who believe police violence is as common as jaywalking and reporters and media love to fan the flames. I don't need to tell you that."

"So bottom-line it for us, Norm," Crawford said.

Rutledge stroked his chin. "Bottom line is I want to talk to Chase," he said, referring to the mayor of Palm Beach.

"Isn't the bottom line that you got no one else to take on the case?" Crawford said. "It's kind of like when my ex-wife got killed. Ordinarily, I wouldn't have been on that one either, but you don't have anyone else."

"I know. I know," Rutledge said, glancing out his window. His eyes came back to first Ott, then Crawford. "Where were you guys when it happened?"

Crawford shot an incredulous look at Ott, then Rutledge. "I can't believe you're actually asking us that. I mean, do you really think—"

"Hey, hey, take it easy," Rutledge said. "It's a question that's gonna be asked by everybody."

He had a point. "Okay, well first of all, we don't know when he was shot. Probably last night. And I was either sleeping, or watching the tube, or having one of my nutritious Healthy Choice dinners."

Ott turned to him. "You *eat* that shit?"

"It was delicious. Grilled Chicken Marinara."

"Okay," Ott said to Rutledge. "And I was pretty much doing the same thing. Except I had a tasty Domino's pizza."

"You eat that shit?" Crawford echoed his partner.

"Ha ha," said Ott.

"Were you with anyone?" Rutledge asked them.

Ott shook his head. Crawford did the same. "No alibis," he said.

Rutledge stroked his chin again.

"Hey, look at it this way," Crawford said. "Who's gonna be more motivated to find Kressy's killer than us?"

"Yeah," Ott added. "You think we want people goin' around saying, 'Those were the same cops who kicked him in the nuts. Bet those vicious sons-of-bitches killed him, too'?"

"True," Rutledge said. "All right. I'm meeting with Chase a little later, I'll get back to you."

"You always remind us how the first forty-eight is so critical," Crawford said. "So don't sit on this."

"Yeah, yeah, don't worry," Rutledge said, standing up abruptly as if to say, *All right, we're done here.* "I'll let you know in an hour or so."

*****

"So what are we supposed to do now," Ott said on his way back to their offices. "Sit around and twiddle our thumbs waiting for Rutledge?"

"Yeah, whatever the hell you were doing before Kressy bought it," said Crawford.

Ott nodded. "Yeah, which was sitting around and twiddling my thumbs, waiting for a dead body to turn up."

"Well, we got one now."

"Yup."

"Trust me. The mayor's on our team."

*****

They didn't have to wait long. Rutledge, true to his word, which wasn't always the case, called Crawford an hour and a half later to say the case was theirs. He quoted Mal Chase as saying, "I don't care what Kressy said on the stand at his trial, Crawford and Ott would never do what he claimed. I mean, *torture room*... what bullshit. Torture room in his imagination. Our *interrogation room* is actually a little bigger and a little better than most. But, hey, it *is* Palm Beach."

"So we're good?" asked Crawford.

"Yep. All Mal said was 'Tell 'em to wrap it up quick.' Then he thought about it a sec and said, 'Nah, on second thought, don't bother. They've heard that a million times.'"

FIVE

Norm Rutledge called Frank Witmer and Joe Mendez and told them to come to his office immediately. Five minutes later, the two officers walked in and sat down.

"So I want to talk to you two about something very sensitive," Rutledge said.

Judging by the blank looks on the faces of Witmer and Mendez, they had no idea what that would be, but they both nodded.

"As I understand it, you two were first on scene at Maynard Kressy's house this morning, correct?"

The pair nodded again.

"Okay, then Crawford and Ott got there, right? Singly or together?"

"Together," Witmer said.

"Okay, now think about this and be very specific: what were their reactions when they first walked in and saw Kressy's body?"

Witmer glanced at Mendez, then back to Rutledge. "I'm not exactly sure what you mean by 'their reactions,' Chief."

Rutledge, never long on patience, arched his eyebrows and opened his hands. "Come on, man. Did they looked surprised? Did they look...matter-of-fact? You know like, *just another homicide*? Or did they look...in some way, I don't know, satisfied maybe. Like the bastard had it coming or something?"

Witmer rubbed his forehead. "I don't really know. This was the first time I've ever been at a crime scene with those two. They just studied the body first, took a lot of camera shots, and went about their business as, I guess, they always do."

"Yeah, professional as hell was my reaction," Mendez chimed in.

"Hey, I'm not looking for you to grade 'em," Rutledge said exasperated. "What about, did they say anything at all about the vic himself?"

Mendez turned to Witmer and shrugged. "Not that I can remember."

Witmer raised his hand. "I remember something Ott said when he saw that Kressy's computer was open to a page of that…child porn, I guess it was."

"What did he say?" Rutledge asked.

"'Up to his old tricks,' something like that. I could barely make it out," Witmer said.

"Referring to Kressy looking at porn, you mean?"

"Exactly."

"What did Crawford say?"

"He didn't say anything. He was just snapping off a lot of photos with his iPhone."

Rutledge tapped his desk a few times. "So nothing at all jumped out at you about Crawford and Ott's reactions when they first got there. No looks on their faces that might have been some kinda tell? Nothing at all like that?"

Both men shook their heads.

"Okay," Rutledge said, standing up. "Now I want to be very clear about one thing: this meeting never took place. I never asked you any questions and you never gave me any answers. You never, ever, mention a word of this to anyone, especially Crawford and Ott. If I ever hear you did, your next job'll be riding on the back of a sanitation department truck. You understand?"

"I understand," said Mendez.

"Yeah, chief," said Witmer. "Loud and clear."

TO KEEP READING VISIT:
https://www.amazon.com/dp/B0BXLWGJXR

Audio Books

Many of Tom's books are also available in Audio...

Listen to masterful narrator Phil Thron and feel like you're right there in Palm Beach with Charlie, Mort and Dominica!

Audio books available include:
Palm Beach Nasty
Palm Beach Poison
Palm Beach Deadly
Palm Beach Bones
Palm Beach Pretenders
Palm Beach Predator
Charlie Crawford Box Set (Books 1-3)
Killing Time in Charleston
Charleston Buzz Kill
Charleston Noir
The Savannah Madam
Savannah Road Kill

About the Author

A native New Englander, Tom Turner dropped out of college and ran a Vermont bar. Limping back a few years later to get his sheepskin, he went on to become an advertising copywriter, first in Boston, then New York. After 10 years of post-Mad Men life, he made both a career and geography change and ended up in Palm Beach, renovating houses and collecting raw materials for his novels. After stints in Charleston, then Skidaway Island, outside of Savannah, Tom recently moved to Delray Beach, where he's busy writing about passion and murder among his neighbors. To date Tom has written eighteen crime thrillers and mysteries and is probably best known for his Charlie Crawford series set in Palm Beach.

Learn more about Tom's books at:
www.tomturnerbooks.com

Made in United States
North Haven, CT
27 March 2023

34627623R00146